Praise for Patricia Wentworth

'Miss Silver is marvellous'
Daily Mail

'. . . some of the best examples of the British country-house murder mystery'
Alfred Hitchcock Magazine

'Miss Wentworth is a first-rate storyteller'
Daily Telegraph

'You can't go wrong with Miss Maud Silver'
Observer

'Miss Wentworth's plot is ingenious, her characterization acute, her solution satisfying'
Scotsman

'I had forgotten how much I enjoyed Patricia Wentworth – the elegance of her style and the classic neatness of her solutions.'
Alice Templeton

ALSO BY PATRICIA WENTWORTH

The Case of William Smith
The Benevent Treasure
The Listening Eye
Grey Mask
The Catherine Wheel
Miss Silver Comes to Stay
Miss Silver Intervenes
Eternity Ring
Latter End
The Case is Closed
The Chinese Shawl
Out of the Past
The Fingerprint
The Gazebo
The Key
Through the Wall
The Alington Inheritance
Vanishing Point
The Girl in the Cellar
The Watersplash
The Silent Pool
The Brading Collection
The Ivory Dagger

ABOUT THE AUTHOR

Patricia Wentworth was born in India and after writing several romances turned her hand to crime. She wrote dozens of bestselling mysteries and was recognised as one of the mistresses of classic crime. She died in the late Sixties.

PATRICIA WENTWORTH

THE CLOCK STRIKES TWELVE

First published in Great Britain in 1945 by Hodder and Stoughton
This edition published in 2006 by Hodder and Stoughton
A division of Hodder Headline

A Hodder paperback

3

A CIP catalogue record for this title
is available from the British Library.

ISBN 0 340 68262 0

Typeset in Sabon by Hewer Text UK Ltd
Printed and bound by
Mackays of Chatham Ltd, Chatham, Kent

Hodder and Stoughton Ltd
A division of Hodder Headline
338 Euston Road
London NW1 3BH

ONE

MR JAMES PARADINE leaned forward and took up the telephone receiver. Birleton had not yet adopted the dial system. He waited for the exchange to speak, and then asked for a personal call to Mr Elliot Wray at the Victoria Hotel, after which he remained in the same position, waiting for the call to come through. The table at which he sat was a large and handsome piece of furniture carried out in mahogany, with a crimson leather top. All the furniture in the room was large and handsome. There were nests of drawers, filing cabinets, and bookshelves. There were chairs and armchairs of the same family as the writing-table – the best leather, the best wood, the best workmanship. A very deep crimson carpet covered the floor. Heavy curtains of the same warm shade were drawn across the windows. Above the black marble mantelpiece hung a life-size portrait of the late Mrs Paradine, a fair, spacious lady in ruby velvet and diamonds – a great many diamonds. In spite of them she managed to give the impression of having been a kind, housewifely sort of person. Nothing in the room was new, nothing was shabby. Everything appeared to partake of the vigorous and dignified quality of Mr James Paradine himself. A massive gilt clock beneath the portrait gave out four chiming strokes and then struck the hour of seven. As the last stroke died, there was a crackling in the receiver, a girl's voice from the exchange said 'Your call', and immediately upon that Elliot Wray was heard to say 'Hello!'

James Paradine said, 'That you, Wray? James Paradine speaking. I want to see you. Here. At once.'

'Well – sir—'

'There's no well about it. I want you to come out here at once. Something's happened.'

At the other end of the line Elliot Wray's heart turned over. He took a moment, and said, 'What?'

'I'll tell you when you get here.'

Another pause. Then Elliot, very controlled, 'Is anything wrong?'

In spite of the control there was something that made old James Paradine smile grimly as he said, 'Wrong enough. But it's business – nothing personal. Come right along.'

'I'm dining with the Moffats, sir.'

'You'll have to cut it out. I'll ring them and say I'm keeping you.'

Elliot Wray stood frowning with the receiver at his ear. James Paradine was Robert Moffat's partner, head of the Paradine-Moffat Works. He wouldn't make him break a dinner engagement, and a New Year's dinner at that, unless the matter was urgent. He said, 'All right, sir, I'll come out.'

James Paradine said, 'All right', and hung up.

The River House was three miles out of Birleton

– four miles from the hotel. Allowing for the blackout, it would take Elliot all of twenty minutes to get here.

He went over to the door and switched off the two brilliant ceiling lights, and then, crossing the dark room, passed between the heavy curtains. The curtains ran straight across in continuance of the wall, but behind them was a deep bay with windows to right and left and a glass door in the middle. Mr Paradine turned a key, opened the door, and stood upon the threshold looking out. Two shallow steps gave upon a wide terrace. The parapeted edge showed dark against the moonlit scene beyond and far below. The house stood on a height above the river from which it took its name. James Paradine looked down upon a silvered landscape which passed from low wooded hills on the right, through the river valley, to the dark clustering mass of Birleton on the left. The moon lighted it, almost full in a cloudless sky. Wray would make better time than the twenty minutes he had allowed him with all this brightness abroad. The edge of the terrace stood out as clear as day below the window, and beyond it the deep, steep drop to the water's edge.

He stood there looking out, pleased with the view but not thinking about it – thinking of other things, thinking his own sardonic thoughts – pleased with them, savouring them. Presently he turned the watch on his wrist. He could read the dial easily enough – a quarter past seven. He parted the curtains again, came back through the room, and put on the lights.

Exactly three minutes later Elliot Wray walked in, his face set hard, his fair hair ruffled, and his eyes as cold as ice. He had come, but he was damned if he was going to stay one split second longer than he need. He had not known how much he would mind coming into the house until he got there. What difference did it make – New York or London, Birleton or Timbuktu – it was all the same, wasn't it? As far as he was concerned Phyllida was dead. He hadn't known till he came into the River House how damnably her ghost could walk – all the way up the stair beside him, whispering.

He shut the door and came over to the far side of the writing table, every bit of him taut with protest.

'What is it, sir?'

James Paradine looked at him across the table, leaning back in his swivel chair with a hand upon either arm.

'You'd better sit down,' he said. 'Those blueprints have disappeared.'

Elliot's two hands came down on the table flat. He leaned on them and said, '*What?*'

James Paradine nodded slightly.

'They've gone,' he said. 'You'd really better sit down.'

Elliot took no notice of that.

'How can they have gone?' He straightened up and stepped back a pace. 'I left them with you this afternoon.'

'Precisely. Cadogan sent you up with them

yesterday. Bob Moffat, Frank, and I had a session over them. After a further session you left them with me this afternoon at three o'clock, and at six-thirty I discovered that they were missing.'

'But, sir—'

'Just a moment. I think you will agree that your dinner engagement must go by the board. I have told Bob Moffat that I am keeping you on business. Now listen to me. Don't worry too much. The prints are gone, but we shall get them back. This is a family matter, and I propose to deal with it in my own way. In order that I may do so I shall require you to stay here tonight. Your old room is ready for you.'

Elliot's face set harder still.

'No, sir – I can't do that.'

'You propose to go back to Cadogan and tell him that the prints have gone? I tell you I'm going to deal with it in my own way, and I can guarantee – yes, *guarantee* – that the prints will be back in our hands before the morning.'

The two pairs of eyes met, both bright, and hard, and angry. If there was a contest of wills, there was nothing to show which way it went.

Elliot spoke first.

'You said it was a family matter. Will you explain that?'

'I am about to do so. You handed me the prints at three-thirty in my office at the works. I left at a quarter past four. During that three-quarters of an hour the prints were inside an attaché case on my office table, and the room was never unoccupied. I myself left it three times. On the first occasion I was away for about five minutes. You will remember that I walked along the corridor with you, and that we met Brown, the works manager, who wanted a word with me. During that time my secretary, Albert Pearson, was in the office. When I got back I sent him to Bob Moffat with some figures which he had asked for. Shortly after that my stepson, Frank Ambrose, came in with my nephew, Mark Paradine. I was away for about a quarter of an hour whilst they were there. When I came back Frank had gone and Mark was just leaving. Lastly, my other nephew, Richard Paradine, looked in, and I asked him to stay whilst I went and washed my hands. He did so. When I came back I took the attaché case and drove out here. At half-past six I opened the case and discovered that the blueprints were missing. You asked why I said that this was a family affair. I am telling you that no one outside the family had any possible opportunity of taking those prints.'

Elliot moved abruptly.

'Your secretary, Pearson?' he said.

James Paradine's fine black eyebrows rose.

'You didn't know that he was a cousin? A distant one, but kin is kin. No, it's all in the family, and I propose to deal with it in the family. That is why I am including you.'

Elliot stiffened noticeably.

'I'm afraid I can't claim—' he began, and was met with a curt, 'That's enough about that! Don't ride your high horse with me! You'll do as I say, and for the simple reason that we've got to get the prints back, and I suppose you don't want a scandal any more than I do. As to punishment, you needn't be afraid. It will be – adequate.'

There was a silence. Elliot stood there. It seemed to him that he had been standing there for a long time. He thought, 'What's behind all this – what is he up to – what does he know?' He said, 'Aren't you rather jumping to conclusions, sir? After all, the case must have been here in the house for a couple of hours. Aren't you rather pinning it on the family? What about the servants?'

James Paradine leaned back. He laid his hands together fingertip to fingertip and rested them upon his knee. He said in a quiet, ordinary tone, 'I'm afraid not, my dear Elliot. You see, I know who took the prints.'

TWO

GRACE PARADINE CAME out of her room and stood hesitating for a moment with her hand on the knob of the door. It was a very white hand, and it wore a very fine ruby ring. The passage upon which she had emerged was lighted from end to end and thickly carpeted with an old-fashioned but most expensive carpet, a riot of crimson, cobalt, and green. Mr James Paradine liked his colours bright. The fashions of his youth admitted of no improvement. They had been there when he was a boy, and as far as he was concerned, there they would remain. If anything wore out, it must be replaced without any variation from this standard. His only concessions to modernity were of a practical nature. The house bristled with telephones, blazed with electric light, and was most comfortably warmed from a furnace in the basement.

Miss Paradine withdrew her hand and moved a step away from the door. Standing thus under the bright unshaded ceiling light, she appeared a fine, ample figure of a woman – not handsome, but sufficiently imposing in a black dinner-gown and a light fur wrap. There was a diamond star at her breast, and a pearl dog collar with diamond slides about her throat. Her dark hair, which was scarcely touched with grey, swept in broad waves from a central parting to a graceful knot low down on her neck. Her hair and her hands had been her two beauties. In her late fifties they still served her well. For the rest, she had widely opened brown eyes and a full face with some effect of heaviness in repose. She was James Paradine's sister, and had kept his house for the twenty years which had elapsed since the death of his wife. As she looked back down the passage now her expression was one of frowning intensity. It was obvious that she was waiting and listening.

And then, with an almost startling suddenness her face changed. The frown, the tension, the heaviness were gone. A wide and charming smile took their place. She turned quite round and moved to meet the girl who was coming out of a room at the end of the passage. The girl came on slowly – slowly and without an answering smile. She was tall and pretty, a graceful creature with dark hair curling on her neck, and the very white skin and dark blue eyes which sometimes go with it. When the black lashes shadowed the blue as they were doing now the eyes themselves might very well have passed for black. It was only when they were widely opened or when they took a sudden upward glance that you could see how really blue they were – as blue as sapphires, as blue as deep-sea water. She was Grace Paradine's adopted daughter, Phyllida Wray, and she was twenty-three years old.

She came along the passage in a long white dress. She wore the string of pearls which had been her twenty-first birthday present – fine pearls, very carefully matched. They were her only ornament. The pretty hands were ringless. The nails had been lacquered to a bright holly red.

Grace Paradine put a hand on her shoulder and turned her round.

'You look very nice, my darling. But you're pale—'

The black lashes flicked up and down again, the blue of the eyes showed bright. It was all too quick to be sure whether there was anger under the brightness. She said in a perfectly expressionless voice, 'Am I, Aunt Grace?'

Miss Paradine had that tender, charming smile.

'Why, yes, my darling – you are.' She laughed a little and let her hand slide caressingly down the bare arm to the scarlet fingertips. 'Just between ourselves, you know, I think you might have put a little less on *here*, and given yourself some roses for our New Year's party.'

'But Christmas roses are white.' Phyllida said the words in an odd, half-laughing voice.

She began to walk towards the head of the stairs, Miss Paradine beside her. Phyllida had disengaged herself. They went down together with the width of the stair between them. Grace Paradine kept a hand on the heavy mahogany rail.

'It was terrible, their keeping you on duty over Christmas,' she said.

'I volunteered.'

Miss Paradine said nothing for a moment. Then she smiled.

'Well, my darling, it's lovely to have you now. How long can you stay?'

Phyllida said, 'I don't know.'

'But—'

The girl stood still, threw a look which might have meant appeal, and said in a hurry, 'I can have a week if I like, but I don't know that I want it. I think I'm better working.' A note of rebellion came into her voice. 'Don't look like that – I didn't say it to hurt you. It's just – well, you know—'

Miss Paradine had stopped too. Her hand tightened on the banister. She was making an effort. She made it very successfully. Her voice was full of sympathy as she said, 'I know. You mustn't force yourself, but after all this is your home, Phyl. There's something in that, isn't there? He can't spoil that or take it away from you. It was yours before he came, and it will be yours long after we have all forgotten him.'

Phyllida moved abruptly. Something in the words had pricked her and pricked her sharply. She said in a strained undertone, 'I don't want to talk about it. *Please*, Aunt Grace.'

Miss Paradine looked distressed.

'My darling, no, of course not. How stupid of me. We won't look back. It's a New Year for us both, and you're home for a holiday. Do you remember how we used to plan every moment of the holidays when you were a schoolgirl? They were never half long enough for all the things we wanted to do. Well, tonight of course it's all family – Frank and Irene, and Brenda. They've made up the quarrel and she's staying with them, but I don't know how long it will last. Lydia is with them too.' She laughed a little. 'Prettier than ever and just as provoking. Then there'll be Mark, and Dicky, and Albert Pearson. I don't like ten very much for a table, but it can't be helped.'

They were descending the stairs again. Phyllida said in a relieved voice, 'What is Lydia doing?'

'I really don't know – she talks such a lot of nonsense. She's somebody's secretary, I believe. You had better ask her. I do hope she'll be careful tonight. James never did like her very much, and nonsense is a thing he just doesn't understand. I've put her as far away from him as possible, but she has such a carrying voice.'

They crossed the hall and came into the drawing room, where two young men stood warming themselves before the fire. Both were Paradines, nephews of old James Paradine. They were cousins, not brothers, and they bore no resemblance either to one another or to their uncle. Mark, the elder, was thirty-five – a tall, dark man with strong features and an air of gloom. Dicky several years younger – slight, fair, with ingenuous blue eyes and an unfailing flow of good spirits.

Whilst Mark was shaking hands and greeting his aunt and Phyllida with the fewest possible words, Dicky was kissing them both and rattling off compliments, good wishes, and enquiries.

'You're a smash hit in that dress, Aunt Grace –

isn't she, Mark? I say – you've got 'em all on too, haven't you? The old diamond star well to the fore! Do you remember when you tied it on to the top of the Christmas tree and Phyl nearly cried herself into a fit because she wanted it for keeps?'

'I didn't!'

'Oh, yes, you did. You were only three, so we won't hold it up against you. You were awfully pretty then – wasn't she, Aunt Grace – pretty enough to stick on the Christmas tree with the star?'

Grace Paradine stood there smiling with Dicky's arm at her waist. Praise of Phyllida was the incense of which she could never have enough.

Dicky burst out laughing.

'Pity she's gone off so – isn't it, darling?'

And then the door opened and Lane announced Mr and Mrs Ambrose, Miss Ambrose and Miss Pennington. They all came in together – Frank Ambrose, big and fair, with a pale, heavy face; his pretty dark wife, Irene, with her air of having dressed in a hurry; his sister, Brenda, mannish, with thick cropped hair as fair as his and the same very light blue eyes. One of the very worst quarrels, which periodically shook the Ambrose household, had followed upon a suggestion by Irene and her sister, Lydia Pennington, that Brenda's appearance would be very much improved if she would darken her almost white eyelashes. Lydia had most obligingly preferred experienced help, but the whole affair had gone up in smoke.

Lydia's own lashes bore witness to her skill.

Nature had made them as red as her hair, but she had no idea of sitting down under anything of that sort. Her grey-green eyes now sparkled jewel-bright between lashes as dark as Phyllida's own. For the rest, she was a little bit of a thing who always managed to look as if she were about to take part in a mannequin parade. The latest clothes, the latest shoes, the latest way of doing the hair, the latest and most startling lipstick and nail-polish – these were Lydia. She made talk wherever she went. Men dangled and pursued, but never quite caught up with her. Dick Paradine proposed to her every time she came to stay. She fluttered up to him now and deftly evaded a kiss.

'Hello, Dicky! Hello, Phyl! I believe you've grown. I must get higher heels on my shoes. You're such an immense family. Look at Mr Paradine, and Aunt Grace, and Frank, and you – and Mark! Miles up in the air, all of you – so remote!'

Dicky had an arm about her.

'Not me, darling. You mayn't have noticed it, but I'm quite nice and near.'

She leaned back, laughing up at him.

'I never do notice you – that's why I love you so passionately.' Then, with a turn of her head which brought it against Dicky's shoulder, she was looking up at Mark.

'Happy New Year, darling.'

He made no answer, only turned and pushed at the fire with his foot. A log crashed in, and a flurry of sparks went up.

'Snubbed!' said Lydia in a mournful tone. Then

she disengaged herself and ran across to Miss Paradine. 'Will I do, Aunt Grace? Or is he going to be shocked as usual? I wanted to come in my new brocade trousers – gorgeous furniture stuff and no coupons – but Frank lectured me and Irene lectured me till my spirit was broken, so here I am all *jeune fille* in a skirt.'

'You look very nice, my dear,' said Grace Paradine. She smiled and added, 'You always do.'

The skirt cleared the floor and stood out rather stiff. It was of heavy cream satin, and there was nothing at all *jeune fille* about it. It was worn with a top of cream and gold brocade, high in the neck and long in the sleeve. The red hair was piled as high as it would go in an elaborate arrangement of puffs and curls.

Beside her, her sister Irene looked dowdy and washed out. She had been in the middle of telling Grace Paradine just how much cleverer her Jimmy was than any of the other children in his class at the kindergarten. As soon as Lydia turned away she resumed her narrative.

Lydia caught Phyllida by the arm and swung her round.

'Look at Irene in that old black rag! Isn't she an awful warning? If I ever begin to feel myself slipping, I just take a good strong look at her and it does the trick. She's still pretty, but it won't go on – she's going down the domestic drain just as fast as ever she can. Come along over here and tell me all about everything. Golly – isn't this an awful room for me – my hair and all this crimson! Pity I didn't go the whole hog and sport the emerald trouserings. One might as well be hanged for a sheep as a lamb.'

'Uncle James would have had a fit,' said Phyllida. She pulled down a fat velvet cushion with gold tassels which was balancing on the back of one of the brocaded couches and sank gracefully against it. 'You can't really wear anything but black or white in this house. I made up my mind to that years ago.'

The room was very large and very lofty. Its three tall windows were draped in ruby velvet. Between them and over the white marble mantelshelf hung mirrors heavily framed in gold. A ruby carpet covered the floor. Couches, chairs, and stools all flamed in red brocade. Two large chandeliers dispensed a brilliant light broken into rainbows by elaborately cut lustres and drops. Vulgarity had been avoided only by a hair's breadth, yet somehow it had been avoided. The effect was heavily old-fashioned – a scene from some mid-Victorian novel – but for all the colour, the marble, and the gilding, it had a kind of period dignity. Queen Victoria might have received in it. Prince Albert might have sat at the grand piano and played Mendelssohn's Songs without Words.

Lydia leaned across from the other corner of the couch.

'Go on – tell me everything! Quick – before someone tears us apart! They will in about half a second. What are you doing? I thought you'd prized yourself loose and gone off on your own.'

'Only to Birleton,' said Phyllida. 'I'm secretary of the Convalescent Home there.'

She did not look at Lydia, but Lydia looked at her – a green, determined glance.

'Why didn't you go right away – into one of the Services or something? I nearly screamed with rage when Irene wrote and said you'd got caught up in this convalescent show and were doing it from here on a push-bike.'

Phyllida looked down into her lap.

'It was too far,' she said listlessly. 'Aunt Grace wanted me to try, but I couldn't keep it up in the blackout – she saw that. So I live at the Home now. I've got a week's leave if I want it, but I expect I shall go back in a day or two. I'd rather be doing something.'

Lydia darted another of those glances.

'Aunt Grace hates it, doesn't she?'

Phyllida nodded.

Lydia went on.

'How many times a week does she come along and take you out to lunch?'

There was nothing in the words, but the tone was a challenging one. Phyllida looked up, her eyes dark and hurt.

'She misses me – she can't help that. She's been very good. Lydia, you know what she's done for me.'

'Well, what has she done for you? She adopted you, but you don't suppose she did it to please you, do you? People don't adopt a baby for the baby's sake. They do it for exactly the same reason that they get a puppy or a kitten – because they want something to pet. Nobody asks the puppy or the kitten if it wants to be petted – nobody asks the baby.'

Phyllida put out a hand.

'Lydia – please – you mustn't! She loved my father and mother. They were her greatest friends – faraway cousins too. I don't know what would have happened if she hadn't adopted me. There wasn't a penny, you know. Nobody wanted me. I do owe her everything.'

Lydia caught the hand and pinched it lightly.

'All right, chicken. Don't overpay your debts – that's all.'

Phyllida drew back. She opened her lips as if she were going to speak, shut them again, and then said in a hurry, 'Why don't you like Aunt Grace? She's always very nice to you.'

Lydia's eyes were all indignant fire.

'Darling, I adore her – just the same as I adore featherbeds, and bubbly, and pouring myself out in a heart-to-heart talk with someone who makes me feel I'm the only pebble on the beach. I just don't think it's frightfully good for one, that's all. Minute doses and at long intervals, yes, but every day and all day, absolutely and definitely no.'

Phyllida jumped up. She didn't want to quarrel with Lydia, but if she stayed any longer she would have to quarrel – or agree. She went over to where Irene was telling Miss Paradine all about a spot on little Rena's chest.

'It only showed this morning, and of course I

took her temperature at once, and it was normal. I sent for Doctor Horton and he said he didn't think it was anything. Of course he hasn't got young children of his own, and I don't think he takes them seriously enough. I didn't really want to come tonight. The spot had gone, but of course you never can tell, can you, and I knew you'd understand. But Frank was so dreadfully cross that I thought I had better get dressed after all. You know, I think he's really unreasonable about the children. He would be the first to complain if I neglected them, but he seems to think that I can go here, there, and everywhere with him just as I used to before we had a nursery. I do wish you'd speak to him.'

Grace Paradine laid an affectionate hand on her arm. She said, 'You're a very devoted mother, my dear.'

And then Phyllida came up. Irene turned to her.

'Oh, Phyl, I've been so worried all day! It was Rena – she had a spot on her chest, and of course I took her temperature at once . . .'

Grace moved a little away. Frank Ambrose joined her.

'Irene been boring you with the kids' ailments? She's always at it. They're perfectly healthy children, but she worries herself to fiddle-strings over them. If it isn't one thing it's another. She's got a good nurse, and she doesn't trust her a yard. Look here, Aunt Grace, can't you put in a word about it? There isn't anyone else she'd take it from.'

'She's young,' said Grace Paradine in an indulgent tone.

'She won't be if she goes on like she's doing. She can't do this, and she can't do that, and she won't do the other, and it's always the same excuse – Jimmy's nose wants blowing, or Rena's had a sneeze, or a hiccup, or a cough. Why, it was all I could do to get her here tonight.'

Grace Paradine turned a sympathetic look upon him.

'Poor old Frank,' she said.

Lydia, glancing across at them from the other side of the hearth, watched the sulky look fade out of Frank's face. The heavy lines relaxed. He talked. Miss Paradine listened. Every now and then she smiled.

Lydia shot a sparkling glance at Dicky.

'The *best* butter—' she murmured.

But when he stared and said 'Hello – what's that?' she only laughed and said, 'Alice in Wonderland, darling.'

And then the door at the end of the room was opened and three people came in. James Paradine first, very imposing. The black and white of evening dress confers an undue advantage upon those to whom much has already been given. Mr Paradine stood six-foot-five in his shoes. He carried his height with ease and dignity. His fine head was thickly covered with silver hair, but his eyebrows and the eyes over which they arched were as dark as they had been when he was twenty. The ruby and gold of the room became merely background when he came in. A little behind him on his left was his secretary, Albert Pearson, a bun-faced young man in horn-rimmed spectacles and the kind of dress suit which suggests a peg in a bargain basement. On his other side, Elliot Wray.

Everyone stopped talking. Everyone looked at Elliot. Mr Paradine came up to his sister and observed with smiling malice, 'My dear, you will be charmed to know we have another guest. You were complaining only this morning that ten would not make at all a good table. Well, here is Elliot Wray to make the number up to eleven. We had some business together, and I have prevailed upon him to stay.'

THREE

ELLIOT WRAY, COMING into the room, looked down the length of it to the group of black and white figures about the glowing hearth. They were small and far away – black figures and white figures of the women, black-and-white figures of the men, with the dazzle of firelight behind them and a brightness of gilding and shimmering glass overhead. The three black figures were Grace Paradine and Irene and Brenda Ambrose, the two white ones were Lydia Pennington and Phyllida. His mind named them in this order because he held it to the task. He held his eyes to each in turn before he let them rest on Phyllida. She was pale, she had grown thinner. She wore a white dress and Grace Paradine's pearls. She stood between Mark and Irene, and she was looking up at Mark. Elliot had come more than halfway up the room behind James Paradine before she turned and saw him.

It was something in Mark's face that made her turn. Those gloomy, brooding eyes of his had waked up, become startled, interested. Phyllida turned to know why, and saw her husband. She hadn't seen him for a year, and she couldn't believe that she saw him now. The sheer unbelievable shock of it made her put out a hand and clutch at Mark Paradine's arm. And then, before she had time to think, everything in her raced and sang – her blood, her heart, the thoughts which she could neither understand nor control. Colour and beauty rushed upon her. She had one of those moments which are outside time and reason.

Elliot Wray went past her to his hostess and gave her a formal greeting which was as formally received. He shook hands with Irene and Brenda, found Lydia stretching up on tiptoe to kiss him on the cheek, and came to a standstill before his wife. His brief, 'Hello, Phyllida!' might have been spoken to the merest acquaintance. Then he turned back to Lydia. Lane opened the door and announced that dinner was served. James Paradine offered his arm to Irene, and the others fell in behind them, Phyllida with Mark, Brenda with Elliot, Lydia with Dicky and Albert Pearson, and Grace Paradine with Frank Ambrose.

In the large dining room more colour, more gilt, more bright unshaded lights. A wallpaper of sealing-wax red was mitigated by a row of gloomy family portraits – three generations of Paradines in black broadcloth, and the wives of two of them in velvet and brocade. All had the appearance of being tolerably uncomfortable in their best clothes and large, expensive frames. They all stared downwards at the company taking their seats.

James Paradine remained standing for a moment at the head of the table. His eye travelled round it. He inclined his head a trifle and said in a conversational voice, 'For what we are about to receive may the Lord make us truly thankful.' After which he too sat down, and Lane placed a massive silver soup tureen before him. In this, as in other matters, Mr Paradine preferred the elder fashion. He liked to ladle out the soup for his guests, and to carve for them at the head of his own table. He intended to do both tonight. He liked to see the board spread with a snowy damask tablecloth, the naked mahogany reserved ceremonially for the dessert and wine, and what he liked he had.

Elliot found himself on the left of the table between Brenda and Lydia. There was a monstrous silver epergne between him and Phyllida on the other side of the table. The decoration afforded brief views of her when she turned, now to Mark on her left, and again to Albert on her right. A chance-caught glimpse of dark curling hair, of the turn of a cheek no longer pale but vividly coloured – these came his way, but not much more. In the face of sharp exasperation he told himself that what he was feeling was relief. Why should he want to look at Phyllida? There was more between them than a clutter of vegetation. He turned to Lydia. Her eyes were sparkling up at him.

'Why did he say grace? He doesn't as a rule, so we all sat down. Do you suppose we're going to receive something very special?'

'I shouldn't wonder.'

'Do you know what it is?'

He said drily, 'Wait and see.' And then, 'Where have you been, and what are you doing?'

'Been? All over the place. Doing? My duty of course. Don't I always?'

'Well, shall we say, what form has it been taking? You're not a WAAF, or a Wren, or an AT, are you, by any chance?'

The green eyes looked mournful, the red head was shaken.

'I feel I might go off pop if I signed papers and promised to do what I was told. I just sit in an office and translate things.'

'What sort of things?'

'Ssh! Not a word! What would you say if I told you I could read Icelandic at sight?'

Elliot laughed.

'I should say you were lying.'

'And you'd be too, too right. What it is to be a brain! How many things have you invented since 1940? It was 1940 the last time I saw you, wasn't it?'

'It was.'

She nodded.

'Last New Year's Eve. I kissed you under the mistletoe. Perhaps I will again if you're good.'

'I don't feel at all good, I'm afraid.'

She raised her brows which were becomingly darkened to match the darkened lashes.

'How odd, darling! How do you think Phyllida is looking?'

If she hoped for a rise she didn't get one.

'I haven't had much opportunity of judging, have I?'

Lydia darted a glance at him.

'No, you haven't, so I'll tell you. She's too pale, she's too thin. She's unhappy, she's bored, and she's tied up hand and foot. What are you going to do about it? You can be thinking up the answer whilst I talk to Dicky. And don't stab me in the back, because it'll make a mess of my brocade, and I can't afford a funeral this month anyway – not after paying my income tax and the rent of my flat.'

The last words were said over her shoulder. Before they were fairly out of her mouth Dicky was saying, 'Look here, fair's fair. I took you in, didn't I? You've got to talk to me till Aunt Grace is done with Frank.'

Elliot addressed himself to a sulky and offended Brenda. It took so little to offend her that on any other occasion he might not have bothered to bring her round, but in the circumstances he had to be talking, to be interested, occupied – anything but the discarded husband lingering superfluous on the scene. He exerted himself to such purpose that Brenda relaxed sufficiently to inform him that she was thinking of joining the Women Police.

'What a marvellous idea!'

She stared suspiciously.

'What do you mean by that, Elliot?'

'What should I mean? I think it's a perfectly splendid idea.'

Brenda sniffed.

'Well, I can't say that I do, and I can't say I'm looking forward to it. But if you grant the necessity for women police you will agree that they require a personnel, and that being the case, I feel it my duty to apply for enrolment.'

'I expect you'll enjoy it.'

The pale eyes stared aggressively from between those very light lashes. He found himself thinking, 'Why on earth doesn't she dye them?' and then remembered that there had been a row, a really epic row, because Lydia suggested her doing so. Phyllida had told him all about it. Echoes of her voice – the way she had looked . . . He stiffened, and heard Brenda disclaim any intention of enjoying herself.

Dicky was saying to Lydia, 'I suppose you know that you're giving me palpitations every time I look at you.'

'"*Heart-throbs*" – by Richard Paradine.' Lydia gazed back at him soulfully. 'What a pity you can't work it off in verse. It would get it out of your system beautifully, and I'd love to have a book of poems dedicated to me. White leather, I think, with a little gold tooling and "To Lydia" inside – or perhaps just "To L—". What do you think?'

'The critics might get ribald about "To L—". What about "To Lydia whom I adore"?'

'"Because she is never a bore",' said Lydia. 'Which would you rather be, Dicky – hideously, revoltingly ugly and very amusing, or frightfully beautiful and dull? I've never been able to make up my mind.'

'You don't have to – you've got the best of both bargains.'

She sketched a kiss and blew it at him.

'Thank you, darling – and all the nicer because it isn't true. If it wasn't for my hair and my complexion and the fact that I dye my eyelashes, I'd be nothing but Irene's younger sister – "a plain little thing, but not her fault, poor girl, so we must be kind to her". And so much better for my moral character, because I would simply have *had* to go in for the domestic virtues – the only refuge of the plain.'

Dicky's head swam a little. It always did when Lydia looked at him like that. He said, 'Look here, do you want me to propose to you whilst you're eating turkey? Because that's where you're heading.'

'I don't know—' said Lydia, in a meditative tone. 'It would be a new experience – no one's ever done it before. But a man did once tell me he adored me when we were having mulligatawny soup, and he choked in the middle and very nearly passed out. It was rather unnerving, and my soup got cold whilst I thumped him on the back. So perhaps not. I'd hate to spoil the turkey.'

Phyllida was between Albert Pearson and Mark Paradine. Conversation with Albert was instructive rather than entertaining. He was always ready to tell you the distance from Saturn to the earth and from Colombo to Singapore, or the exact number of vitamins in the new margarine, or the origin of coal, or all about who invented steel – a mine of information produced in such a manner as to rob it of any possible spark of interest.

Long practice enabled Phyllida to smile and let instruction pass her by.

When he had finished telling her a few facts about concrete, she turned back to Mark, and thought as she turned how unhappy he looked. Irene on his other side was talking to James Paradine. Mark was for the moment unattached. His face in repose was so gloomy that it worried Phyllida.

She said, 'What are you thinking about?' and smiled.

The heavy lines relaxed.

'Nothing worth talking about, Phyl.'

'Well, what shall we talk about? Have you been reading anything good lately?'

He took the opening with relief. They talked about books, about films, about music. To Elliot on the other side of the table they seemed very deep in conversation. The epergne screened them, but once when Phyllida leaned sideways he saw her shining eyes and brilliant cheeks. The champagne in her glass was untasted – it was something else which had lighted all her candles. As he pursued a rather laboured conversation with Brenda he was wondering just what had lighted them. His first sight of her in the drawing-room had showed her pale and listless. Or was that just his imagination? No, it wasn't. His heart had turned over because she looked so pale.

Brenda Ambrose was staring at him with an air of offence.

'*Really*, Elliot – I don't believe you heard what I was saying!'

He dragged his thoughts from Phyllida and made the best amends he could.

The turkey disposed of, a flaming plum pudding was set before James Paradine, while Lane and a parlourmaid handed jellies and mince pies. It was when Phyllida was helping herself to a spoonful of jelly that the turn of her body brought her into Elliot's view. He saw her and looked away. The eyes which he had wrenched from her face became fixed upon the hand with which she was steadying the proffered dish. It was her left hand, and it was as bare as the day she was born – a bare hand and a bare arm – nothing to break the line from shoulder to wrist, from wrist to fingertips. The painful colour rushed into his face, burned there, and receded slowly, leaving him cold. It had not occurred to him that she would take off her wedding ring. Catching him unprepared like that, it was like a slap in the face.

When the hot blood had sunk, he was as coldly angry as he had ever been in his life.

FOUR

GRACE PARADINE FACED her brother down the length of the table. She had had her moment of blinding anger, but for all that anyone could see it had passed. She was the charming, gracious hostess, friend and confidante, of all the family. For twenty years it had been, 'Ask Aunt Grace – Aunt Grace will know', whenever there was anything to be done. Only Elliot Wray had stood aloof, made her no confidences – had asked her for nothing at all and had taken Phyllida. She thought of him always as a thief. He had stolen, he had robbed, but he hadn't been able to keep what he had taken. Phyllida had come back. That James should have brought Elliot here, and tonight of all nights in the year; that Elliot should be so lost to all sense of decency as to come – these were things which were hardly to be believed. The anger which had shaken her had been the sharpest that she could remember. She had controlled it. If her colour was high, it became her well enough. She talked perhaps a little less than usual, but how charmingly she listened to Dicky as he spoke of Lydia, to Frank Ambrose as he pursued a long complaint about Irene, about Brenda.

'It's an extraordinary thing women can't get on together. Those two girls are always sparring.'

'I know. I'm so sorry.'

'Men don't have these senseless quarrels. After all, Brenda is ten years older than Irene. You'd think she'd be glad to have her advice about the children, about the house. After all, Brenda and I did keep house together for nine years. You'd think Irene would be glad of her experience, but no, it's hands off at every turn. Of course Brenda resents it, and I feel she's been driven from her home, or what used to be her home. Don't you think you could get Irene to see that?'

Grace Paradine looked grave.

'I don't know, my dear. Irene doesn't care about advice. It might do more harm than good.'

He reddened.

'She's utterly unreasonable.'

Grace Paradine smiled.

'Young wives very often are. You must just be patient, Frank.'

Lane and the parlourmaid were removing the cloth. The epergne was lifted to the sideboard, to be replaced upon the bare mahogany by a ritual display of hot-house grapes, stem ginger, and apples on silver dishes. Heavy cut-glass decanters with port, sherry, and madeira were placed in front of James Paradine.

Across the empty board Elliot saw Phyllida. She was lovely. She had been his. She was a stranger. A lovely stranger with Phyllida's hair and Phyllida's eyes, and the lips which he had kissed. There wasn't anything left, there wasn't anything left at all – she was a stranger. In the coldness of his anger he looked, and looked away. Lane reached between him and Lydia and set the epergne in its place again.

James Paradine gave Irene the thimbleful of port which was all that she would take, poured half a glass of sherry for Brenda on his left, and sent the decanters coasting. They went down to Grace Paradine at the other end of the table and came back again. Lane and Louisa had withdrawn. James Paradine pushed back his chair and rose. Standing there with the light shining brightly upon him, he bore a remarkable resemblance to the portrait immediately behind him, that of Benjamin Paradine, his grandfather, founder of the family fortune and of the Paradine Works. There was the same great height, the same contrast of silver hair and bold black eyebrows, the same keen glance, the same clear-cut features, dominant nose, and hard, sharp chin. Not a handsome face, not even an attractive one, but the face of a man who knows what he wants and gets it.

James Paradine stood with his back to the portrait and addressed the assembled family.

'Before we drink our usual toasts I have something to say. It has been my custom to celebrate New Year's Eve with a family gathering. It has not been my custom to interpose a speech at this particular juncture, but tonight I ask your indulgence. I can promise you two things – I shall be brief, and you will not be bored.' He paused here, saw that they were all looking at him – carelessly, intently, with surprise – and continued. 'The matter is personal, but unfortunately not pleasant. This is a family party. Everyone here is a member of the family, everyone here is connected with it either by blood or by marriage.' His eyes travelled round the table. 'Brenda – Elliot – Lydia – Richard – Grace – Frank – Albert – Phyllida – Mark – Irene – here you all are, as you were last year. And what I have to say to you is just this – one of you has been disloyal. A family holds together because of its common interests. If these interests are betrayed, there can be no security. I am stating as an incontrovertible fact that one of you has betrayed these interests. I am not saying this in order to surprise the guilty person into some sign of guilt. I need no such sign, for I know who this guilty person is.'

He paused again, and again looked round the table. Nobody's expression had changed, but there was in every case an intensification, a hardening, as if stiffening muscles had caught and held it. Brenda's light eyes stared aggressively, Elliot had a look of cold control, Lydia a smile which had caught a tinge of incredulity and kept it because her lips were stiff and could not change their curve. Dicky frowned, his eyes as fixed as Lydia's smile. Grace Paradine sat upright in her chair, a hand on either of its arms, her head just resting against the tall carved back. Frank Ambrose had an elbow on the table, a big pale hand half covering mouth and chin as he leaned upon it. Albert Pearson had taken his glasses off. Without them his shortsighted eyes blinked at the light and the blur of faces. He polished them in a fumbling sort of way and put them on again. Phyllida's hands were clasped together in her lap. They were as cold as ice. Her eyes, wide and frightened, looked away from old James Paradine, looked for Elliot Wray. The epergne was between – she couldn't see him. She leaned sideways, but all she could see was his hand about the stem of a wineglass. The knuckles of the hand were white. She did not know that she was touching Mark, leaning hard against his shoulder. She couldn't see Elliot's face. Mark Paradine was the one who seemed least affected. His air of gloom remained. He looked straight in front of him, and felt Phyllida lean against his shoulder. Irene had uttered a faint gasping cry. She sat back in her chair and gazed at her father-in-law with an expression of terror. James Paradine, who had always thought her a very silly young woman, now had his opinion confirmed. That Irene was behaving exactly as he would have expected her to behave was gratifying. He continued his speech.

'I don't want there to be any mistake about that, so I will repeat it – I know who the guilty person is. I take this means of communicating the fact for several reasons. Punishment is one of them. That person is not in a very enviable position. That person is wondering at this moment whether I am going to name him – or her. Well, I am not going to do that – not at this time, not just now – perhaps not at all. That will depend upon the person himself – or herself. I am inclined to clemency, whether from family feeling, from the desire to wash dirty linen in decent privacy, or for some other reason. I therefore state that after we rise from this festive board I shall be in my study until midnight. The person whom I have refrained from naming will find me there, and find me prepared to make terms. This is all that I have to say. We will now proceed to drink our usual toasts. I give you the Paradine-Moffat Works coupled with the names of John Cadogan and Elliot Wray, to whose outstanding designs the whole country owes so much. May output continue on an ever ascending curve and invention lead the way.' He lifted his glass.

There was no answering stir about the table. Irene took a choking breath. It was very nearly a sob. Frank Ambrose said 'Sir!' on a protesting note. Grace Paradine alone leaned forward and took up her glass.

James said incisively, 'No one except the guilty person can have any objection to drinking this toast. I am afraid I shall regard abstinence in the light of a public confession. I gave you the Paradine-Moffat Works.'

This time every glass was lifted. Phyllida's just touched her lips and was set down again. Irene's hand shook so much that the wine spilled over and left red drops upon the bright mahogany. Somewhat belatedly, Elliot responded with a 'Thank you very much, sir.'

James Paradine lifted his glass again.

'To absent friends.'

The tension, which had almost reached breaking point, slackened a little. There was to be no immediate, irremediable disaster.

The third toast followed.

'Sweethearts and wives.'

James Paradine gave it out with a subtle change of voice and manner. There was the suggestion of a challenge. He looked from Irene to Frank, from Phyllida to Elliot Wray. He looked at Lydia and Dicky. He went on smoothly, 'With this toast I couple the memory of my wife.' This time he drained his glass and sat down.

A breath of relief went round. The worst was over. Grace Paradine looked at Irene and pushed back her chair.

FIVE

THE DRAWING ROOM was a haven. With the door shut upon them, the women looked at each other.

'What is it all about?' Brenda's voice was at its bluntest. 'Has he gone mad?'

Miss Paradine showed distress.

'My dear, I don't know any more than you do.'

'He must be mad!' said Brenda. 'To get us all here to a party and then say a thing like that! It's the limit!'

Irene had been trembling. She now burst into tears.

'I know he thinks it's me – and I haven't done anything – I really haven't. And I didn't want to come – Frank will tell you I didn't. He was angry with me because I wanted to stay with my baby, and I wish – oh, how I wish – I hadn't listened to him! What does he think I've done? And why does he think it's me? I don't even know what he was talking about. Why shouldn't it be anyone else?'

After a good deal of groping she had managed to produce a handkerchief. It was unfortunate that a pause in the process of dabbing at her eyes should have disclosed them apparently fixed upon her sister-in-law. Brenda stared angrily back.

'Meaning it might have been me, I suppose. Thank you very much, Irene! Frank will appreciate that, won't he?'

Grace Paradine put out a hand to each.

'My dears – my dears – we really mustn't! Irene – Brenda! This is quite bad enough without our doing anything to make it worse. I feel that there must be some terrible mistake. If we think of it that way we can help each other, and help to set things right. Don't you see? And we mustn't lose our heads or say anything we're going to be sorry for tomorrow. Now, Irene, dry your eyes. Would you like to go up to Phyllida's room? . . . No? Well, I'm sure Lydia can give you some powder. Lane will be coming in with the coffee, and you mustn't look as if you had been crying. Phyl darling, you and Lydia can look after Irene. Of course no one suspects her of anything – it's too ridiculous. Brenda and I are going to have a nice talk. How long is it since we had one, my dear? Not for months, I do believe. Come along over here.'

Brenda was only too glad to have an audience. Her grievances were many, and she minced no words in stating them.

'What on earth do men want to marry for? Frank and I were perfectly happy together. And look at him now! Irene thinks of nothing but the children. Of course that's what's wrong with her – she's stupid. Why, she can't even keep house. The bills are double what they were, and nothing to show for it.'

Grace Paradine smiled.

'Well, my dear, we can't all be such good housekeepers as you are. Frank is always saying how marvellous you were.'

'Yes – *were!*' Brenda's tone was dry and bitter. 'Why couldn't she let us alone? Frank would never have thought about her if she hadn't thrown herself at his head. And now she's got him she doesn't want him.' A dull, ugly red was clouding the sallow skin. The hard mouth twitched.

Grace Paradine experienced some alarm. It was really going to be exceedingly difficult to get through the evening without a scene. On the other side of the hearth she could see Irene, still dabbing at her eyes and ignoring the powder puff and compact which Lydia was holding out. She took a sudden decision, laid a hand on Brenda's shoulder, and stood up.

'My dears—' the movement and her voice caught everyone's attention – 'my dears, I had a little remembrance for each of you. I'm just going to run upstairs and get them. I don't see why a stupid contretemps should prevent me from giving my presents. Phyl, you come over and talk to Brenda. I shan't be a moment . . . No, darling, I'd rather get them myself – I know just where they are.'

Turning at the door to look back, she felt relief. Irene was powdering her nose, and even Brenda would find it difficult to quarrel with Phyl. But she must be quick. It wouldn't do to risk anything. In spite of stately proportions she was light on her feet. She picked up her dress and ran up the stairs almost as quickly as Phyllida would have done.

She was down again before Irene had finished doing her face, and while Brenda was still answering Phyllida's questions about some mutual friends. She came in with four little parcels tied up in Christmas paper – gold holly leaves and scarlet berries on a white ground, with different coloured ties, silver for Irene, scarlet for Brenda, green for Lydia, and gold for Phyllida.

'Only little things,' she said in a deprecating voice.

They were unwrapping them, when the door was thrown open and Lane came in processionally, bearing a vast silver tray set out with the coffee equipage and followed by Louisa with a massive cake-stand.

Miss Paradine drew a breath of satisfaction. No scene could have been more natural or more pleasantly familiar – herself gracious and charming, with her gifts dispensed; the four girls unfolding the bright paper; the tray set down on the low walnut table; the heavily moulded silver coffee-pot, milk jug and sugar basin; the old Worcester cups, dark blue and gold. It might have been any New Year's Eve in any other year.

Louisa set down the cake-stand, which contained a Christmas cake in the bottom tier, and in the other two mixed biscuits and chocolate fingers. Everything had a secure, established look. Everything was time-honoured and according to custom – Lane with his twenty years of service, his portly presence, his bald head with its fringe of fine grey hair; Louisa, a worthy second-in-command, upright in character as in carriage, her figure restrained by the stays of an elder fashion, her hair done over a cushion and supporting an authentic Edwardian cap. The picture was reassuring in the extreme.

The procession withdrew. Aunt Grace was kissed and thanked. Lydia's favourite bath salts – 'Where *did* you get them?' A torch for Brenda – 'That's what I call really useful.' A snapshot of Jimmy and Rena, enlarged and framed, for Irene – 'Oh, Aunt *Grace!*' And for Phyllida half a dozen handkerchiefs, cobweb-soft and fine, with her name embroidered across a corner – 'Oh, darling, you shouldn't! Your coupons!' They were all clustering about her, smiling, chattering, when the door opened again and the men came in.

But only five of them. The tall, dominant figure of James Paradine was not there.

SIX

MISS PARADINE HAD more gifts to distribute – unwrapped this time, and most unobtrusively slipped into the hand of each of the four men for whose presence she had been prepared. The fact that there was a fifth guest was quite smoothly ignored. Elliot Wray was ignored. The others received a small pocket diary each, compact and useful, with pencil attached – brown leather for Frank, scarlet for Dicky, blue for Mark, and purple for Albert Pearson. Not by look or word was the fact so much as glanced at that an uninvited guest was present.

Elliot found himself with a twinge of bitter amusement which passed rapidly into anger. It wasn't taking very much to make him angry tonight. The present occasion was trivial, but beneath its triviality, like the tide beneath a floating straw, there was an unanswerable weight, a cold opposing force. He had discerned it always, but he had never been so conscious of it as now. Sharply across a surge of resentment, that bitter humour expended itself in a zigzag flash. Did he get any coffee, or was he just not here at all?

Hard upon that, Lydia came over to him with a

cup in her hand. Their eyes met. Hers flashed. He said, 'But this is yours.'

'I'll get another.'

On the edge of the group, voices low against the background of talk, they might have been alone – the coffee cup between them; Lydia's hand raised to offer it; Elliot's just touching the saucer but not yet accepting; she looking up, her green eyes bright; he looking down with the smoulder of anger in his.

She said, 'Don't be a fool.' And he, 'I was a fool to stay.'

'Why did you?'

'He made a point of it. A matter of business.'

The pronoun held no ambiguity. *He* in that house was James Paradine.

The long dark lashes flickered.

'Only that?'

'What else?'

She laughed.

'I don't dot other people's 'i's for them. Here, take your coffee! *And don't be a fool.*'

She left the cup in his hand and was gone.

After a moment he followed her, skirting the group about the coffee tray until he came to Phyllida. Standing behind her, he heard Miss Paradine say with resolute cheerfulness, 'We've all got to be as normal as possible – go on just as usual – not give the servants anything to talk about. I do feel that so strongly. Don't you all agree with me? It may not be easy, but I really do think we must just go on as if nothing had happened. I don't know, I can't think, what has put this idea into James's head, but if we allow ourselves to be disturbed by it, he – oh, don't you see, if anyone behaves differently, he'll think it's because the thing he said is true. So we mustn't behave differently – nobody must. Everything must be just as it was last year.

Elliot Wray said at Phyllida's shoulder, 'On the strength of that, suppose we sit down and talk. That was what we did last year, wasn't it?'

She turned, startled, not by his nearness which she had felt, but by a quality in his voice which was new. Of all the tones it had taken for her between love and anger, this one was new. The words were lightly, easily spoken, but they had a cutting edge. It hurt, and just because of that she smiled. The days were gone when she would let him know that he had power to hurt her. She smiled and turned away with him, going towards the couch where she had sat with Lydia. It was only a little way in distance, but it had the effect of isolating them.

Elliot felt a disproportionate elation, but it centred, not about Phyllida, but about Grace Paradine. He had walked his wife away from under her nose, and she couldn't do anything about it. A very pleasing circumstance – very salutary for Miss Paradine. Everything must be just as it was last year? Very well, she should have good measure. Last New Year's Eve he and Phyllida were just back from their honeymoon. A week later they had parted. In that one week their house had crashed down upon their heads. But they had been hand in hand when they saw the New Year in – they had looked for it to bring them happiness. Because of these things he was mindful that he had a debt to pay. He said in that new tone which hurt, 'What shall we talk about?'

But this time Phyllida was ready. When you are pressed hard you use whatever weapons you can. Whether from instinct or from choice, she took the simplest, the least expected, the oldest weapon of all. She smiled and said, 'You. Won't you tell me what you've been doing? I haven't heard anything for so long.'

It was very disarming, but he was not to be disarmed. His resentment held.

'I didn't think you would be interested.'

'Oh, yes.' She spoke quite simply. 'There's so much I want to know. The thing you were working on – did it come out all right? You were worried about it.'

'James Paradine is in the best position to tell you about that.'

She shook her head.

'No. He never talks – you know he doesn't. Besides . . . Did it come out all right?'

'No – we had to scrap it.'

'Oh, what a pity!'

'Not really. We've got something better – much better. That's what I'm up about now.'

Insensibly they were slipping into something easier. She was looking at him with the serious, half-wistful attention which had always touched some spring of confidence and compunction – like a child who is trying very hard but not sure whether it is trying hard enough. He remembered her saying, 'I do love all your things when you talk about them. But I'm not clever – I don't understand them. You won't mind, will you?' And he had said, 'Anyone who likes can be clever. I only want you to be sweet.'

Where had it all gone? They were looking at each other across a blank, lost year. It was gone. How suddenly the path had crumbled before their feet and left them separate.

But Phyllida went on speaking as if there were no gap.

'Where are you living?'

No – if the gap had not been there, she would not have needed to ask him that – 'Where thou lodgest I will lodge . . .'

He answered without any noticeable pause.

'I'm with the Cadogans. It's very good of them, and of course it's very convenient. Only Ida complains that John and I never stop talking shop.'

He thought bitterly, 'So she didn't even know where I was – didn't care. What are we doing, making conversation like this? It's like talking over a grave. She isn't Phyllida – she's a ghost trying to get back into the past. And you can't do it, so what's the good of trying?'

She said, her voice tripping and hesitating, 'Why do you – look like that? What is it?'

'I was thinking you were a ghost.'

Her eyes were on him. He saw them widen a little and wince. Something in him was savagely glad because he had hurt her. He had seen a man look like that when he had had a sudden blow. She said, quick and low, 'Do I look – like a ghost?'

'No.'

She was all colour and bloom, her eyes deep blue and shining, carnation in her cheeks and on her lips – vivid colour which ebbed and flowed. She said, 'Why did you say that? I don't like it.'

'Isn't it true?'

She bent her head, not in assent, but as if she could not look at him any longer. The brilliant colour rose.

'What are you?' she said.

'I wonder—'

'Another ghost?'

He gave a short laugh.

'Ghosts don't haunt each other – or do they?'

'I don't know.' She looked up again. 'Elliot—'

'Yes?'

'Couldn't we just go on talking – about – about ordinary things?'

Something got under his guard. He said, 'I don't know, Phyl. It's a bit late in the day.'

'*Please*, Elliot—' She dropped to her lowest tone. 'It's all been – frightful – hasn't it? This evening, I mean. Irene's been crying, and everything's bad enough without making it worse. *Please*, Elliot—'

'All right, Phyl – without prejudice.'

'Of course. Elliot, what did he mean – what is it all about? Do you know?'

'Well, he was fairly explicit.'

She was leaning towards him.

'Do you think it's true? Do you think someone has really – oh, I don't see how it could be true!'

'Yes. I think it's true.'

The brilliant colour faded. Her eyes were puzzled – frightened. She said, 'What is it?'

And then, before he could answer, Grace Paradine was calling, 'Phyl, darling – Phyl!'

Nothing for it but to go back to the others.

Miss Paradine's smile was a faint one. Her manner showed distress.

'Phyl, they think we ought to break up the party. Frank thinks so. He wants to take Irene home. And perhaps – I did think we ought just to go on, but Irene is very upset, and Frank thinks . . . It's very difficult to know what is best.'

Frank Ambrose stood beside her frowning.

'It's no good, Aunt Grace. You can pretend up to a certain point, but there are limits, and I've reached mine. I'm going home, and I'm taking Irene. Brenda and Lydia can do just as they like.'

'Well, you don't expect us to walk, do you?' said Brenda bluntly.

For once Lydia found herself in agreement. The sooner they all got home the better. Aunt Grace could put a perfectly good face on it with the staff. Nobody did that sort of thing better – 'Mrs Ambrose was anxious about the little girl – she didn't seem quite the thing this afternoon – and as Mr Paradine isn't very well—' She could just hear her doing it, and Lane being respectfully sympathetic.

Goodbyes were said. The Ambrose party trooped away.

Miss Paradine spoke her piece to Lane. It would have amused Lydia very much, because it was almost word for word as she had imagined it – Mrs Ambrose is feeling anxious about her little girl, and the rest.

Ten minutes later Mark and Dicky said good-night. The party was over.

SEVEN

THERE REMAINED IN the big drawing room Elliot, Phyllida, and Grace Paradine, with Albert Pearson as a buffer. It was impossible to say whether he realised the position and found it untenable, or whether he was merely being conscientious when he said that he had work to do and thought he had better be getting down to it. He did not appear nervous, but then Albert never did. Whether he had ever felt unequal to any occasion in the course of his twenty-nine years, was known only to himself. To the world he presented an obstinate efficiency which was sometimes irritating. Infallibility requires a great deal of charm to carry it off. Unfortunately, Albert was deficient in charm. Yet on this occasion three people watched him go with regret.

There was one of those pauses. Phyllida stood by the fire looking down into it, half turned away from the room, her pose one of graceful detachment, her colour high. Grace Paradine had not resumed her seat. A couple of yards away Elliot, with the expression of a polite guest masking some embarrassment and some sarcasm. If she was waiting for him to speak first, she could wait.

They all waited, Phyllida withdrawn, Miss Paradine momentarily more indignant. He had the insolence to come here, to force himself upon them – upon Phyllida! She was going to find it hard to forgive James for abetting him – very hard indeed. The shock to Phyl was unforgivable. And what was he waiting for now, when everyone else was gone? She made a quick movement and said, 'I think we had better say goodnight. Lane will show you out.'

At this moment, which should have increased it, any embarrassment that Elliot had been feeling went up in smoke. He was suddenly so angry that he didn't give a damn. He found himself saying cheerfully, 'Oh, didn't Mr Paradine tell you? I'm afraid I must apologise, but I'm staying the night. We're in the middle of some rather important business, and he insisted on it.'

Miss Paradine was speechless. The blood rushed to her face. Words rushed clamouring to her tongue, driven by the rage which filled her. But for the moment she held them back. Stronger than her resentment, stronger than anything else at all, was the consciousness that Phyllida was listening, and that she must not put herself in the wrong. No matter what the provocation, there must be nothing said or done to swing Phyllida's sympathies over to Elliot's side. She refrained those crowding words and, choosing among them, said, 'No, he did not tell me. I think that I should have been told.'

Elliot could admire what he disliked. He disliked Grace Paradine a good deal, but he had never despised her as an adversary. They had fought for Phyllida, and she had won. Anger over that barren victory swept any faint admiration away.

'I quite agree. But you mustn't hold me responsible. Mr Paradine requires my presence rather urgently – I am certainly not here of my own choice. I have to see him now, so I will say goodnight,' he said.

Grace Paradine inclined her head and stepped back a pace. Elliot looked towards Phyllida, and all at once she turned from the fire and came over to him.

'Goodnight, Elliot.'

He said, 'Goodnight,' and having said it, waited – to see what she would do, or because he found it hard to look away.

She came right up to him, still with that gentle, dreamy air, and put up her cheek to be kissed. It was done so simply, so naturally, as to make his response an involuntary one. His lips just touched her, and withdrew as she withdrew. She looked over her shoulder and said, 'Goodnight, Aunt Grace,' and so went down the room and out of the door.

He had no impulse to follow. Everything in him was shocked into stillness. They had been lovers, and they had parted. They had met as strangers and talked as mere acquaintances. To what remote distance from all their passion of love and anger had Phyllida withdrawn that she could come up to him and offer the kind of kiss you gave your grandfather? His mind was shocked quite numb. He stood where he was and watched Grace Paradine follow Phyllida.

EIGHT

THE NUMBNESS LASTED through his interview with James Paradine. It was not a long one. He had, in fact, made an excuse of it. James was neither expecting him nor desirous of keeping him. He sat grim and sarcastic at his writing table and said, 'Come to confess, have you? Go away! I'm busy, or I'd tell you just what a fool I think you are.'

'Thank you, sir – Lydia has been telling me that.'

'She's too free with her tongue. Wants a husband who'll keep her in order. Richard won't. But I'm talking about you. You're a fool to come visiting me tonight. It's compromising, that's what it is – damned compromising.' He gave a short, hard laugh. 'If anyone saw you, your character's gone. They'll be sure you came to confess.'

'To what?'

'Folly of some kind,' said James Paradine. 'There are more fools than wise men, and I've come to the conclusion that the devil made the fools. Anyhow, be off with you! You'll get your plans in the morning.'

Elliot went out, and was aware of Albert Pearson in the offing, looking earnest.

'If I might have a word with you, Wray—'

Nobody in the world with whom Elliot less desired to have a word than Albert, but impossible to refuse. He did say, 'I thought you had work to do,' but it produced no effect. Albert merely remarked that he could do it later and followed Elliot to his room. It was on the farther side of the bedroom floor, and was the same which had always been assigned to him before he married Phyllida – a fair-sized room which would have looked larger if it had not contained so much furniture. Mahogany bed, wardrobe, chest of drawers, dressing table and wash-stand encroached upon the floor space. There was a writing table, an armchair, and two or three smaller chairs.

Albert came in, shut the door, and said, 'Do you mind if I stay here till after twelve?'

'*What?*'

Albert repeated the horrible remark.

'Do you mind if I stay here till after twelve? You see, he's made it very awkward for me, living in the house. It's all very well for the Ambrose lot – they can go home and be alibis for each other, and so can Richard and Mark. Miss Paradine and Phyllida can stick together if they want to. But what about me after what he said? "I'll be in my study till twelve" – well, who's going to say I didn't go and have an interview with him and confess to what he was hinting about at dinner? I'm the one the family would rather see in a spot than any of themselves – wouldn't they? If you can't see them tumbling over one another to put it on me, I can.

And I'm not having any. My character is my capital, and I'm not risking it. I'll have a witness to prove that I didn't go near him till the time was up.'

Elliot leaned against the footrail of the bed with his hands in his pockets and said with a spice of malice, 'Well, you had a minute or two to confess in before I came along – didn't you?'

Albert shook his head.

'No, I didn't. Lane was in the study when I got there, putting out a tray of drinks – he can speak to that. And I wasn't there half a minute behind him. I suppose nobody imagines I had time to confess to whatever it is in about thirty seconds.'

'It would be quick work.'

'Very well. Then if I stay here till after twelve, they can't put it on me.'

Elliot raised his eyebrows. The hands on the clock on the mantelpiece pointed to a quarter past ten. He had never cottoned to Albert, he was not cottoning to him now. Nearly two hours of Albert neat was a stupefying prospect. Of all things in the world, he desired to be alone. He said in the driest tone at his command, 'I should cut it out and go to bed.'

Albert looked obstinate. All the Paradines could be obstinate, but it was his mother, born Millicent Paradine, who had been nicknamed Milly the Mule.

'I have my character to consider.'

Elliot produced an agreeable smile.

'I could always lock you in and take away the key.'

Albert's resemblance to the late Mrs Pearson was intensified. He walked over to the easy chair and sat down.

'I might have another key. I'm not taking any risks. Besides, have you thought about your own position? Cousin Grace doesn't exactly love you, you know, and what goes for me goes for you. If we sit here together, she can't put anything on either of us. See? I can say you weren't in long enough with him to do any confessing. So it will be all OK for both of us.'

The situation could hardly have been more tersely summed up. The facts were as stated. That there was a certain humour attaching to them was obvious to Elliot. He resigned himself to the inevitable.

Albert having annexed the only armchair, he seated himself upon the bed and prepared to endure. He would at least not be called upon for very much in the way of conversation. No one in England could better sustain a monologue than Albert. A competent analysis of Japanese foreign policy for the last twenty years led on by a natural transition to a résumé of the personal history and career of Marshal Chiang Kai-shek. The words flowed over Elliot without really impinging upon his mind or impeding the processes of his thought. They were even vaguely soothing. Albert's voice rose and fell. There was not the slightest need to listen to what he was saying. Elliot did not listen.

He came to the surface at intervals and was aware of Albert discoursing on Communism, on

Proportional Representation, on the life history of the eel, but for the most part he remained submerged beneath the flow of his own thoughts and of Albert's persistent monologue.

NINE

AS SOON AS Phyllida had closed the drawing-room door behind her she picked up her long white skirt and ran like the wind, up the stair, along the passage and into her room which was at the end of it. Before she so much as switched on the light she was turning the key in the lock. Nobody was going to come and talk to her tonight, not for anything in the world. The door was locked, and locked it would remain.

She put on the light and looked about her with relief. After the crimson and mahogany of the rest of the house the room was charming – cream walls, and pale blue curtains with a delicate pattern of shells; quite modern furniture, silver-grey and polished only by hand; a silver bed with pale blue sheets and pillows and a blue and silver eiderdown; a grey unpatterned carpet. Everything in it was fresh and simple. Everything in it had been chosen by Grace Paradine.

Phyllida stood in the middle of the room hesitating. She was waiting for what she knew would come – the tap on the door, the voice speaking her name.

'Phyl – darling – won't you let me in?'

She could see the handle turn and turn back

again. She said quickly, 'Oh, is that you, Aunt Grace? I'm just rushing into bed—'

'I only wanted to say goodnight.'

'Goodnight, Aunt Grace.'

There was a pause before the footsteps withdrew. Phyllida took a long breath. Now she was really alone. The first thing she did was to switch on all the lights, one over the dressing table, another lighting the long wall mirror. The room glowed – cream and silver and forget-me-not blue, and Phyllida in her white dress.

She stood looking into the glass and saw the room and herself as if she were looking through a narrow panel with a silver frame at another girl in another room. So much light and brilliance, so much colour and bloom. This wasn't the girl she had seen in the glass every day for a year. 1941 was going out, taking that girl with it. Phyllida never wanted to see her again. This was someone else. She looked and looked, and came up close to see into that other Phyllida's eyes. And then all at once she turned away, went slowly over to the door, and put out all the lights except the shaded one beside the bed. Still slowly, she came over to the fire and sat down beside it on a small low chair. A quarter of an hour went by.

At last she got up, crossed over to the door, and opened it. The passage stretched before her, dark and empty, the bright overhead light switched off and just a twilight glow coming up from the well of the stairs. Everything was quiet. She stood listening, and could hear no sound at all.

When a full minute had gone by she came out of the room and, shutting the door noiselessly behind her, began to walk along the corridor. Two doors on this side, a bathroom and Grace Paradine's bedroom and sitting room on the other. Then a short flight to the central landing and wide steps going down into the hall.

On the bottom step she stood again and listened. One light burned in the hall all night. It showed the dining-room and drawing-room doors on her left, the library door and the baize door leading to what was called the west wing on the right. This west wing contained the set of rooms which James Paradine had arranged for his wife when she became an invalid – bedroom, sitting room, bathroom, and dressing room. They looked upon the terrace and the river, and were entered from a passage which lay between them and the library and billiard room. At the far end a staircase led to the bedroom floor above. The room which had been Mrs Paradine's bedroom had never been occupied since her death, but James Paradine used the bathroom, slept in the dressing room, and had turned the sitting room into a study.

In this study he sat and waited, his eyes on the door, his ears alert to catch the slightest sound. On the writing table in front of him an orderly arrangement of blotting pad, pen tray, writing block, and the handsome silver inkstand presented to him by his employees on the occasion of his marriage. Across the corner of the table on his left *The Times*.

He had been sitting like this for some time almost without moving, when the faintest of faint taps sounded upon the door. It was so small a sound that it might easily have passed unnoticed. As if he had been waiting for it, James Paradine said, 'Come in!'

Impossible to say whether the appearance of Phyllida was a surprise to him or not. She came in almost with a rush, and then, as if the impetus had spent itself, stood leaning against the door, still holding on to the handle.

'Can I speak to you, Uncle James?'

He was looking at her with that keen, bright look of his which had frightened her when she was a little girl. It came very near to frightening her now. Her breath quickened and her eyes had a startled look.

James Paradine said, 'Certainly, Phyllida. Come and sit down. If you will just turn the key, we can make sure that we are not disturbed.'

She turned it, came to the other side of the table, and took the chair in which Elliot had sat an hour or two before. For a moment that wide, startled gaze remained fixed on James Paradine's face. Then she flushed deeply and looked away.

His lips moved into a faint sarcastic smile.

'Well, Phyllida – have you come to confess?' he said.

She looked up again at that.

'I suppose I have, Uncle James.'

'And what are you going to confess?'

She said quickly, 'When you said that at dinner – you didn't – you didn't mean Elliot?'

'And what makes you think that?'

'Because he wouldn't – he *couldn't*—'

'Very proper sentiments, my dear. A wife should always be convinced of her husband's integrity.'

As if the cynicism in his voice was a challenge, Phyllida's head came up. She said with simplicity and pride, 'You think I haven't the right to speak for Elliot any more. Perhaps I haven't. But there are some things I know he wouldn't do.'

James Paradine nodded.

'Quite right, my dear, and admirably put. To relieve your mind, I will assure you that I am not expecting a confession from your husband. Now what about yours?'

She looked down again.

'It isn't really a confession – except that I think – I have been – I don't know how to say it—'

'A fool?' suggested James Paradine.

He got a fleeting glance, startled again, but with a faraway hint of rueful laughter.

'Perhaps – I don't know. That's what I wanted to talk to you about.'

'And why to me? I thought Grace was the universal confidante.'

Phyllida said in a desperate voice, 'She cares too much. I want to talk about it to someone who doesn't care—' She paused and added, 'like that.'

James Paradine surveyed her with an odd glint of humour in his eyes.

'The detached point of view. I see. Well, go on.'

She said, 'I don't know what Aunt Grace told you last year – about Elliot and me.'

His black eyebrows lifted.

'Let me see – you came back from your honeymoon, spent Christmas in London with the Lionel Wrays, and came on to us on the thirtieth of December. We had our usual party on New Year's Eve, and on the sixth – or was it the seventh – of January, Grace informed me that you had parted.'

'Did she say why?'

'She said' – James Paradine's voice was extremely dry – 'to the best of my recollection she said that he had "proved himself utterly unworthy", and she intimated that you had grounds for a divorce. It seemed rather early in the day. May I ask whether you are going to tell me what really happened?'

Phyllida said, 'Yes.' She lifted her eyes and looked at him. 'I haven't talked about it to anyone. People care too much, or they don't care enough, and they want to give you advice.'

'A damnable habit,' said James Paradine. And then, 'I appreciate the compliment.'

Phyllida kept her eyes on him.

'Aunt Grace has done everything for me – everything in the world. I'm *very* grateful. But sometimes when people love you so much it makes you feel as if you couldn't move without hurting them. When I got engaged to Elliot I felt like that – I was hurting Aunt Grace, and I was going to hurt her more, and I couldn't help it. She didn't like him.'

James Paradine nodded.

'No, she didn't like him. I may say, my dear, that there wasn't a millionth chance of her liking anyone you proposed to marry.'

She had that startled look again.

'It made me very unhappy, but I couldn't help it. We were married, and we went away on our honeymoon. Two days afterwards Aunt Grace got a letter which had been delayed in the post. It was from a friend of hers, that Mrs Cranston whom I never liked, and it was about Elliot.'

'Women have a remarkable talent for interfering in other people's affairs,' said James Paradine.

'She said she thought Aunt Grace ought to know that he – that he—'

'Yes, my dear?'

She had turned rather pale. She said, 'There was a motor accident. He had a girl with him and she was hurt. She was taken into the Cranstons' house – that's how Mrs Cranston knew about it. Elliot was driving. Of course they had to give their names and addresses. The girl's name was Maisie Dale. Mrs Cranston said they'd been staying at a roadhouse.'

Mr Paradine again raised his eyebrows.

'Is that all?'

'No, of course not. It's just – I haven't ever talked about it – it's not very easy.'

'I see. Will you go on?'

She nodded.

'Yes. There was a lot more. I didn't see the letter – I didn't want to. I think she's a horrid woman, but I think she just wrote down what people were saying – about Elliot and the girl. Aunt Grace was dreadfully upset. We were married. Mrs Cranston said that Elliot was keeping up with the girl. I don't know how she knew.'

'She's the sort of woman who makes it her business to know,' said James Paradine. 'By the way, was the girl badly hurt?'

'Oh, no, Mrs Cranston said she wasn't – just knocked out. She said she was quite all right as soon as she came round.'

'I see. Go on.'

Phyllida coloured high. Her eyes avoided him.

'Aunt Grace – she wanted to find out – whether it was true. She got someone to make enquiries.'

'How extremely – enterprising.'

'She – she thought she was doing the right thing. When we came back I saw that she wasn't happy. I didn't know what to do about it – I thought it was just because I had gone away. Then one day she came into my room and told me. She read me Mrs Cranston's letter, and just as she was finishing it Elliot came in. You see, I hadn't any time to think. It all happened like an accident does – one minute you're all right and the next minute everything crashed. Elliot said, 'What's going on?' and Aunt Grace said, 'Phyllida would like to know what you have to say about Maisie Dale.' She didn't even give me time to speak.'

'I suppose not.'

She was looking at him again, her eyes bright and her colour high.

'Elliot was very angry – they both were. Aunt

Grace said, "You spent a weekend with her at Pedlar's Halt, in June," and he said, "It's none of your business if I did." Then she said, "Will you deny that you are keeping her?" and he said, "That isn't your business either." Then she said, "Will you deny that you visited her only last week, on the afternoon of December 26th?" and he said, "I won't deny anything. And now will you get out of here and leave me to talk to my wife!"'

'And did she – get out?'

Phyllida shook her head.

'She said, "You think you can talk her round".'

'And what did you say, Phyllida?'

'I didn't say anything – I didn't say anything at all. It sounds idiotic, but even when I go over it in my mind – and I've been over it hundreds of times – I can't think of anything to say. Everything goes numb – I don't even seem to feel anything, or to want anything, or to be able to speak. I just felt as if I had come to the end of everything. It still feels like that when I think about it. I could hear them saying dreadful things to each other. And then Elliot said, "I'm off. Are you coming, Phyllida?" Aunt Grace came and put her arms round me and said, "No," and Elliot went out of the room and banged the door, and – it was very stupid of me – I fainted. I thought he would come back, but he didn't, and I thought he would write, but he didn't. And Aunt Grace said he had gone to *her*.'

'Are you sure he didn't write?'

'What do you mean?'

'Well, I should have expected him to write.'

'He didn't.'

'I think I should ask him about that if I were you.'

She said, 'Ask him?'

'Why certainly. Now that he is here, you surely don't intend to let him go again without talking things over?'

'Oh—'

James Paradine leaned back in his chair and contemplated her.

'The whole affair has been a little totalitarian up to date, hasn't it? The prosecution very ably represented, but no counsel for the defence, and the accused not given a hearing.'

Phyllida said 'Oh—' again. And then, 'Uncle James, let me go on. I want to tell you about tonight.'

'By all means.'

'When Elliot came into the room—'

'Yes, my dear?'

'I've been very unhappy – I didn't know one could be as unhappy as that – but when Elliot came into the room it all went. As soon as I saw him it all went away. I was *frightfully* happy.'

'So I observed.'

'Oh—'

'My dear, you can't fly all your flags and not expect anyone to notice them.'

They were flying now. She said in a soft, sighing voice, 'It didn't seem to matter any more – I just didn't care.' Then, very earnestly, 'That's why I had to come and talk to you. Is it just because I'm so tired of being unhappy? I mean, is it just letting go and not caring about the things one ought to care about? That's what I want to know. You see, Aunt Grace cares too much, and I care too much, and I don't know whether Elliot cares at all. Perhaps he doesn't now.'

'I should ask him,' said James Paradine briskly. He leaned forward, pulled out one of the writing-table drawers, and produced a tin box with a patriotic design upon the lid. Opened, it disclosed boiled sweets in variety. James selected a lemon drop and offered the box to Phyllida.

'Have a lollipop, my dear, and stop thinking about yourself. There's Elliot, you know. Even accused persons have rights – and feelings. I should give him a hearing. Someone's been at these sweets of mine – I've been suspecting it for some time. Albert? No, I don't think so – too human a failing. I often have serious doubts as to whether Albert is really human. Whom would you suspect? What's the name of the apple-cheeked child who turns puce when I meet her in a passage?'

Phyllida laughed a little shakily.

'Polly Parsons. She's only sixteen. I expect she likes sweets.'

'I shall have to allowance her. How do you suppose she would react to a two-ounce packet laid in the top of the box and marked "Polly"?'

Phyllida pushed back her chair and got up.

'I should think she'd be scared to death,' she said, and with that the handle of the door behind her moved and the lock was jarred.

James Paradine's expression changed, sharpened. He called out, 'Hold on a minute – I'll open the door!'

After which he put a finger on his lips and with the other hand waved Phyllida in the direction of the unoccupied bedroom next door. As she hurried towards it she heard him cross the floor, and as she closed the connecting door behind her she heard something else – the key turning back in the lock of the study door.

The room into which she had come was dark – pitch dark. Phyllida could not remember that she had ever been inside it before. She had stood once or twice at the door and looked in, but no more than that. When she was a child it was forbidden ground. Glimpses from the passage provided a rather terrifying memory of heavy dark red curtains, a very large four-post bed covered with dust-sheets, and enormous mahogany furniture. There was a wardrobe which took up all the space between this door and the left-hand window.

She stood now and tried to remember where the rest of the furniture was. She had to reach the door which opened upon the passage, and she had to reach it without blundering into anything. She thought there was a chest of drawers . . . Yes, that was it – a tall and massive chest of drawers, on the right of where she was standing now. If she took five steps forward and then turned and walked straight ahead, that ought to bring her to the door.

As she moved to take the first step, the sound of voices came to her from the study – James Paradine's voice and another. Both these voices were familiar to her. She took five quick steps into the darkness, turned, and went forward with her hands stretched out before her until they touched the panels of the bedroom door.

TEN

SOMEWHERE ROUND ABOUT half-past eleven Elliot Wray came broad awake. His mood of drifting acquiescence broke. Albert was well away with the migration of eels to the Sargasso Sea with a view to increasing and multiplying there, and quite suddenly the flow of that instructive voice had become sharply intolerable. Like the continual falling of a drop of water upon one spot, it had produced an inability to endure what had by insensible degrees become a torture. He stood up, stretched himself, and said, 'Let's have a drink.'

Albert stared, his mind for the moment infested by eels. Through the thick lenses which screened them his eyes bore a strong resemblance to the smaller kind of bull's eye. They were just the same shade of brown, and they bulged. If you can imagine a bull's eye with an offended expression, you have Albert.

Elliot grinned.

'Come on! Lane used to leave a tray in the dining room. Let's prospect.'

The rooms on this side of the house lay immediately over James Paradine's suite and the library and billiard room. To reach the dining room they could either descend the stair at the end of the passage, or, turning left, come out upon the main staircase, and so down into the hall. This was the way they had come up and the quicker way. It also made it unnecessary to pass the study.

Elliot turned to the left and walked down the short flight which led to the central landing. For the first half-dozen steps a view of the hall below was largely obscured by the massive gilt chandelier. Its lights extinguished, it was just a black shape hanging in mid-air against a single lamp which burned below. Just short of the landing the hall came into view, and with it the big double mahogany door which led to the lobby and the porch beyond. The right-hand leaf of the door was in movement. Afterwards Elliot had to press himself very hard on this point – how sure was he that the door had been moving? And like the late Galileo he found himself obstinately of the opinion that it moved. By the time he was on the landing and had turned to make the further descent, the movement had ceased. He reflected that if James Paradine had had a visitor it was none of his business, and perhaps as well to have been just too late to see who that visitor was.

As they came into the hall there was a sound of some sort from the upper floor. Like the movement of the door, it was more of an impression than a certifiable fact.

He proceeded into the dining room, where he had a mild whisky and soda and watched Albert Pearson make himself a cup of cocoa over a spirit lamp. A disposition on Albert's part to go on talking about eels was countered by the statement that he had taken in all the information he could hold, and that he would cease to provide an alibi if he had to take in any more. Whereupon Albert looked superior and solaced himself with cocoa.

As they left the dining room, Elliot tried to analyse his impression of that second sound. There had been a sound, he was quite sure of that – a sound from upstairs, from the part of the house over the drawing room. Grace Paradine slept there, and Phyllida. Each had a sitting room and bathroom. Nobody else slept in that part of the house. The servants' quarters were beyond, in a separate wing. If anyone moved there, it must be Phyllida or Miss Paradine. The sound was like the sound of somebody moving. When he had to press himself on this point too, he could get no nearer to it than that. What he had heard might have been a footstep, or it might have been the opening or the closing of a door. His impression was featureless, without detail. He had heard a sound – he thought that he had heard somebody move. He went back to his room and saw that the hands of the clock on the mantelpiece were pointing to eight minutes past twelve.

It was 1942. Albert no longer required an alibi.

ELEVEN

A LITTLE EARLIER than this, whilst Elliot Wray and Albert Pearson were in the dining room, James Paradine was still sitting at his writing-table in the study. It was three hours since he had flung his bomb into the family circle. If he felt either reaction or fatigue he did not show it. He had, on the contrary, the air of a man for whom the time has passed quickly and not without entertainment. As he sat there waiting for the clock to strike twelve and release him from the obligation to which he had pledged himself, he appeared to be on good terms with himself and his surroundings. It is true that a frown drew his brows sharply together as his eyes dwelt for a passing moment upon a cardboard cylinder conspicuous on the left of the table, but quickly enough his look changed. The frown was gone, his rather sarcastic smile flashed out. His glance had passed to a small leather-covered diary on the farther side of the table. It lay open, face downwards, the bright blue cover making it conspicuous against the dark red leather of the desk. He reached across, picked it up, looked quizzically at the date exposed, February 1st, and let it drop again, closed this time, upon the blotting pad.

After which he appeared to lose himself for a time in pleasurable thought.

Presently he pushed back his chair, took a bunch of keys from his right-hand trouser pocket, and going over to the filing cabinet on the left-hand side of the hearth, pulled it away from the wall and opened the safe which it served to conceal. What he took out was a number of old-fashioned cases in red leather with the initials CP stamped upon them in gold. The leather was faded and the gold was dim, but inside the diamonds shone very brightly indeed. The necklace which could be used as a tiara; the solitaire earrings; the rings – half-hoop, cluster, solitaire, marquise; the bracelets; the breast ornament; the brooches – they flashed as brilliantly after their twenty years in the dark as they had done when Clara Paradine had worn them to sit for the portrait above the mantelpiece.

He looked from the real jewels to the painted ones appraisingly. It was a good portrait, very like Clara, and the diamonds were very well done. They were good diamonds. He had paid a pretty penny for them. Nobody had worn them since Clara died. It had never even entered his head to give any of them to Brenda or Irene. Clara's daughter and daughter-in-law maybe, but the diamonds had come from the Paradine side and they were part of the Paradine capital.

He put the cases back in the safe, locked them away, and pushed the cabinet against the wall. Then, with the keys in his hand, he came over to the hearth to look at the clock. Two minutes to twelve . . . Well, he supposed that no one would come knocking at the study door now. New Year's Eve was almost gone. A singular evening, but not, he thought, ill spent.

He went over to the door as he had done earlier in the day and switched off the lights. Then, repeating what was obviously a habit, he passed between the heavy curtains which screened the bay and unlatched the door to the terrace. Looking out, he observed the change which had come over the landscape since he had stood there before dinner. There was still a glint of moonlight away to the left, but the moon itself was out of sight. The wind was up, driving black clouds before it. In a moment the light would be gone. Behind him in the room the clock on the mantelpiece gave out the first of the four strokes which announced the hour. James Paradine stepped out upon the terrace, walked over to the parapet, and stood there looking down. The last of the moonlight struck a sparkle from the river where it bent by Hunter's Lea. He thought vaguely about the diamonds he had locked away. Then it was dark.

As the last stroke of twelve died in the empty room, the black clouds opened and the rain came down.

TWELVE

HALF AN HOUR later all the sounds in the house had ceased. The sounds of footsteps going to and fro in the wing above the study, the noise of water running into the bath and out of it, the gurgling and murmuring in the pipes as the cistern filled again – all these were past. Refreshed by his bath, Elliot had fallen asleep almost as soon as his head touched the pillow. The house lay in that profound silence which falls upon a place of human habitation when conscious thought and movement are withdrawn. There is a special quality about this silence of a sleeping house. It is a silence of life, as different from the empty stillness of a deserted dwelling as sleep is different from death.

Phyllida had dreamed that she was walking in a garden and it was dusk. The air was full of the scent of roses, and she knew that Elliot was there. She could feel his arm about her, but she couldn't see his face. Then a woman in a long black veil came out of the dusk and took him away. Phyllida couldn't see her face either because of the veil, but she thought it was Maisie Dale. In her dream all the pride was melted out of her. She ran after them, calling to Elliot, but he wasn't there, and the woman in the veil turned round and threw it back.

And she wasn't Maisie Dale, but Grace Paradine. And she said, 'I'll never let you go.'

Phyllida woke up with a sound in her ears like the sound of a cry. She didn't know whether it was really a cry or not. She woke up in the dark, and she was frightened. A breathless sense of danger just escaped had followed her out of the dream.

She reached out her hand and switched on the bedside light. At once the charm and security of the room closed her in. The dream was gone. She blinked at the light and saw that the hands of the little chromium clock stood at just past twelve. This horrible year was gone. She was glad that there had been no need to sit up and see it go. Let it slink away and be forgotten, like a guest who has stayed too long and whom nobody regrets.

She put out the light again and began to think about seeing Elliot in the morning. This time there must be no risk of someone else between them. She thought, I'll ask him to come up to my sitting room. Deep down under the thought a little laughter stirred. Funny to be planning an assignation with your husband – funny, and nice. The feeling of having left all the unhappy things behind was strong upon her. Presently she drifted off into a dreamless sleep.

It was Lane's custom to enter Mr Paradine's room at half-past seven precisely. The procedure never varied. Advancing a dozen steps, he put down the tray which he carried, after which he closed the open window, drew the curtains across it, and switched on the light. On the first morning of 1942 he observed his usual routine, but as he turned towards the bed he was surprised to find it empty.

His first impression was just that and no more – the bed was empty. But hurrying upon this came peturbation and dismay because the bed had not been slept in. There were the covers neatly folded back, there the undinted pillows, and the red and white striped pyjamas laid ready but unworn. He was so much startled that he found it necessary to verify what he saw by coming close up to the bed and touching it, after which he hastened to the bathroom, his mind full of the idea that Mr Paradine might have had some sudden seizure. But in the bathroom everything was in order – too much in order – the bath mat unruffled, the bath showing no water-mark, toothbrush and toothpaste shut away.

In a state of considerable distress, he proceeded to the study and approached the windows, passing between the curtains to the long door in the centre, and at once he began to be very much afraid, because the door was unlatched and stood ajar with a cold wind blowing in. It blew right in his face, cold and a little wet. It must have rained in the night. The smell of rain came in with the wind. He pushed the door wide and stood there looking out.

It was very dark. There would be no daylight for another hour. He could see nothing. Even though he knew just how far the terrace ran out to the low parapet which guarded it, he could not discern the edge.

He passed back into the room, found a torch, and switching it on, came out upon the terrace. It must have rained hard in the night. Wherever the stone had worn away water stood in a pool. The beam of the torch dazzled on the wet flags, and dazzled the more because for all his trying Lane could not hold it steady.

He came to the parapet, no more than two foot high, and stood there with his lips moving and the torch hanging in his hand.

'I always said so. Lizzie will bear me out – I always said so. 'Tisn't safe having a drop like this and no more than a two-foot wall – I always said so.'

The words made no sound. His lips moved on them but made no sound.

Presently he lifted the torch and sent the beam down over the wall – down the long drop to the path beside the river. There was something there – a huddle of darker clothes, the sprawled shape of a man as immovable in the fading beam as the path on which it lay or the rock beyond it.

Lane stopped shaking. A dreadful certainty steadied him. On the extreme right of the terrace a flight of steps led down to a little lawn from whose farther side a rustic path wound to the river's edge, sometimes running straight for a yard or two, sometimes breaking into wooden steps, slippery now with the wet. He came down it with accustomed feet. It was a path to tread in sunny weather, going down to the boathouse on a summer afternoon – not like this, not in the dark of a

January morning. He remembered that it was New Year's Day.

And then he came out on the river path and focused the torch on that dark, sprawled shape. It was James Paradine, and he was dead.

THIRTEEN

PHYLLIDA WOKE IN the dark to a knock on the door and murmured a sleepy, mechanical 'Come in!' The door opened and shut, the ceiling light snapped on, and there, coming towards her, was Elliot, hastily dressed, his fair hair rumpled, his face drawn and grim. At the very first sight of him all her new happiness was gone. A dreadful conviction of disaster caught at her heart. It didn't even seem strange for him to be there. She was out of bed in a flash, her hair about her shoulders.

'Oh! What is it? Elliot – what is it?'

'Bad news, I'm afraid.'

She was shaking. She caught at his arm to steady herself.

'It's Mr Paradine – he's had an accident.'

'An accident—'

She was clutching him hard. It seemed quite natural to both of them. He said, 'I'm afraid he's dead.'

The tears began to run down Phyllida's face.

Elliot said, 'You'd better sit down. And look here, Phyl, you've got to pull yourself together. It's going to matter very much what we do and say – all of us. We've got to pull ourselves together, and we've got to keep our heads.' He took her over to the bed, and they sat together on the edge of it. 'Look here, I'll tell you about it. Lane found him. He'd fallen from the terrace. He was right down there on the river path. You know how he always went out the last thing to take the air and look at the river – he never missed, wet or fine. Well, he must have turned giddy and gone over the parapet. His bed hadn't been slept in, and the study door was open. Lane went out with a torch and found him. Then he came to me, and I got Albert. I've left him ringing up all the people who've got to be told – Moffat, Frank Ambrose, Mark and Dicky, Dr Horton, and the police.'

She was still holding him. Her grasp tightened. 'The police—'

He said in a curious restrained voice, 'Because of its being an accident – you have to notify the police when there's been an accident.'

A long shudder went over her. She let go of him and turned so that they were facing one another.

'What did you mean – when you said – it mattered so much – what we said—'

Elliot did not answer her for a moment. Instead he got up, fetched the pale blue dressing gown which lay over a chintz-covered chair, and came back with it.

'You'd better put this on.' Then, when he had put it round her, he said soberly, 'I think you'll have to tell Miss Paradine. And I think we shall all have to make up our minds what we are going to say to the police.'

They were both standing now. With her hands

on the cord she was knotting at her waist, she looked up and said in a startled voice, 'What do you mean?'

'I mean what happened at dinner last night. It did happen, and we can't behave as if it didn't. A lot of people heard what he said. If they're going to hold their tongues about it, they'll all have to hold their tongues. If they're going to talk – if any one of them is going to talk – the police will have a good many questions to ask.'

She finished tying her girdle before she said, 'What are you going to do?'

Their eyes met. His were hard, angry, antagonistic. He said, 'I don't know.' Then, after a sharp break, 'Was it an accident?'

'Oh—'

He went on looking at her with those hard eyes.

'*Was* it? You don't know – I don't know. If it was, it was a lucky accident for someone. You heard what he said – we all did. Someone in the family had let the family down, and he'd got it in for them. He'd got his own ideas about punishment, and he meant to keep it in the family, but whoever had done it wasn't going to get off light. And he knew who it was. That's the crux of the thing – he knew who it was. And he was going to be in his study till midnight. Confess and take the consequences – that's what he said, wasn't it? So someone goes along and confesses. And there aren't any consequences, because James Paradine has an accident. That's about the size of it, isn't it?'

There was no colour at all in Phyllida's face.

'How do you know – that someone – went to confess?'

Elliot said, 'I know.'

'How – *how?*'

After a pause he said, 'Something was taken. Well, it had been put back.'

'What was taken?'

He shook his head.

'I can't tell you. I'm only telling you that I know someone did go to the study last night.'

Phyllida looked at him in a very direct and simple manner and said, 'I went there.'

His hand came down on her shoulder almost with the force of a blow.

'Do you know what you're saying?'

She nodded.

'Of course I know. I went down to the study because I wanted to talk to Uncle James.'

'After what he said at dinner, you were damned fool enough to go to the study?'

It was extraordinarily heartening to have Elliot swearing at her. Polite strangers don't swear at you. This was Elliot – angry. Something very homely and familiar about it.

'Oh, don't be silly! I wasn't thinking about all that. I wanted to talk to him,' she said.

No man can really believe how irrelevant a woman's mind can be. Elliot stared.

'He said all that at dinner, and you weren't thinking about it – you just wanted to talk? What did you want to talk about?'

'About us.'

He let go of her, walked away until the dressing table brought him up short, and then stood with his back to her fingering the odds and ends which lay there – nail-scissors, a powder-puff, a little pot of cream, a pencil.

'Why did you want to do that?'

Phyllida's smile came out just for a moment, showed, trembled, and was gone again. Her eyes were wet. If he had looked into the mirror he would have seen these things. But his eyes were on the foolish trifles which somehow plucked at his heart and made it hot and angry.

She said, 'Oh, I just thought I would.'

And with that he swung round and came back to her.

'Did anyone see you – coming or going?'

'I don't think so.'

'What time was it?'

'I don't know – some time after ten o'clock. I suppose I was there about twenty minutes, but I don't really know. I didn't look at the time – then.'

'How do you mean, *then*?'

A frightened look came over her face. She came nearer.

'It was afterwards. I went to sleep – and I woke up – I had a horrid dream – and just as I woke up I thought there was a cry. Oh, Elliot, do you think—'

He said quickly, 'Did you look at the clock then? What time was it?'

'Just after twelve – about half a minute past. I put on the light and looked. Oh – was it then?'

'Sounds like it. Now look here – you hold your tongue about all this. You went to your room just before ten, and you went to your bed, and you slept all night. You didn't hear anything and you don't know anything – that's you. Close as a clam – do you hear?'

She said, 'I – don't – know—'

He took her by the shoulders and shook her.

'Oh, yes, you do! You hear what I say, and you'll do what you're told! I'm not going to have you mixed up in this, and that's flat!'

Something inside Phyllida began to sing. If he didn't care he wouldn't be angry like this. He was frightfully angry. His chin stuck out about a mile, and he had bruised her shoulder. She looked down to hide the something in her eyes which she didn't want him to see. And right at that moment the door opened and Grace Paradine came in.

She had knotted up her hair, but she wore a plum-coloured dressing gown and bedroom slippers trimmed with fur. What she saw was certainly capable of misconstruction – Phyllida with her eyes cast down and Elliot's hands just dropping from her shoulders. It might have been the end of an embrace – or the beginning. Her eyes fairly blazed as she said, 'What does this mean?'

It was a source of some regret to Elliot that decency forbade any of the replies which sprang readily enough to his mind. You cannot score off a woman who is just going to be told that her brother has met with a fatal accident. He said,

'Phyllida will tell you, Miss Paradine,' and walked past her out of the room.

Grace Paradine came up to Phyllida and put her arms round her.

'Oh, my darling, don't look like that! I never dreamed – How dare he come in here – it's outrageous! But you mustn't let it upset you. I shall see that it doesn't happen again.'

Phyllida did not look up. She said quite gently, 'It wasn't Elliot who upset me, Aunt Grace.'

Grace Paradine stiffened.

'What do you mean?'

Phyllida made an effort. If she had to do it she must do it quickly. She steadied herself and said, 'Something has happened. Elliot came to tell me. It's something dreadful. It's – it's – Uncle James—'

'*What?*' said Grace Paradine on a sharp note of fear.

Phyllida said, 'Oh, Aunt Grace – he's dead!'

FOURTEEN

THE FAMILY HAD assembled in Miss Paradine's sitting room, a pleasantly furnished room with deep blue curtains and upholstery. There was a fine old walnut bureau and some Queen Anne chairs, and half a dozen moderately good water-colours on the plain cream walls. But what took the eye and held it were the photographs in every size and aspect, from babyhood to what magazine articles call present day, of Phyllida. There was, to be sure, one remarkable omission. Phyllida in her wedding dress was not represented by so much as a snapshot. The photographs ceased with Phyllida Paradine. There was none of Phyllida Wray. It was only a stranger, however, who would have been struck by this. The family were too used to it to take any notice, and it was the family who were assembled – Grace Paradine, Frank and Brenda Ambrose, Mark and Richard Paradine – sister, stepson and daughter, nephews – and Phyllida.

Miss Paradine was speaking as Elliot Wray came into the room. He shut the door behind him and surveyed the scene – Grace Paradine and Phyllida on the sofa; Mark at the window with his back to the room; Frank Ambrose and Dicky on the hearth, Frank with an elbow on the mantelpiece, Dicky fiddling with a bit of string, both of them shocked and strained; Brenda bolt upright in one of the Queen Anne chairs, her black felt hat tipped crooked.

Grace Paradine took no notice of the opening and shutting of the door. She went on with what she was saying in her deep, full voice.

'I don't see how there can be any question about it. He wasn't himself at all. I don't know when I was so shocked. It is not only quite unnecessary for it to be mentioned – it would really be a great injustice to his memory. He could never have said what he did if he had been himself. It was' – the deep voice vibrated as if it were about to break – 'it was terribly painful. We all felt that, and I think we want to forget about it as soon as we can. We don't want to remember him like that.' She forced a tremulous smile and looked from one to the other.

Mark's back gave no clue to what he was thinking. Brenda looked obstinate, Frank Ambrose grave and doubtful. In Dicky alone she discerned a response. Elliot had been very markedly excluded, but it was he who spoke. He came forward, joined the group by the fire, and said, 'I gather that you are discussing whether to say anything about what happened at dinner last night.'

'Why should we?' said Brenda defiantly. This was so unexpected that everyone stared at her. 'I don't see that it's anyone's business.'

Dicky nodded.

'Of course it isn't. Why should it be? The whole thing's perfectly ridiculous – I don't know why we're discussing it. Aunt Grace has said anything that needs to be said. He wasn't himself last night – anyone could see that. I thought he'd gone off his head – I suppose we all did. Very painful and upsetting – the sort of thing they call a brain-storm, I suppose. Then he went out on the terrace like he always does to have a look at the river and fell over. Turned giddy or something. It's a bad business, but we don't want to make it worse, cooking things up.'

Frank Ambrose said, 'Yes, it's a bad business.' And then, 'I don't suppose they'll ask any questions that would be difficult to answer – why should they?' There was no ring in his voice, and no conviction behind the words. They fell discouragingly upon the room.

There was a flat silence which lasted until Elliot said, 'They'll ask whether he was just as usual last night, and they'll want to know who saw him last.'

This time the silence was not flat, but electric. Again it was Elliot who broke it. He said what he had said to Phyllida.

'If we're going to hold our tongues, we'll all have to hold them. Better look at it squarely. There were ten of us at dinner last night besides Mr Paradine. He made a serious charge against one of us. He didn't say who it was, but he said he knew. He also said he meant to punish the person in his own way, and that the amount of punishment would depend on whether he got a full confession before midnight. He said he would be in his study until then. Everyone knows that he didn't say things unless he meant them. If he said he was going to stay in his study until twelve, then he did stay there until twelve. And everyone knows that he never went to bed without crossing the terrace to look at the view. We've all heard him talk about it and say that he hadn't missed a night for fifty years except when he was away from home. Well, if those three things are put together, I think we're all going to be asked some questions we don't particularly want to answer. We would all rather hold our tongues, but the thing is, if one of us doesn't we are all going to be in the soup. The thing that's got to be decided here and now is whether those ten people can be depended upon.'

Grace Paradine looked past him and said with a good deal of emphasis, 'It is a matter for the family to decide.'

The implication was too plain to be missed – Elliot Wray was mixing in matters which did not concern him. It took him no time at all to understand and accept the challenge.

'It's a matter which will have to be agreed upon by all the ten people to whom Mr Paradine spoke last night. Pearson's making himself useful – he'll be along presently. What about Irene and Lydia? Can you answer for them, Frank? There isn't much time, you know – the Superintendent will be wanting to see Miss Paradine. What about it?'

He addressed Frank Ambrose, but it was Brenda who replied. She gave a short laugh entirely devoid of merriment and said, 'Lydia and Irene! I don't suppose either of them could hold their tongues if they tried! I can't say I've ever seen either of them try!'

Frank Ambrose was frowning heavily. He said, 'They'll have to – that's all about it.'

'If they don't?'

'They'll have to.' He gave himself a kind of shake and straightened up. 'I would like to say that I think too much is being made of what happened last night. I agree with Aunt Grace that he wasn't himself – he couldn't have been. The whole thing was extremely painful, and I can't think why anyone should want to talk about it. I suggest that we stop doing so. It has nothing whatever to do with the police, and it has no possible bearing on the Governor's accident. I propose that we now drop the subject.'

Grace Paradine said, 'I quite agree.'

After which there was a pause which was broken by Brenda Ambrose, who said in her most downright voice, 'I wonder what put it into his head. And I wonder if anyone did go and see him in the study last night.'

The colour ran up into Phyllida's face. Elliot saw it because he was looking at her. And all mixed up with being angry and wondering whether anyone else had seen her flush, he was thinking that Lydia was right – she had got thin. And he hated that grey dress – it made her look like a ghost. But he supposed she would have to wear it. Insensate custom, mourning – barbaric. His eyes met hers and forbade her to speak. Then he swung round on Brenda.

'That's another thing the police will want to know – which of us saw him last? I was with him for a minute or two after I said goodnight in the drawing room. If nobody saw him later than that, I suppose it rests with me.'

Grace Paradine's glance just flickered over him.

'*You* went to see him in the study?'

'I did.'

'Do we ask why?'

'You do if you like – I don't at all mind saying. He asked me to stay here last night because we had business together. I went to the study to say goodnight to my host. I wasn't there three minutes, as Albert can testify. He saw me go in, and waited for me to come out again.'

Brenda fixed her light gaze upon him and said in the tone of one who makes a discovery, 'Albert – now that's an idea! I don't mind betting that it was Albert whom the Governor meant – I don't mind betting it was. I wonder what he's been up to – letting out official secrets, or hanky-panky with the cash? When you come to think of it, Albert's much the most likely person.'

Elliot laughed.

'That, my dear Brenda, is exactly what Albert thought. That is why he was waiting for me. He said with perfect frankness that the family would try and put it on him, and he wanted an alibi. So he clung to me till well after midnight. It was rather like sitting up with the *Encyclopaedia Britannica*. But I'm in a position to say that he never got a chance of going anywhere near the study until after the accident must have happened.'

'But no one knows when it happened – not exactly. How can they?' said Dicky.

Elliot looked round at him.

'Well, as a matter of fact they can, because it began to rain just after twelve, and the ground under the body was dry. The Superintendent says it was coming down hard. Albert and I were having drinks in the dining room about then. It was nearly ten past twelve when we got back to my room and said goodnight. So I'm afraid it's no good picking on Albert for the family skeleton.'

Brenda said, 'Pity—' and with that the door opened and Albert Pearson came in.

'The Superintendent would like to see Miss Paradine.'

Grace Paradine got up.

'Perhaps I had better see him here. What do you think?'

Elliot said, 'Shut that door, Albert! Look here, we've agreed that it's no use saying anything about what happened at dinner last night.'

Albert said, 'Oh, quite – let sleeping dogs lie and all that. But it's not going to be so easy – is it?'

For the first time, Mark Paradine turned round. He had stood looking out over the wet gravel sweep, the frost-burned lawn and wet, dark shrubberies which were all that were to be seen from this side of the house. It was Phyllida's sitting-room which looked upon the river and had the view. Miss Paradine had contented herself with the lesser prospect.

It is to be doubted whether Mark knew what he had been looking at. He turned, and Elliot was conscious of some degree of shock. The dark skin had a greenish tinge. There was a tension of every muscle. The line of the jaw was rigid. The eyes had certainly known no sleep. He said harshly, 'What do you mean?'

Albert came a little farther into the room.

'Well, you see, it's going to be awkward.'

'What do you mean?'

'Well, they're not satisfied. I've been there with them, and I've done my best, but they're not satisfied.'

'How do you mean, they're not satisfied?'

Mark's hands were deep in his pockets. Elliot guessed at fists clenched hard. Everything about him seemed to be clenched. He began to have cold feet. He liked Mark.

Albert said in the voice which always sounded a little smug, 'Well, they're not. They're not satisfied about its being an accident.'

'What else could it be?' said Grace Paradine in deep indignant tones.

Albert turned to answer her.

'Well, they haven't said, Miss Paradine, but it's plain enough that they're not any too satisfied. You see, there are a lot of scratches and abrasions which must have been due to his striking the parapet. Dr Horton says he must have come up against it hard, and they don't seem to think he'd have done that if he'd turned giddy. I'm afraid it's going to be awkward.'

FIFTEEN

SUPERINTENDENT VYNER CAME in with something of the air of a docile bull in the traditional china shop. He was, as a matter of fact, uncomfortably conscious that his boots were not only large but muddy, and that the whole situation was, as Mr Pearson had put it, awkward. Previous contacts with Miss Paradine had been over such pleasant matters as the provision of police for the marshalling of cars at social functions. There had also been handsome donations to police dances and police charities. Business was business of course, and duty was duty. He found it in his heart to wish that Dr Frith, the police surgeon, was less positive about those cuts and bruises. Dr Horton, now, he was all for making things easy for the family – hadn't been their doctor best part of twenty years for nothing. But when Frith up and put it to him – well, there was no mistaking it, he didn't see his way to contradicting him, not out and out. He'd have liked to, but he didn't see his way to it. Cautious, and got his reputation to think about. Frith was one of the cocksure sort, but the way he put it you couldn't help seeing he'd got sense on his side. If a man turns giddy he goes down in a heap, blundering. He don't come up against a two-foot parapet hard enough to cut his trousers and take a bit out of his knee, to say the least of it. And when Frith says and sticks to it that those cuts and bruises were made before death, and you can see for yourself where the stone's been knocked from the parapet – well, it's no wonder. Dr Horton won't go farther than to say that he don't feel called on to express an opinion. The plain English of it was that it looked uncommon like Mr Paradine having been pushed over that parapet, and the next thing after that was – who pushed him? There was no getting from it, it was awkward.

With these thoughts occupying his mind, he advanced into the room, and was aware of Miss Paradine, tall and dignified in a plain black dress. She inclined her head, bade him good morning, and asked him to be seated. Looking about for a chair, he selected the one upon which Brenda Ambrose had been sitting, and wished the interview well over. The family had been dismissed. Miss Paradine was alone and gravely at her ease.

'This is a very sad accident, Superintendent,' she said.

Something in the way she said it gave him just that hint of opposition which puts a man's back up. Mr Pearson knew well enough that Dr Frith wasn't satisfied about it being an accident. Very outspoken about it Frith had been, and nothing was going to persuade Superintendent Vyner that Mr Pearson had held his tongue. Why, it wasn't in nature that he wouldn't have passed on what he'd heard. Frith shouldn't really have talked so free. But there it was, he'd said right out in front of the butler and Mr Pearson that it wasn't an accident, and it was a hundred to one that Mr Pearson would have passed that on. So when Miss Paradine got off with its being a sad accident it just naturally put his back up, because it looked like she was trying to come it over him. And he was in his duty.

He sat up straight in the Queen Anne chair, and he looked at the lady and said right out, 'Dr Frith doesn't think it was an accident.'

She had a handkerchief in her hand. She might have been crying, or she might not. She touched her lips with it, sitting up very straight on the sofa, and said, 'Dr Frith? What do you mean? Dr Horton was my brother's doctor.'

The Superintendent nodded.

'Dr Frith is the Police Surgeon. It's his opinion that it was no accident.' He told her why.

She listened with increasing distress.

'But, Superintendent – I can't believe it. You mean you think – no, Dr Frith thinks – that my brother was pushed?'

'That's what he makes of the evidence, and I'm bound to say that's how it looks to me.'

She was staring at him with a horrified expression.

'But who – there's no one – it's too dreadful—'

'That's what we've got to find out. I take it you will give us all the assistance you can.'

'Of course.'

'Then perhaps you won't mind answering a few questions.'

'Oh, no.'

He sat forward a little – a big man, heavily built, with grey hair beginning to recede from the temples, and a square, weather-beaten face. The hair had once been fair, and the rather deep-set eyes were astonishingly blue. He said, 'I would like to ask whether there is anyone you might suspect.'

'Indeed there isn't.'

'No one with a motive – no one who might have wanted him out of the way? No quarrels? No threats or threatening letters?'

'None that I knew about.'

'No differences of opinion in the business – or in the family?'

Miss Paradine's tone was very cold as she replied, 'Certainly not.'

Vyner said with a shade of apology in his voice, 'You mustn't mind my asking these questions – they have to be answered. Now, you had a family party here last night. These are the names as your butler gave them to me. Staying in the house, besides yourself and Mr Paradine, there were Mr and Mrs Wray and Mr Pearson. Mr and Mrs Ambrose, Miss Ambrose, and Miss Pennington, Mr Mark Paradine, and Mr Richard Paradine dined here. Is that correct?'

'Quite.'

'At what time did you dine?'

'Eight o'clock is our dinner hour, but we were a few minutes late. Mr Wray's visit was on business. We were not expecting him, and the meal was delayed.'

'I see. Can you tell me when you left the dining room?'

'At about nine o'clock, I suppose – I didn't notice particularly.'

'The party broke up rather early, didn't it?'

'Mrs Ambrose was anxious about her little girl. They left at about half-past nine.'

'And Mr Mark and Mr Richard?'

'Soon afterwards.'

'Did Mr Paradine join you in the drawing room after dinner?'

'No.'

'Was that usual?'

Miss Paradine hesitated. Then she said, 'I don't think I know quite what you mean.'

The Superintendent looked at her very straight.

'You had a New Year's Eve party. Mr Paradine did not join you in the drawing room. He went straight from the dining room to his study. Wouldn't that be unusual?'

She said, 'I don't think he was quite himself.'

'You mean that he was ill?'

'Oh, no – not ill – I didn't mean that. He just didn't seem quite himself, and when he didn't come into the drawing room, I thought he wanted to be quiet. He had had a lot of business all day. Mr Wray was with him right up to dinner-time, I believe. And he wasn't a young man.'

He thought, she's doing a lot of explaining. He asked, 'Did you see him at all after you left the dining room?'

She said, 'No.' The handkerchief went to her lips again.

'Not when the party was breaking up?'

'No.'

'He didn't come out of the study when Mr and Mrs Ambrose and the others were going away?'

'No.'

'Did they go into the study to say goodbye?'

She said, 'No,' again.

He shifted his weight on the chair.

'Wouldn't that be rather unusual, Miss Paradine?'

Her face showed only offence, but on the hand which was holding the handkerchief the knuckles stood up white.

'No – I don't know. I think we all took it for granted that he didn't wish to be disturbed. It was a family party. There was no need to stand on ceremony.'

'Then did none of you see him again?'

'Not that I know of. Oh, I believe Mr Wray did.'

'Oh, Mr Wray did? Yes, I remember he said so – he went in to say goodnight. Did anybody else do that?'

'Really, I can't say.'

'Mr and Mrs Ambrose didn't – or Miss Ambrose – or Mr Mark – or Mr Richard?'

'No.'

'Or yourself?'

'I did not think that he would wish to be disturbed.'

'Or Mrs Wray?'

'Oh, no. She went upstairs before I did.'

He leaned forward.

'Miss Paradine, you must realise that all this has a very unusual sound. I feel obliged to ask you whether there was anything to account for this break-up of the party, and no one except Mr Wray having seen Mr Paradine to say goodnight. I am bound to tell you what it looks like to me, and that is a family quarrel.'

'There was no quarrel.'

'No difference of opinion? No unpleasantness of any kind? Nothing to make Mr Paradine go off to his study? Nothing to account for the party breaking up at half-past nine without saying goodnight to him?'

She sat up very straight and said coldly, 'The party broke up because Mrs Ambrose was anxious about her little girl.'

'A case of serious illness?'

'Oh, no. She is apt to be over anxious.'

'Miss Paradine, you must see that this does not account for the whole party breaking up before a quarter to ten. And it doesn't explain why no one said goodnight to Mr Paradine. Do you really wish to maintain that nothing had occurred which would account for these things – nothing of an unpleasant nature?'

She looked him straight in the face and said, 'There was nothing.'

SIXTEEN

THE FAMILY WERE just across the passage in Phyllida's sitting room. The instinct to keep together, to avoid being singled out, had taken them there – the old primitive herd instinct. This time no one sat down. Mark leaned on the mantelpiece and looked into the fire, his shoulder turned upon the room. Dicky still twisted a bit of string. There was one of those horrid silences which no one breaks because no one wants to be the first to voice the common thought. The fact that Albert was at a loss for words was enough to keep anyone else from speaking. It had never happened before, and would probably never happen again. He stood there, the last into the room, looking for all the world like something out of the family album. There was the same stiffness, the fixed regard, the attempt at an easy pose.

It was Brenda who spoke for everyone present. In blunt and heartfelt tones she exclaimed, 'I wish we knew what Aunt Grace was saying to him.'

Her brother turned a frowning look upon her.

'She'll say what we agreed to say – why shouldn't she?'

Albert Pearson came a little farther into the room.

'It's most unfortunate that we hadn't a little longer to talk things over. Dr Frith was being very positive about it not being an accident, and when they got it out of Lane how early the party had broken up, I could see they were going to ask a lot of questions. Of course, we don't want to say what isn't true, but we don't want to stir up trouble either.'

Brenda said, 'What about Irene – and Lydia? Suppose he goes and talks to them? Hadn't you better ring up and tell them to be careful what they say?'

Frank Ambrose said, 'No.'

'Well, I should.'

'Too risky. Besides, the telephone's out of order – at least it was last night.'

Brenda hunched her shoulder.

'Then I don't mind betting they give the show away.'

'Lydia's got too much sense,' said Dicky.

Brenda laughed unpleasantly.

'And Irene hasn't any sense at all!'

In quite a quiet undertone, Frank Ambrose said, 'Hold your tongue, will you!'

Elliot Wray surveyed the room with a sense of impending disaster – Phyllida's pretty pastel room which he hated because it wasn't Phyllida's room at all. It was the setting devised by Grace Paradine – her taste, her furniture, her idea of what a young girl's room should be; sweet pea colouring, a little mauve, a little pink, a touch of purple, and a great deal of blue. He thought, we've bitten off more than we can chew – that's about the size of it. If he goes through the whole ten of us one at a time, somebody's bound to crash.

Then Phyllida had her hand on his arm and was saying in a voice which was only meant for him, 'Elliot, I'm no good at telling lies – I don't think I can.'

He turned his eyes on her with a spark of angry humour.

'Oh, you can't, can't you?'

She shook her head.

'Why can't we just tell the truth?'

His hand came down over hers. He said almost inaudibly, but with an extraordinary effect of anger, 'You're not to say you went down to the study – do you hear?'

'Well, I won't unless he asks me.'

'He won't ask you – why should he?'

'I don't know – he might.'

'Then you'll say "No"!'

She shook her head.

'I can't, Elliot – honest I can't.'

'George Washington complex?' His grip was hurting her. 'Don't be a damned fool, Phyl!'

She said, 'You're hurting me,' and got a hard 'I'd like to wring your neck!'

He was not prepared for her looking up at him with a smile. What can you do when a creature looks at you like that? And what business had she to smile at him when he had just called her a damned fool and said he would like to wring her neck? He let go of her abruptly as Brenda repeated her opening remark, 'I do wish we knew what Aunt Grace was saying.'

Superintendent Vyner, having finished with Miss Paradine, was considering whom he would see next. He had no intention of allowing her to rejoin the rest of the family, and had devised a plan for preventing it. Sergeant Manners was called in and told that Miss Paradine had kindly consented to make a statement. Even without previous instructions Manners could be relied upon to take an almost unbelievable time over this routine exercise, being a slow writer and very punctilious about getting everything down correctly. People who tried to hustle him came out of the encounter rather the worse for wear.

The Superintendent's own plan was to select the next person to be interviewed and proceed to the study. But he had only taken a couple of steps along the passage, when he heard the sound of voices from the hall. What he saw when he looked over the balustrade sent him downstairs without further ado. As he came down the last of the flight he encountered Mrs Frank Ambrose and her sister coming up. Both ladies had made some attempt at mourning, Mrs Ambrose wearing a fur coat and a small black turban, and Miss Pennington having on a grey tweed coat and skirt and a white scarf. She had nothing on her head but her own bright copper curls. The Superintendent stopped them, blocking the way.

'Good morning, Mrs Ambrose. I am very sorry to be here on such a painful errand. Can you spare me a few minutes of your time? If you will do so, I can take your statement and get it over.'

Irene's eyes opened very widely indeed.

'My statement?'

'Why, yes, Mrs Ambrose. In the case of a sudden death like this I would like to have a statement from everyone who was dining here last night. If you wouldn't mind coming into the study – I needn't detain you for more than a few minutes—'

She opened her mouth and shut it again. Two steps higher up Lydia looked down at them. She was pale and she wore no make-up. Without it she appeared a little, insignificant creature. The thought passed through the Superintendent's head. Then he met the steady grey-green eyes and changed his mind. She was all there, and she'd got spunk. Not so much change to be got out of Miss Lydia Pennington. He turned back to Irene, standing there with her mouth a little open, and considered that he'd picked the right sister. Well, he'd best get her along to the study before anyone had a chance of telling her what to say.

Lydia's voice pursued him, 'Don't you want me too?'

It gave him a good deal of pleasure to reply, 'Not at present, thank you, Miss Pennington.'

SEVENTEEN

LYDIA RAN ON up the stairs, stood listening in the passage for a moment, and then, catching the sound of voices from Phyllida's sitting room, opened the door and walked in. Everyone had the same question. Frank, Brenda, and Dicky asked it.

'Where's Irene?'

'With the large policeman. He met us in the hall and took her off to the study to make a statement. Why?'

Brenda said, 'That's torn it!' and Dicky, 'Gosh, Frank – hadn't you better go down? You might be able to stop her if she starts talking too much.'

Frank shrugged his shoulders.

'Anyone ever tried to stop Irene when she wants to say anything? She doesn't take hints – especially not from me. Besides, what would it look like? Vyner would be on to it in a moment.'

'You ought to have rung her up,' said Dicky.

'I tell you the telephone's out of order.'

'Well, someone managed to ring you up with the news, didn't they?'

'Albert rang the Brethertons next door and got them to take a message. Do you suggest that I should have got on to Jack Bretherton and asked him to tell Irene to hold her tongue?'

Dicky said, 'All right, all right—'

Lydia had come into the middle of the room. She stepped between them.

'Frank, what is all this about? Elliot – what is it?'

But it was Mark Paradine who answered, turning upon the room and saying with the extreme of harshness, 'Frith says it's murder.'

No one had said the word before. It came crashing into the midst of them like a stone through a window. The silence splintered. There was a general sound of protest, and, coming through it, Lydia's 'Mark!'

'Well, it's true. You've all been hushing it up and covering it over, but that's what it amounts to. Frith says he was pushed. Two and two make four, don't they? Add it up for yourselves. If he was pushed, it was murder,' he said.

Lydia stood where she was and looked at him. After a moment she turned to Elliot Wray.

'Dr Frith says he was pushed?'

'Yes, he does.'

'Why?'

He told her.

She said, 'I see—' and then, 'But who – *who*?'

'That's what Vyner is trying to find out.'

'If Irene tells him what the Governor said last night, he'll be pretty well bound to think it's one of us,' said Brenda Ambrose.

Lydia said, 'I see—' again. Then she went up to Mark, took him by the arm, and walked him off through the connecting door into Phyllida's bedroom.

Brenda said, '*Well!*'

Behind the closed door Lydia kept her hold on Mark.

'What's the matter with you?'

He stared at her.

'Mark, what is it – why do you look like that?'

He said, 'How do you expect me to look? He's been murdered, hasn't he?'

'Yes, my dear. But you mustn't make things worse, must you? That doesn't do any good.'

No one could have believed that Lydia's voice could sound so soft. She put up her other hand and began to stroke his arm.

'It's been a most dreadful shock. You must pull yourself together. Do you hear, Mark – you *must*! He isn't here to help us any more – we've got to look to you. It would have happened some day. It's happened suddenly like this. You've got to take his place – do what he would have wanted. Don't you see?'

He said, still in that harsh voice, 'You don't see anything at all.'

'What do you mean, Mark?'

He pulled away from her and went over to the window. With his back to her he said, 'You're right about one thing – it falls on me. I can't see any farther than that. I meant to get away. That's gone too. I've lost my chance. Now I'll have to stay.'

She came slowly up to him, but did not touch him again.

'Why were you going away?'

He said in a tone of despair, 'I can't go now. I've lost my chance. I shall have to stay.'

The room was warm, but Lydia's hands were cold. After a moment she said, 'What are you going to do, Mark – about what happened at dinner last night? What sort of questions have been asked?'

'Nothing yet. Vyner hasn't seen anyone except Aunt Grace. She didn't mean to say anything. I don't know how hard he pressed her. It was her idea that we should all hold our tongues. Personally I don't think it's practicable. It would have been all right if it had really been an accident – they'd have asked Aunt Grace and old Horton about his health, and that would have been the end of it. But if Frith says it's murder, they'll sift through everything that happened in the house last night. Ten of us heard that speech of his. One of them is Irene. Do you suppose for a moment that it's possible to keep it dark? Something is bound to come out. And when things start coming out you don't know where they're going to stop.'

At any rate he was talking now. That dreadful brooding silence had been broken. She said, 'Come back to the others and talk it over. What does Elliot say?'

'I don't know – I wasn't attending very much – I think he thought we should hold our tongues. But that was before Albert came in and told us what Frith was saying.'

'Albert?'

'Yes, he came in and told us. Right on the top of that Vyner came along to see Aunt Grace, and we all cleared out. We don't know what she's said to him. We don't know what he's asked her.'

The colour came suddenly into Lydia's face and burned there. He had turned from the window. She caught his arm and shook it.

'Why are we talking like this? Why should we tangle ourselves up with a lot of lies? We haven't got anything to hide.'

'Haven't we?' His tone was sombre.

'Why don't we tell the truth?'

She was looking up into his face. His eyes avoided her. He said, 'Do you know what it is?' Then, almost violently, 'Have you forgotten what he said in that damned speech of his? He accused one of us of a crime. That's what it amounted to, didn't it – he accused one of us – one of the ten people who'd been dining with him. And he said he'd wait in his study for one of us to come and confess. Well, he waited, and he was murdered. Do you think Vyner's going to look outside of those ten people for the murderer?'

She said, 'I suppose not.' And then, 'I don't think it's going to help us to tell lies about it.'

He said with great bitterness, 'It's a million to one we don't get away with it if we do. Which gets us back to "Honesty is the best policy" and all the other copybook maxims. I've had all I can swallow. Let's go back and preach to the others.'

EIGHTEEN

IRENE PASSED NERVOUSLY into the study, threw a shrinking glance about her, and sat down as far from the writing table as possible. To the Superintendent's invitation to come a little nearer she responded with obvious reluctance. So very, very odd to see him sitting there in Mr Paradine's place. No one else had ever sat there or used the table. She had the feeling that he might walk in suddenly and surprise them, and be very, very angry. The thought of it made her feel as if cold water was running down her back, like the drip from an umbrella. She did hope this statement business wasn't going to take long.

The Superintendent was looking at her quite kindly and politely. He said, like an echo of what she was thinking, 'I won't keep you long, Mrs Ambrose. I just want you to tell me what happened last night.'

'Last night?'

'Yes. There was a New Year's Eve party here, wasn't there? You, and your husband, and Miss Ambrose, and Miss Pennington came to it?'

'Oh, yes.'

'Dinner was at eight, I think, or just a little later. You were in the dining room till about nine. At half-past nine you and your party went home. Now why was that?'

Irene brightened.

'Oh, yes – my little girl wasn't well – at least I was afraid she might be sickening for something, but she's quite all right today. You see, she had a spot on her chest, and Dr Horton said it was nothing, but you never can tell with spots, and though she didn't have a temperature or anything, or of course I shouldn't have dreamed of leaving her, I was naturally anxious to get back. I didn't want to come out at all, but my husband really insisted. And of course Mr Paradine wouldn't have liked it if any of us had stayed away.'

Superintendent Vyner said, 'Quite so.' And then, 'So it was on your little girl's account that you went home so early. It wasn't on account of anything that happened at dinner?'

Irene's expression changed. The interest with which she had been talking about little Rena faded out. She appeared disconcerted. She put up her hand and fumbled inefficiently with a straggling lock of hair.

The Superintendent repeated his question.

'Something did happen at dinner, didn't it? You wanted to get home to your little girl. But your husband wouldn't have broken up the party just for that. There was something more, wasn't there?'

Irene never found it easy to switch her mind from one topic to another. She seized upon what seemed to her to be a connecting link.

'Oh, but he didn't mind a bit,' she said. 'It was

really his own idea – I wouldn't have liked to go as early as that. It was Frank who suggested it – it really was.'

It was no use, the piece of hair wouldn't tuck in. She left it straying, put her hands in her lap, and gazed earnestly at the Superintendent. She wasn't nervous now. He seemed a very nice man. She wondered how old he was. Perhaps he had grandchildren like Jimmy and Rena. If she got a chance she would ask him. He had rather nice blue eyes. She did hope Rena's eyes were going to be blue—

And then he was saying, 'Mr Ambrose wanted to go home because of what happened at dinner?'

Her mouth fell open. Frank wouldn't want her to say yes. She said in a confused voice, 'Oh – I don't know—'

'Well, Mrs Ambrose, it couldn't have been pleasant for any of you. I expect Mr Ambrose thought it would be better to break the party up.'

'Oh, I don't know—'

He said briskly, 'Mr Paradine came straight here from the dining room and didn't appear again. He didn't come into the drawing room, did he?'

'No – he didn't—'

'It must have been very trying for you.'

'Oh, it was!'

If a shade of triumph entered his thought, his manner gave no sign of it. He leaned a little towards Irene across the table and said, 'Now, Mrs Ambrose – I wonder whether you would tell me just how it all struck you. Different people get different impressions of the same thing. I would very much like to have your version of what happened in your own words, if you don't mind.'

Irene went through the process which she called thinking. A number of uncoordinated and confused impressions strayed to and fro in her mind. Frank must have told the Superintendent about last night – somebody must have told him – if it wasn't Frank, Frank would be angry . . . The straying thoughts were not really as formulated as this. She did nothing to formulate them. She let them stray.

She said in a hesitating manner, 'Oh, I don't know that I can—'

'Will you try, Mrs Ambrose? Just begin at the beginning. What started it?'

'Well, I don't know – it just seemed to happen. He stood up, and we thought he was going to give us a toast – at least I did – I don't know about the others. But it wasn't that at all.'

'I see. Now I wonder how much you remember of what followed. Just give it to me in your own words.'

She said, 'Oh, I don't know—'

'You mean you don't remember?'

'Oh – I remember—'

'Then just see if you can help me. How did he begin?'

Irene looked doubtful.

'I can't remember it all. He said we shouldn't be bored – and then he said it wouldn't be pleasant – and then he said things about our all being related, or connected by marriage, and families had to hold together, and all that sort of thing—'

'And after that?'

'Well, I don't know if I ought to say – I don't think—'

He said quietly, 'I am afraid I must ask you to go on. Just tell me what you can remember.'

'Well, he used a lot of long words – I can't remember them. And I don't know—'

'Please, Mrs Ambrose – just what you remember.'

Sitting there in her fur coat, Irene shivered. She began to feel sure that Frank was going to be angry. She didn't see what she could do about it. If you didn't answer the police they would think you had something to hide. But she didn't like having to answer, because now when the actual words came crowding back they weren't the sort of words you want to repeat to the police or to anyone else. She faltered as she repeated them.

'He said – someone – had been – disloyal. He said someone had – betrayed – the family interests. He said it was – one of us—'

The blood came up behind Vyner's tan. His thoughts shouted, 'By gum, he did – *by gum!*' He looked down at the blotting pad and saw a little leather-covered diary lying there – just one of those pocket diaries, bright blue, with 1942 stamped upon the cover in gold. He looked at it because he wanted to keep his eyes from Mrs Ambrose. Mustn't startle her – mustn't startle her . . . He managed his voice and said, 'Did he say who this person was?'

'Oh, no, he didn't.'

'Do you think he knew?'

'Oh, yes – he said so.'

'He said someone had betrayed the family interests, and that he knew who the person was?'

'Yes, that's what he said.'

He was looking at her again now.

'You are doing very well, Mrs Ambrose. What else did he say?'

Irene had now arrived at feeling some pleasurable excitement. She was doing well – she was being praised – it wasn't as difficult as she had thought it was going to be. She said in quite a complacent voice, 'It was dreadful. I'm sure I didn't know where to look. And I was sitting next to him. It really was dreadful. We all thought he must have gone out of his mind.'

'Did he seem to be excited?'

'Oh, no. That's what made it so dreadful – he was absolutely *calm*. I don't know how he could be when you think of the things he was saying, but he *was*.'

'Will you go on telling me what he said?'

'Well, all that sort of thing. And then he said he would wait in the study till twelve o'clock, and if anyone had anything to – to confess, he would be there, and – well, I can't remember exactly, but – I think he meant that he wouldn't be too hard on anyone if they confessed. I *think* that's what he meant, but he did say something about punishment too.'

'Can you remember what he said?'

Irene looked vague.

'No – I don't think I can. It was something about the person being punished.'

'I see. It must have been quite a relief when the party broke up.'

'Oh, it was!'

'You didn't see Mr Paradine again?'

'Oh, no.'

'None of your party saw him again to say good-night?'

'Oh, no.'

'You all went home together?'

'Oh, yes.'

'You must have got home at about a quarter to ten. As far as you know, did any of the party go out again?'

The colour came into her face. Her eyes opened widely. She said, 'Oh!'

Vyner said in his own mind, 'By gum – I've got something!' He looked at her hard and said, 'Which of you went out?'

She was flustered, but not unduly so.

'Well, it was because of Rena – my little girl you know – I couldn't wake her.'

He experienced a slight feeling of stupefication.

'Why did you want to wake her?'

'Well, I didn't, you know – not really. I mean I was very pleased at first when I got home to find she was sleeping so soundly, and then – well, I was talking to my sister for some time, and when I got back and began to go to bed I thought perhaps she was sleeping too soundly.'

'Yes?'

'Well, I got frightened. My sister doesn't know anything about children. I did try to get my husband to come and look at her, but he only said "Stuff and nonsense!" He thinks I'm fussy. But when I picked her up and her head just fell over and she went on sleeping, I got *dreadfully* frightened, and I tried to ring up Dr Horton, but the telephone was out of order – I'd forgotten about that. So when I couldn't get on I thought I'd go and fetch him – it's not any distance really – so I did.'

'You went and fetched Dr Horton?'

She was looking vague again.

'Well, I didn't really, because when I got there he was in his car just starting to go out somewhere. I ran and called after him, but he didn't hear me.'

'So you came home again?'

'Well, I didn't – not at once. I thought perhaps he wouldn't be long. I walked up and down a bit. I didn't like to ring the bell, because Mrs Horton always tells you how she brought up eight children and never fussed over any of them.'

Vyner's face was as expressionless as he could make it.

'How long did you wait, Mrs Ambrose?'

'About half an hour. And then I got frightened again wondering what was happening to Rena so I went home. I ran all the way, but she was quite all right.'

'And was she still asleep?'

'Oh, yes. My husband was so angry.'

'He had missed you?'

'Oh, yes. He was out looking for me when I got back. Then he came in and was frightfully angry.'

'What time did he get in?'

'I don't know – it must have been getting late – I know I was longing to get to bed.'

'Did your husband say where he had been?'

'He said he had been looking for me.'

'He didn't say where?'

'Oh, no.'

'He just said he had been looking for you?'

Irene coloured brightly.

'He was most *unkind* about it,' she said.

NINETEEN

SUPERINTENDENT VYNER SAT in a solid armchair and faced the Chief Constable across a comfortable hearth. The Chief Constable was Colonel Bostock, a wiry little man with a brown wrinkled face, bright twinkling eyes, and a cheerful expression. He was sixty years old, and had the air of having enjoyed every minute of them. Since he was a widower, it is to be supposed that this was not quite the case, but Mrs Bostock had been dead for so many years that any sad memories must long ago have been obliterated. His three daughters, at present serving their country, were healthy and pleasant young women who had never given him a moment's anxiety. One of them was overseas, but the other two had seven days' leave and were spending it at home.

Vyner had just used the word murder. Colonel Bostock was regarding him with the cocked head and bright attention of a terrier to whom someone has just said 'Rats!'

'You don't say so!'

'It's not me, sir – it's Dr Frith. And Dr Horton couldn't contradict him, though he'd have been glad enough if he could. Of course if you put it to me, I'd say that Dr Frith was in the right of it. It was murder all right. He was pushed, and I'd say he was pushed by someone who knew that he'd got the habit of standing by that parapet and having a look at the view. The butler says he did it every night as regular as clockwork before he went to bed.'

'That's all very well but who was to know what time he'd go to bed? Or did that go by clockwork too?'

'Oh, no, sir. But last night, you see, all those ten people who had dinner with him, well, they'd heard him say he'd be sitting up in his study till twelve o'clock. He'd brought a serious accusation against one of them, and he was going to wait in the study for that one to come and confess. Well, there's the motive. We don't know just how serious it all was. The offence may have been a criminal one for all we know. There's no doubt the family were pretty hard hit, and there's no doubt they meant to keep their mouths shut. You've got Miss Paradine's statement there – well, she denies the whole thing. She wouldn't have done that if she hadn't thought the others would back her up. What they hadn't reckoned with was my getting hold of Mrs Ambrose before they'd the chance of telling her what to say.'

Colonel Bostock gave a short, dry sniff.

'Mrs Ambrose? Let's see – she's Irene. Lydia's the red-haired one. Old Pennington's daughters. The mother's dead too. Very pretty woman Mrs Pennington. Danced like an angel. Neither of the girls a patch on her for looks. The red hair comes from the Pennington side. Nice chap old Pennington and a damned good shot. Red as a scraped carrot. The girls went to school with mine. Wait a minute – there was something about one of them . . . Not Lydia – no. Shouldn't have been so surprised if it had been the red-headed one. Never trust a red-headed woman. No, it was the other one, Irene – girl who looked as if butter wouldn't melt in her mouth.'

Vyner considered it time to recall his Chief Constable from these reminiscences. He did so with respect, but firmly.

'Well, sir, you see, once I had got that statement from Mrs Ambrose, it wasn't any good the others holding out. I had the sister in next, Miss Lydia Pennington – a very intelligent young lady, if I may say so – and she saw at once that the game was up. I read her what Mrs Ambrose had said, and she agreed that it was correct so far as it went. Only she tried very hard to get across that Mr Paradine mightn't have meant very much after all – said she was very fond of him and all that, but there was no denying he was very strict and old-fashioned, and that he expected everyone in the family to do just what they were told.'

'Well, that's true enough. Everyone knows that. Very able man – very able indeed. Bit of an autocrat. Bit of a tyrant, I shouldn't wonder.'

'Yes, sir – that's the impression Miss Pennington wanted to give. She did it very well. There's her statement.'

Colonel Bostock ran his eye over it.

'Yes – yes . . . Well, it's all quite true. Who did you have next?'

'Mr Ambrose. You've got his statement there. Very short and to the point. But he didn't like making it. Looked like fury when I read him what his wife had said. She'll be hearing about it, I expect. But he didn't deny it – said he had no idea what his stepfather meant, but thought there wasn't much in it – said Mr Paradine had been overworking, and considered he'd gone off the deep end about something that was probably not very important. When I asked him whether he was out again after he got home, he said yes, he went out to look for his wife. When I asked him how he knew where to look for her he said he didn't, but she might have gone round to the doctor's because she was always getting into a state about the children and the telephone was out of order. It sounds a bit thin, you know, sir.'

Colonel Bostock said, 'Oh, I don't know.' And then, 'Good lord, man, what are you suggesting – that Ambrose trekked all the way back to the River House to push old Paradine off?'

Vyner looked up quickly.

'Well, sir, when you say all the way back – it's not that far.'

'Took them a quarter of an hour to drive it.'

'Yes, sir – to drive it. But it wouldn't be more than six or seven minutes by the footbridge and along the river path.'

Colonel Bostock gave a long whistle.

'The footbridge! No more it would! Of course the Ambroses are in Meadowcroft. It's no distance at all by the footbridge. Did he say how long he was out, or when he came in?'

'He said he couldn't say – said he didn't look at his watch. And that doesn't sound natural to me, sir, because when a man's waiting for a woman, and especially if he's a bit worked up, why, he'd keep looking at his watch all the time – I've done it myself.'

'Mightn't have a luminous dial,' said Colonel Bostock reasonably. 'You're forgetting the black-out.'

'Very bright moon, sir, till a quarter before midnight.'

''Hm! Let's have a look at what the fellow says. Short and sharp. Well, thank the Lord for that.' He scanned the statement and put it down again. 'Well, you know, Vyner, it might have happened just as he says. That girl Irene – Mrs Ambrose – how did she strike you? Is she the sort to go rushing off for old Horton in the middle of the night like she says? A lot depends on that, you know.'

Vyner had allowed himself to smile.

'Well, yes, sir – she struck me that way.'

'Not much of a head on her shoulders? She used to come about the house when my girls were at home, but I don't know that I've said three words to her since she married. Nice people the Penningtons. But there was something about this girl Irene

– I must ask my daughters when they come in. So you think she's a bit of a fool?

The smile lingered for a moment in the Superintendent's eyes.

'Well, yes, sir.'

'All right – there you are. If a woman's a fool she's a fool. Might do anything.'

The Superintendent abandoned Mrs Ambrose.

'Yes, sir. I saw the other four men after Mr Ambrose – Mr Mark Paradine, Mr Richard Paradine, Mr Pearson and Mr Wray. I didn't get anything that you could add to the Ambrose statements. You'll see if you look at them, the wording varies a little, that's all. There isn't any doubt that Mrs Ambrose gave a pretty fair account of what took place. I didn't read them her statement, and they'd had no opportunity of seeing either her or her husband again before I had them in – one at a time of course. So they'd no means of knowing what she had said. I just told each of them that both she and Mr Ambrose had described a painful incident which took place at the dinner table last night. I indicated the nature of the incident, and I invited each of them to give his own version of what had occurred. Well, none of them wanted to do it, but none of them wanted to be the one to refuse. They cut it down as much as they could, and they didn't say more than they could help, but there isn't much in it between what they say, as you'll see. I think they're all telling the truth as far as they go, but of course they're not saying anything they don't have to.'

'Quite, quite. Painful predicament for a family.'

Vyner said drily, 'Yes, sir – especially if one of them pushed him over that parapet.'

Colonel Bostock appeared to be shocked.

'Bless my soul, Vyner – that's a dreadful thing to say!'

'Yes, sir, but that's what it looks like. To get back to those statements – if you'll just run your eye over them you'll see Mr Mark Paradine and Mr Elliot Wray have got the least to say about it – cut it down all they could. Mr Richard, he talked quite a lot – rather fell over himself trying to explain it away. And Mr Pearson – well, very discreet.'

'Hold on, let's get these people straight. Mark and Richard are the nephews. Which is the tall, dark one?'

'Mark, sir.'

'That's it. Someone was telling me about him. Wanted to go into the Air Force, but they wouldn't let him. In the Research Department – can't be spared. The other one – my girls know him. Lively – bit of a ladies' man. By way of making up to Lydia Pennington.'

'Yes, sir.'

'Elliot Wray – he's the fellow who married the adopted daughter – what's her name – Phyllida. Marriage broke up before the honeymoon was over. Extraordinary thing. Nice young fellow – pretty girl. Can't think what young people are coming to. Shouldn't be surprised if somebody had meddled. Grace Paradine for choice. Old maid's daughter – something unnatural about it to my mind. Pity she didn't marry Bob Moffat and have half a dozen. Never could make out why she didn't. All over him one minute, and a flourish about the engagement – everyone as pleased as Punch. And then the whole thing broken off and the families dead cuts. Damned awkward thing to happen with your business partner.'

Vyner said, 'Yes, sir.'

Colonel Bostock picked up Albert Pearson's statement, glanced it through, and said, 'Who's Pearson? How does he come into it?'

'Secretary, sir. Some kind of a cousin as well. Lives in.'

Colonel Bostock rubbed his forehead.

'Pearson – Pearson – yes, of course, he'd be Milly Paradine's son. Big, gawky girl. Some kind of a second cousin. Used to come and stay with the Paradines. Ran away with old Pearson the jeweller's son – made a lot of talk. Old Pearson cut 'em off, and the Paradines cut 'em off. Obstinate girl – very. Pearson got a job – died some years later. I've got an idea that the boy was apprenticed to his father's trade . . . Wait a bit, I'm getting there. Bless my soul, now who was it was talking about Milly Paradine not so long ago? Campion – no, it wouldn't be Campion. Mrs Horton – might have been Mrs Horton. Reminds me of the elephant – she never forgets. That's who it must have been! And she was saying what a good son that young Pearson had been – praiseworthy fellow – worked hard, ambitious – the virtuous apprentice – took night classes – languages, typing, shorthand, all that kind of thing. Mother died a year or two ago. That's him!' He returned with satisfaction to the restrained statement of Albert Pearson.

'You see, sir,' said Vyner, 'Pearson did see Mr Paradine after he went to his study. He was in the drawing room with the others until first the Ambrose party and then the two Mr Paradines went away. He then went back to the drawing room, said goodnight, and proceeded to the study to see if his services were required by Mr Paradine. He found the butler there setting out a tray of drinks. Lane corroborates this. Pearson says he was told he wouldn't be needed, but that Mr Paradine called him back as he was following the butler out of the room and suggested a slight alteration to a letter which he had dictated earlier in the evening. He says Mr Paradine didn't keep him a moment, and that he was about to go up to his room, when it struck him that he was, as he puts it, in a very invidious position. He says he stood there thinking that about this, and thinking it would be a good thing if he could be in company with someone else during the time that Mr Paradine had set for being in his study in case anyone should be wanting to confess. He says he was on the point of going back to the drawing room, when he saw Mr Elliot Wray come through the baize door from the hall. Mr Paradine's rooms are on the ground floor – bedroom, bathroom, study, and his late wife's room which is not in use. Mr Pearson was along the passage from these rooms on his way to a back stair which comes out near his own bedroom. He saw Mr Wray go into the study, and made up his mind to wait. After no more than about two minutes Mr Wray came out again. Pearson then addressed him, telling him frankly that he would like to be in his company till after midnight. After which they went up to Mr Wray's room, which is just across the passage from Pearson's, and stayed there until after half-past eleven, when they went down to the dining room and had a drink. When they got back again it was eight minutes past twelve. Mr Wray went and had a bath, and Pearson went to bed. Their statements corroborate each other and this puts them both out of court as far as the murder is concerned, because Mr Paradine was dead by twelve o'clock. It's an undisputed fact and no getting away from it that a heavy shower of rain started at that time. I can vouch for that myself. We were sitting up to see the New Year in, and we'd the wireless on. With the last stroke of twelve you could hear the rain against the window, and that's when it started, for I'd only just let the dog in, and it was dry then. So there you've got it, sir – he was dead just after the last stroke of twelve.'

Colonel Bostock made the grimace which accounted for his network of wrinkles.

'You make it sound like a damned detective novel. Who says it was eight minutes past twelve when Wray and Pearson got upstairs?'

'Both of them, sir.'

The Chief Constable grunted.

'Very noticing of them. Fellows don't generally look at the clock every time they go into a room.'

'Well, sir, it was New Year's Eve. And Pearson makes no bones about it, he wanted to cover himself over this confessing business – says right out he's the one the family would be glad to pick on if they could.'

'What's he mean – the confessing, or the murder?'

Vyner said, 'Both,' rather drily, and then, 'I'm not going to say he's wrong either. He's only what you might call on the edge of the family, as you may say. But Mr Wray bears him out over the matter of the clock – says it was all of eight minutes past before they separated.'

Colonel Bostock said, 'H'm! What about the clock being wrong?'

'Well, sir, Mr Paradine was very fussy about that – used to have a man up once a week to wind and set the clocks, until labour got scarce, then he did it himself. The butler says he'd have a fit if any of the clocks was half a minute out. I checked them over myself, and they were all the same, and all dead right.'

'All right, let's get on. What about the nephews? Let's see – they went off early too, didn't they?'

'Yes, sir – at about a quarter to ten.'

'Together?'

'Yes, sir – on bicycles. Mr Mark, he's got a service flat in that new block, Birleton Mansions, just as you get into the town. He says he stopped there. Mr Richard lodges farther on, in Lennox Street. Both of them say they left without seeing Mr Paradine. Mr Richard says he didn't go out again. Mr Mark says he went for a walk. As a matter of fact the policeman on duty on the bridge says he saw him. It was bright moonlight up to the time the rain came on. He says Mr Mark passed him, going back in the direction of the River House. He puts the time at ten-twenty or so – says he looked at his watch within a few minutes of seeing him, to see how the time was getting on. I've only just had that, so I've not had the opportunity of putting it to Mr Mark. Well, that's as far as I've got with the nephews. Then there's Mr and Mrs Wray. He's here on business. He and his wife were occupying rooms on different sides of the house.'

Colonel Bostock nodded.

'Marriage broke up. Pity. Surprised he should be staying there. Awkward – very.'

'Well, sir, he says urgent business cropped up, and Mr Paradine insisted. Government business, I understand – confidential.'

Colonel Bostock nodded again.

'Yes, yes – he's in with Cadogan. Bomb sights – all that kind of thing. Very able fellow, I'm told.'

'Yes, sir. He wasn't giving much away – just said he looked in on Mr Paradine to say goodnight. And then corroborated Pearson. But Mrs Wray – well, sir, she admits to having had a conversation of some length with Mr Paradine after the others had gone to bed.'

'What?'

'I don't think there's anything in it, sir. In point of fact she needn't have told me. I just asked her as a matter of form whether she'd seen him again, and she said at once that she had – says she went up to her room and got thinking of something she wanted to discuss with Mr Paradine, so she went down and had a talk with him. She says it lasted about twenty minutes. It was a very friendly talk, and it had nothing to do with what had been said at dinner. She wouldn't say any more than that, but I got the impression that she hadn't expected to meet her husband like that – the butler said none of them expected him – that it upset her a good bit, and that she wanted to talk to her uncle about it.'

'That's natural enough.'

'Yes, sir, that's what I thought – but of course you never can tell. I've left Manners and Cotton taking statements from the staff. I did Lane the butler myself – you've got his statement there. He found the body. Then there's his wife – she's the cook, Mrs Lane – Louisa Holme, housemaid – she's been there fifteen years – and two young girls, Polly Parsons, under-housemaid, and Gladys Huggins, kitchenmaid. None of them in the way of knowing anything, I should say. Miss Holme was waiting at dinner with Lane, but no nearer the study than that. The others wouldn't have any business there either. All their rooms are in the kitchen wing, on the other side of the dining room.

None of their windows opens on to the terrace. The only occupied bedrooms whose windows do look out that way are Mr Wray's at one end of the house, more or less over the study, and Mrs Wray's at the other end. Mr Wray would have been in the dining room, which looks the other way, at the time of Mr Paradine's fall. But Mrs Wray says she woke up with a feeling that she had heard someone cry out. She says she can't be sure just what she heard because she was dreaming, but she woke up with the feeling that she had heard something. She put on the light and looked at the time, and it was just after twelve. I think there's very little doubt that she heard Mr Paradine cry out as he fell.'

Colonel Bostock made a very pronounced grimace.

'Good lord, Vyner, what a girl hears in a dream isn't evidence!'

'No, sir. Well, that's all the statements, except the one we got from Miss Brenda Ambrose. I left her to the last, and I didn't expect to get anything out of her. And now I don't know whether I did or not.'

Colonel Bostock pricked up his ears.

'How's that?'

'Well, sir, you've got what she's put her name to. But there's more to it than that. She'd a kind of manner with her every time she mentioned her sister-in-law, Mrs Ambrose – and it's my opinion she went out of her way to mention her.'

Colonel Bostock whistled. He rummaged out Brenda Ambrose's statement and went through it.

'Not so much the things she says as the nasty way she says 'em.'

'You've got it, sir.'

Colonel Bostock whistled again, softly.

'Well, there was something about that girl Irene—' he said.

TWENTY

MISS MAUD SILVER was shopping. Even in wartime, and with all the difficulty about coupons, children must be warmly clothed. She was planning to make a jersey and pull-on leggings for her niece Ethel's youngest, who would be three next month. Ethel would provide two coupons, but that would not be enough. She would have to break in upon her own spring supply. It was of no consequence – her last summer's dress was perfectly good, and she had plenty of stockings. Of course it was very difficult for girls who wore these extremely thin silk stockings. Really you had only to look at them to see that they couldn't be expected to last. Her own sensible hose were a very different matter – ribbed grey wool in winter, and good strong thread in summer. A great deal more durable.

Having settled the matter of the coupons, she had to decide upon the most suitable wool. There were very good shops in Birleton, really quite equal to London. Hornby's was a very good shop, but of course no one had much choice in wool nowadays. You couldn't really expect it.

The girl at the wool counter, who looked about fifteen, could only offer Miss Silver a choice between dark grey, vivid magenta, and a very bright emerald green. Miss Silver looked disapprovingly at all three of these shades, and for a time seriously considered the question of a wool substitute – very heavy and cottony, in fact not wool at all, but to be obtained in a number of most pleasing colours. It was very seldom indeed that she found it difficult to make up her mind. With the worst of winter in front of them, warmth should come first, and yet that green was really too bright – quite blinding. And dark grey for a child of three – oh, dear me, no!

As she stood by the counter in this unwonted state of hesitation, voices reached her from the other side of a display of brightly coloured scarves. The voices were lowered to that sibilant whisper which has a carrying quality all its own.

'The most shocking affair! Mr Paradine of all people!' That was one voice.

Another, higher and with the suspicion of a lisp, responded eagerly. 'They say it's murder.'

'It can't be!'

'They say it is.'

'Oh, *no!*'

Well, my dear, Mrs Curtin – you know, she works for me—'

'Yes?'

'Well, her niece Gladys is kitchenmaid at the Paradines' and she says all of them are as sure as sure that he'd never have fallen if he hadn't been pushed.'

'Ssh!'

'Well, I'm only telling you what she said – but of course people do gossip so—'

'Yes, don't they? It's dreadful.'

'Isn't it? Ssh! There's Lydia Pennington coming this way.'

Miss Silver made up her mind suddenly. Little Roger should have a dark grey suit with collar, cuffs and belt of the emerald green. She gave the order crisply, handed over her card to have the coupons cut off, and turned to look down the length of the department.

Lydia Pennington was coming towards her dressed in a dark grey coat and skirt. The black felt hat which she had just bought was pulled down over her red curls. The brim threw a shadow across her small, pale face. There was no colour in her cheeks, and her lips were as little made up as was consistent with her ideas of decency. It is possible that Miss Silver, who had only met her once, might not have known her if it had not been for those whispering voices on the other side of the scarves.

Lydia, on the other hand, would have known Miss Maud Silver anywhere. The tidy, dowdy figure in the black cloth jacket and the elderly fur; the hat with its bunch of purple pansies; the neat mousy hair; the neat, inconspicuous features; the air compounded of mildness and self-possession – these, once seen, had somehow impressed themselves and were immediately recognised.

Miss Silver heard her name, and found her hand being shaken.

'Miss Silver! Do you remember me? No, of course you don't. But I did meet you about a month ago. You were with Laura Desborough, and she introduced us. She's a friend of mine. I'm Lydia Pennington.'

Miss Silver gave her little dry cough.

'Indeed I remember you very well, Miss Pennington.'

Lydia said quickly, 'What are you doing here?' Her thoughts were racing, racing. The colour had come into her face.

In her driest manner Miss Silver replied, 'I am buying wool.'

Lydia's colour brightened still more. She lowered her voice.

'I didn't mean that. I meant, are you on a case?'

Miss Silver looked at her with attention.

'Oh, no. I am staying with my niece, Mrs Burkett. Her husband has been transferred to the Birleton branch of his bank. He joined up, you know, but he is not very strong and they have sent him back to his work. So delightful for Ethel. They are such a devoted couple, and they have three children, all boys. They very kindly asked me for Christmas, but I was unable to come to them then, so I have been spending the New Year with them instead.'

As she spoke Miss Silver observed the fluctuation of Miss Pennington's colour and the manner in which she kept herself rather rigidly turned away from the other shoppers. She was not, therefore, much surprised when Lydia said, 'Miss Silver – could I speak to you – would it be possible?'

'There is a nice tea-room here. We could have a cup of tea.'

'I don't know – I don't think so – too many people know me. I just came in to get myself a hat. I hadn't got a black one, and there'll be the inquest, and the funeral. Where are you staying? Could I walk there with you?'

Miss Silver coughed.

'We could walk – yes, certainly. My niece has a flat in Birleton Mansions.'

'What!'

'They are quite new and most convenient – a restaurant on the ground floor, and most reasonable. But of course, with the children, my niece will do most of the cooking upstairs. There is a very up-to-date kitchenette. Perhaps you know the flats?'

'I know someone who has one.'

'Then I will just pay for my wool, and we will walk in that direction,' said Miss Silver.

TWENTY-ONE

IT WAS PERHAPS an hour later that Lydia emerged from Mrs Burkett's flat, which was No 12 Birleton Mansions, and stood for a moment on the landing. She could take the lift, or she could walk down. She wasn't very fond of automatic lifts. She looked past the lift-shaft to the door of No 12A, and thought how surprising it was that Miss Silver's niece should be living just across the landing from Mark Paradine. She wondered if there were any possibility that he would be in, and all at once she wanted him to be in so overwhelmingly that she found herself standing on Mark's threshold and ringing his bell. It would save hours of time. They would be able to talk for once without the family streaming in and out. And he could take her back. He was sure to have to go out to the River House again. Excellent reasons and full of common sense. But the impetus which had taken her across the landing and set her finger on the bell owed nothing to reason.

The bell tinkled somewhere inside the flat. Lydia was sure that he wasn't going to be in. Why should he be in? It was nearly five o'clock. He was probably having tea with Grace Paradine and Phyllida – Elliot and Albert somewhere on the edge of the party, if they hadn't been frozen right off it. Or else he was interviewing solicitors, undertakers, and policemen.

She had reached this point of ultimate depression, when the door jerked open and Mark stood there glowering. She hoped that his really outrageous frown was not for her, and received some confirmation of this from an abrupt, 'I thought you were another of those damned reporters.' At once she was herself again, cool and self-possessed.

'Thank you, darling – I'm glad I'm not. You look absolutely homicidal. May I come in?' she said.

He stepped away from the door.

'Why did you say that?'

'Why did I say what?'

His voice rasped as he said, 'Homicidal.'

Lydia felt quite sick. What had he done to himself? What was he doing, to make him look and speak like this? She slammed the door behind her, leaned against it, and said in a blaze of anger, 'Don't be such a damned fool!'

They stood glaring at each other, until all at once he shook himself, gave a short hard laugh, and turned back to the room from which he had come.

'All right – that's that. Do you still want to come in?'

'Yes, I do.'

She walked past him into an untidy, comfortable sitting room – brown leather chairs, brown curtains, a shabby carpet, walls lined with books, a writing table, an electric fire. She sat down on the arm of one of the chairs.

'Cut it out!' she said. 'I love quarrelling with you, darling, but we haven't got the time. I want to talk. And do you mind sitting down, because you're about a mile up in the air, and I can't speak to people who are scowling over my head. It gives me the same feeling as a long-distance call.'

He came unwillingly down to the arm of the opposite chair.

'What do you want? I'm busy, you know. I came back for some papers.'

'All right, I won't keep you longer than I can help. I won't keep you at all if you'd rather not.'

'Go on – what is it?'

He wanted her to go with everything in him which was set to resist her. He wanted her to stay with all the unruly storm of emotion against which that resistance had been put up. Deep in his consciousness, a voice was calling him what she had called him – a fool – a damned, damned fool.

She said quietly and seriously, 'Mark – will you listen? I do want to talk to you, but I can't unless you listen – I don't mean just with your ears, but with your mind.'

He looked at her, nodded, and looked away again.

'All right.'

'You see, at Meadowcroft or at the River House someone is always coming in. You can't talk like that. I want to talk to you.'

'All right, talk.'

She wasn't looking at him. She was looking at the bright red of the fire, two bright glowing bars framed in bronze. She said, 'Mark, this is a frightful thing. The police think it was one of us.'

'Has that only just struck you?'

'No, of course not. But I don't see any way out of it.'

'Nor do I. So what?'

'We want someone to help us.'

'What do you mean?'

She looked at him now, her eyes brightly intent.

'Well, there's someone who could help us – right here at this moment, in this building. Her name is Miss Maud Silver, and she's a detective. I heard about her from Laura Desborough. You won't know her, but I expect you remember that Chinese Shawl case – well, she cleared it up. And then last autumn those murders at Vandeleur House, when that woman was caught – what was her name – Simpson. The police had been looking for her for ages. That was her again. She's absolutely marvellous, and at this moment she's staying with the people in No 12. Mrs Burkett is her niece.'

Mark's eyes were as intent as her own, but they were dark and bitter.

'And what do you expect this prodigy to do – find a convenient scapegoat outside the family circle? What a hope!'

Lydia said, 'I don't want scapegoats – I want the truth.'

'Whatever it is?'

'Whatever it is. Don't you?'

'I – don't – know—'

She struck her hands together.

'Mark, we've got to know! How can we go on if we don't? It's a thing that's got to be cleared up. How can we go on like this – all of us under suspicion – everyone suspecting everyone else – wondering if people are suspecting us – afraid to be natural – afraid to open our mouths? Look at yourself – at me! I used the sort of word one uses, and you went up in smoke. I could have bitten my tongue out the moment I'd said it, and I'd have boxed your ears if I could have reached them when I saw how you took me up. Are we going to have lists of things we mustn't speak about, words we mustn't say? Are we going to walk round like a lot of cats on hot bricks? I say, whoever it is, it's better to know.'

Mark got up, walked over to one of the bookcases, and stood there fingering the books that faced him.

'Whoever it is?' he said. 'I don't know. That's the sort of thing one says, but when it comes down to brass tacks and you go through the people and wonder which of them it was – well I don't know. Say it's murder – say someone pushed him over – say the police find out, or your Miss Silver finds out who did it – who is it to be? Aunt Grace? Frank Ambrose? Brenda? Irene? You? Me? Dicky? Albert Pearson? Elliot? Phyllida? That's the field. One of them did it. And you say let's find out – whoever it is. All right, the police find out – your Miss Silver finds out – and the murderer hangs.' He turned and came striding back to her. 'One of those ten people hangs – Aunt Grace – Frank – Brenda – Irene – you – me – Dicky – Albert – Elliot – Phyllida. Which is it to be?'

Lydia was standing too. She was as white as a sheet, but she looked up steadily.

'That is what I want to know.'

'You've got no favourites? Of course we'd all rather it was Albert, because we've never liked him very much. But you can't hang a man for being a bore, and unfortunately Albert and Elliot are the only people within measurable distance of having an alibi. If you want to know who the police are going to pick on, I'll tell you – *me*.'

'Why should they?' Her voice was as steady as her look.

He laughed.

'Because I went back.'

'Why?'

'Why do you suppose?'

'I don't know, Mark.'

'You're not being very bright, my dear. You don't seem to be able to put two and two together. But the police can – it's the sort of thing they're good at. They will say I went back to confess to whatever it was Uncle James was hinting about, and from there to saying I pushed him over is as near as makes no difference.'

There was a little pause before she said, 'Do they know you went back?'

His shoulder jerked.

'They will. The Chief Constable was over with Vyner this afternoon. I told them I went out for a walk. A bit of a thin story anyhow, and by this time it's a million to one the chap who was on duty on the bridge has reported having seen me. He knows me quite well. I believe he said goodnight as I passed him. They'll make sure I was going back to the River House.'

'You did go there?'

'Yes, I did.'

'Why?'

'Oh, to murder Uncle James of course – what else?'

She caught his arm and shook it.

'Mark, stop being stupid! It's too dangerous. Don't you see how dangerous it is?'

He twisted away from her, walked to the end of the room, stood there a moment, and then came back.

She said earnestly, 'Call Miss Silver in. We want help – we can't manage this alone. Mark, will you listen to me?'

'Oh, yes.'

'How is everything left? Are you an executor?'

'Yes – I and Robert Moffat.'

'And the house – who gets the house?'

'I do – the house and his place in the firm and the most damnable lot of money. All the motives the police can possibly want.'

She said, 'Rubbish!' And then, 'That is what I wanted to know. You see, if the house is yours and you're an executor, there's nothing to prevent your calling Miss Silver in. You can say she's an extra secretary. Nobody need know.'

'I won't play a trick on the family – it might do for the servants. What is she like?'

Suddenly Lydia relaxed. He was going to do it. The stiff, obstinate temper against which she was pushing had given way. It was odd that at this moment she should begin to shake. She laughed a little and said, 'She's exactly like a governess.'

TWENTY-TWO

MISS SILVER SAT primly at the writing table. An exercise book with a bright green cover lay in front of her upon Mark's blotting-pad. Mark himself sat facing her. Lydia lay back in the most comfortable of the chairs and looked on. The names of the Paradine family connection had been entered in the exercise book, together with such facts as had been elicited about each. The circumstances surrounding the New Year's Eve party and Mr Paradine's death had been repeated.

Mark said abruptly, 'We're putting you to a lot of trouble. I think we should have waited until we had discussed the matter with the rest of the family. They may not feel—'

Miss Silver coughed.

'You are not committing yourself to anything, Mr Paradine – that is understood. I should, naturally, regard anything you have said to me as confidential. At the same time I feel it is my duty to point out to you that resistance to enquiry on the part of any member of the family would be a fact the significance of which could not be overlooked.'

He leaned back frowning.

'People are not necessarily criminals and murderers because they would dislike being cross-examined by a stranger.'

Miss Silver smiled indulgently.

'No, indeed, Mr Paradine. The publicity in which murder involves a bereaved family is truly distressing, but I fear it is unavoidable. I will amplify your remark if I may, and say that it is not everyone with something to hide who is a criminal. One of the complications in a case of this kind is the fact that many people have thoughts, wishes, or actions which they would not willingly expose even to a friend, yet when police enquiries are being made these private motives and actions are brought to light. It is, in fact, a little like the Judgement Day, if I may use such a comparison without being considered profane.'

Mark said, 'Yes, that's true.'

He was in process of surprising himself. After some twenty minutes' conversation with this curiously dowdy little person, in the course of which she had neither said nor done anything at all remarkable, he was experiencing the strangest sense of relief. He could remember nothing like it since his nursery days. Old Nanna, the tyrant and mainstay of that dim early time before his parents died – there was something about Miss Silver that revived these memories. The old-fashioned decorum, the authority which has no need of self-assertion because it is unquestioned – it was these things that he discerned, and upon which he found himself disposed to lean. Miss Silver's shrewd, kind glance – perfectly kind, piercingly shrewd –

took him back to things he had forgotten. 'Not the least manner of good your standing there and telling me a lie, Master Mark. I won't have it for one thing, and it won't do you no good for another.'

There was that effect, but there was also a reassurance that he had not known since the time when he would wake sweating with nightmare to the light of Nanna's candle and the sound of her, 'Come, come now – what's all this?'

He looked up and met her eyes. Something had gone from his. Miss Silver saw in them what she had seen in many eyes before, a desperate need of help. She smiled slightly, as one smiles at an anxious child, and said, 'Well, Mr Paradine, we will leave it like that. You will go back and consult the rest of the family, and then if you wish it, I will come out to the River House and do what I can to help you.'

He said abruptly, 'I don't want to consult them – I'm prepared to take the responsibility. I want you to take the case. I want you to come out to the River House with me now.'

She became very serious.

'Are you quite sure about that?'

He gave a brief impatient nod.

'Yes, I'm quite sure. I want you to come. Lydia's right – we've got to clear this up. Someone inside, in the house, will have a better chance of doing it than the police – I can see that.'

Miss Silver coughed.

'You must understand, Mr Paradine, that my

position will be quite a private one, and that I can be no party to anything to which the police could take exception. May I ask who is in charge of the case?'

'Superintendent Vyner.

An expression of interest appeared on her face.

'Indeed? I have heard of him from an old pupil of mine, Randal March, who is Superintendent at Ledlington. He considers him a very able man.'

She got up with the air of the teacher who dismisses a class.

'Very well, then. I will just go across the landing and pack my case.'

TWENTY-THREE

'YOU HAVE BROUGHT a detective here – *here?*' Miss Paradine was quite white, quite controlled, but her eyes blazed and her voice had a cutting edge.

Mark, standing just inside the door of her sitting room, contemplated his assembled family and said, 'Yes.'

They were all there except Albert Pearson, and they were all looking at him – Frank Ambrose with a heavy frown; Brenda paler than usual, her eyes bolting; Irene with her mouth hanging open; Phyllida startled; Dicky, his lips pursed for an inaudible whistle; Elliot grim; and Grace Paradine with a look of anger which he had seen once or twice before, but not for him. Only Lydia's face held any encouragement. She met his eyes, smiled into them with hers, and then looked quickly away. She thought, It's going to be a dog-fight. Oh, my poor Mark!

They were all standing. Grace Paradine said, 'I don't know what you were thinking about. You must send him away at once!'

Mark stayed where he was by the door. He said, 'No.' And then, 'It's a woman, Aunt Grace – Miss Silver.'

She said again, and with no less anger, 'You must send her away!'

'I can't do that. I'm sorry you don't like it, but I've quite made up my mind. None of you will like it, but there's been a murder. As I see it, the only person who can reasonably object is the murderer. I'm not saying it's one of us. The police are quite sure that it is. I hope it isn't. I've brought Miss Silver here because I think that's our best chance of getting at the truth – I think we've got to get at the truth. At the moment we're all under suspicion. It doesn't seem possible to us because we're right in the middle of it – we can't see what it looks like from outside. The police are going to suspect everyone who hasn't an alibi. They're going to dig about until they can turn up a motive. Miss Silver said just now that a murder case was like the Day of Judgment. She's absolutely right. Most people have got something they don't want to have ferreted out. Well, it's no good – we shan't be able to hide anything. It's damnable, but there's something worse, and that is all going on suspecting one another and being suspected by everyone we know. We've got to find out who did it, and we've got to find out quickly.'

There was a dead silence, broken by a burst of tears from Irene. To her sobbed-out 'How – how can you say such things?' Mark replied curtly, 'Everyone's going to say them.'

Grace Paradine said in her voice of cold anger, 'You're very ready to accuse your relations of murder, Mark. Perhaps you will tell us whom you suspect.'

He straightened himself up and turned a look of bitter amusement on her.

'Well, I gather that the police favour me.'

This time Dicky's whistle was audible. Frank Ambrose said, 'Why?'

'Oh, this and that. I'm not expected to give evidence against myself am I?'

'The police will want to know the terms of the will. Do you know them?'

'Do *you*?'

Frank Ambrose said, 'No,' and said it rather quickly. After a short pause he went on, 'I suppose you do. And I suppose from the way you've taken over that they're very much in your favour.'

'That's one of the reasons why the police are going to suspect me.'

Frank went on doggedly.

'Don't you know how you stand? I think the rest of us ought to know too.'

'Here and now?'

'I think we're entitled to know as much as you do. I'm not asking *how* you know.'

Mark said, 'That's damned offensive, Frank.' Then, in a curiously abstracted voice, 'He gave me a draft. I can't remember everything. Phyllida gets five thousand – he was very fond of her. Dicky gets ten and the Crossley shares. Aunt Clara's diamonds are to be divided between Dicky and myself – two thirds to me and a third to him. Albert gets a thousand pounds free of legacy duty. You and Brenda get two thousand each as a mark of affection. He said he'd settled money on both of you when you came of age. That's all I can remember offhand.'

Frank looked heavily at him.

'Who gets the rest?'

'I do. I'm the residuary legatee.'

'You get the house?'

Mark nodded.

'Yes. You can see why the police are going to suspect me. Let's get back to the question of Miss Silver. She's been extraordinarily successful in other cases. She's easy to get on with – nothing aggressive about her. I'm asking you all to make things as easy for her as possible. I can see how it looks to you, Aunt Grace, and I'm sorry, but you must want this cleared up as much as any of us. As I said before, there's only one person who doesn't want it cleared up. I don't suppose anyone wants to fit the cap on, so I take it you'll all do what you can to help.'

Nobody answered him.

When the silence had lasted long enough to make it clear that nobody was going to answer he turned and went out of the room, almost running into Albert upon the threshold. A collision having been narrowly avoided, Albert advanced and approached Miss Paradine.

'Mr Moffat is below. He asked whether you would see him.'

TWENTY-FOUR

GRACE PARADINE WAITED for Robert Moffat. She had moved nearer to the fire, and stood there facing the door through which he would come. She had not been alone in a room with him for thirty years – not since the brief bitter interview in which she told him that she knew about Carrie Lintott, and gave him back his ring. Across the gap of the years it still pleased her to remember that it was he who had wept, not she. It was just a month before the day which had been set for their marriage. Her wedding dress hung, covered with a sheet, in the room which was Phyllida's now. Her wreath and veil reposed in the top long drawer of the tallboy. But it was Robert Moffat who contributed all the emotion to that interview. He had gone down on his knees and clutched at her skirt. He had abased himself in penitence. He had begged, implored, protested. She was remembering these things now, as she had remembered them every time she had seen him in the last thirty years.

You cannot live in the same place and never meet. Robert Moffat's father was a partner in the Paradine-Moffat Works. In due course Robert succeeded him. They were bound to meet. She went away for a time, and then she came back.

They were bound to meet. The first time was at the County Ball. She had a new dress, she was looking her best. She bowed and smiled. It was he who flushed and turned away. After that, many chance meetings – in the street; coming out of church; coming out of the theatre; at balls, receptions, bazaars. He ceased to change colour, but she never ceased to remember that she had had him on his knees to her. When he married, she paid a formal call upon the bride, leaving her father's cards. Mrs Moffat, a pleasant rosy little person, smiled and dimpled, and made herself very agreeable. Miss Paradine was not at home when the call was returned. Meetings between the two households were few and formal. Never till this moment had there been any approach to a personal relationship.

The door opened and he came in – a big, bluff man, fresh-coloured and hearty. He came up to her with an outstretched hand. He was both shocked and horrified, but he was plainly nervous too. Even a murder in the family didn't prevent him from thinking how formidable Grace Paradine looked, and what an escape he had had. Extraordinary to think that he had once been so madly in love with her. Thought the world had come to an end when she turned him down. Something in him chuckled. He'd been much better off with his comfortable Bessie. Kind, that's what she was – comfortable and kind. A woman ought to be kind.

Miss Paradine ignored the outstretched hand. To his 'This is a terrible thing!' she replied that it was very good of him to have come. He thought how impassive she was, how controlled. He would have thought the better of her if she had broken down. And then, as she turned a little and the light from the farther window struck her face, he was shocked at her pallor and the dark marks under her eyes.

'It's been a horrible shock. If there is anything that we can do. . . . It's a terrible break-up for you, Grace. I can't think what it's going to be like without him – I can't realise it at all – he has always been there. And it's worse for you – I don't know what to say about it. I hope you've got Phyllida here – she'll be a comfort. Elliot's with you too, isn't he? James rang me up last night and said he was staying. Threw our table out, and if it had been anyone else he'd have had the rough side of my tongue, but as it was, we were only too glad, Bessie and I. Dreadful thing for young people to separate like that. James felt it, I know – wanted to see it made up. Hope he had the satisfaction of knowing he'd brought them together again. Never could understand what went wrong myself. She's a charming girl. I'm glad you've got her with you.'

Grace Paradine said in her deep, controlled voice, 'Yes, I have got Phyllida.'

Then she moved a step and rang the bell.

'You will like to see Mark, Robert.'

TWENTY-FIVE

MARK HAD REACHED the head of the stairs, when Elliot Wray caught him up.

'Here – wait a minute.'

'What is it?'

'Where have you put this woman?'

'In the study. I've told Lane she's to have the bedroom next to yours.'

Elliot said abruptly, 'I want to see her.'

'All right, come along. Do you want me to come too?'

Elliot considered.

'I don't know . . . No, I'll see her alone. How much does she know?'

'Lydia saw her first – I don't know what she said. I told her what happened last night, and told her the names of the people who were there and the way they were related – things like that.'

Elliot stood for a moment as if he were in two minds whether to say something or not. In the end he laughed grimly and said what he hadn't thought about at all.

'Well, you seem to have inherited a bomb-throwing tendency along with the rest of it.' After he went off down the stairs and round the corner towards the study, just missing Robert Moffat, who had emerged from the drawing room on the other side of the hall.

Elliot's first view of Miss Silver gave him a shock of surprise. She wasn't in the very least like anything he had expected. Just what he had expected, he didn't know. Something hard and efficient – a stony eye and a mouth like a trap – certainly not this mild, decorous little person in clothes which must have been out of date when he was born. He was reminded of an Edwardian period film seen recently enough to bob up at the sight of her.

He said, 'Miss Silver?' and received a pleasant smile and a slight inclination of the head.

She was seated at the table with a green copybook before her. It was curious to see her there in old James's chair. The police had occupied the room all the morning. Photographs had been taken both here and on the terrace, everything had been gone over for fingerprints. Now the room was straight and tidy again. The police had done with it. Mr Paradine had done with it. Except for the fact that this little governessy person was sitting at his table, everything was just as it had been last night. The chairs had been put back in their accustomed places. The table, the ink-stand, the blotting pad were just as usual, except for the green copybook in front of Miss Silver and, a little way off on the left, one of those small pocket diaries which Miss Paradine had been handing out last night. It was the blue one. He wondered how it had got there. He couldn't remember who had had the blue one – he hadn't been noticing. He thought it would be Mark, or Richard. He came over and picked it up. As he turned it in his hand, it fell open, as a book will do when it has been bent back to mark a place. A date sprang into view – February 1st.

With the diary still in his hand, he was aware of Miss Silver saying, 'Is it the date that interests you, or the book?'

He put it down at once.

'Oh, neither. Miss Paradine was giving these diaries as presents last night. I wondered—'

'To whom this one had been given? You think not to Mr Paradine?'

'I don't know.' There was some finality in his tone.

He took a chair and sat down.

'I believe you have a list of all our names. I am Elliot Wray. Mark Paradine said I could come and talk to you.'

'Oh, certainly.'

Her voice was the voice of a gentlewoman, pleasant in tone, a little prim. As he was thinking this, she said, 'What do you want to talk to me about, Mr Wray?'

Something prompted him to say, 'I was wondering how much you know.'

Miss Silver smiled. Rather a rugged-looking young man – intelligent – not so obviously under strain as Mr Mark Paradine. Her excellent memory provided her with the reflection that he was one of the two members of the family circle fortunate enough to have an alibi for the time of the murder. She smiled at him.

'Not so much as I should like to know, Mr Wray. Perhaps you will add to my knowledge. I may say that I am very glad to see you. Will you mind if I ask you some questions?'

'Not at all.'

'Well then, Mr Wray – you do not live in Birleton?'

'No.'

'And you are engaged on confidential work in connection with aeroplane construction?'

'Yes.'

'These things are common knowledge? And so is the fact that your present visit to Birleton was connected with work being done for the government at the Paradine-Moffat Works?'

'I shouldn't say that it was common knowledge.'

Miss Silver coughed.

'Will you agree that this knowledge was common to the party dining here last night?'

He gave her a glance of quick surprise.

'Yes, I would agree to that – at least to this extent that they could all have known as much, if they had been interested. I don't suppose any of the women would have bothered about it.'

Miss Silver coughed again.

'Suppositions are not always reliable, Mr Wray. But let us continue. You stayed here last night, I believe, but not the night before. Had you expected to stay here at all?'

She saw his fair brows draw together in a frown as he said, 'No.'

'Had you expected to dine here last night?'

'No.'

'Will you tell me what occasioned the change in your plans?'

He said with an assumption of carelessness, 'Mr Paradine rang me up at seven o'clock. He said he wanted to see me on a matter of business.'

'And when you came out here he insisted on your remaining for dinner and staying the night. May I ask how you had intended to spend the evening?'

He gave her a curious look.

'I was dining with Mr Moffat, Mr Paradine's partner.'

'And you broke the engagement?'

'Mr Paradine broke it for me.'

Miss Silver said, 'Dear me—' and then, 'I am going to ask you a question which you may not wish to answer. Miss Pennington and Mr Mark Paradine have given me an account of what took place at the dinner table last night. It must have been a very trying experience, especially for the guilty person. I understand that Mr Paradine actually used that expression, "the guilty person", but beyond stating that the family interests had been betrayed he gave no indication of the nature of this betrayal. The police will, of course, have made enquiries on this point. I have no means of knowing what information they may have obtained, or what conclusions, if any, they may have arrived at. I should just like to ask you whether you brought any papers or plans with you on this visit. I feel sure that you must have done so.'

'Naturally.'

'You had entrusted these papers to Mr Paradine?'

'What makes you think that?'

Miss Silver smiled.

'I feel sure of it, Mr Wray. I also feel sure that when Mr Paradine summoned you at seven o'clock last night it was in order to inform you that these papers, or some of them, were missing.'

Elliot jerked back his chair and sprang up.

'Who told you that? Was it Mark?'

Miss Silver regarded him with intelligent interest. Then she said primly, 'I do not imagine that Mr Mark Paradine knows.'

Elliot was leaning towards her across the table.

'Then it was Lydia – Lydia told you.'

Miss Silver shook her head.

'I am quite sure that Miss Pennington does not know either.'

'Then how the devil do you know?'

Miss Silver gazed at him in reproof. To his extreme astonishment he found himself flushing beneath this gaze.

'I beg your pardon! But would you mind telling me who did tell you?'

Her look became one of forbearance. He felt himself the backward boy to whom a teacher patiently explains the obvious.

'The evidence told me, Mr Wray. You will forgive me if I touch on what may be painful. There had been a breach between you and Mr Paradine's family for a year. Your dining and spending the night here could only mean one of two things – a reconciliation, or an emergency of such gravity as to cause all other considerations to be set on one side. There was no evidence of a reconciliation. Your appearance in the drawing room just before dinner startled everyone. It was obviously quite unexpected even by Miss Paradine – even, pardon me, by Mrs Wray. I had therefore to consider the other alternative, an emergency so sudden and urgent that Mr Paradine himself cancelled your dinner engagement and was able to induce you to cooperate in a plan which necessitated your joining the party at dinner and staying the night. Taken in conjunction with his remark about betrayal and his statement that he knew who the guilty person was, this led me to the conclusion that Mr Paradine had missed some important paper or papers, that he knew who had taken them, and that he believed he could put sufficient pressure on this person to secure their return. On this assumption your acquiescence and the scene at the dinner table fall naturally into place. 'A very serious motive is also supplied for the murder of the person who possessed such damaging information.'

Elliot dropped slowly back again into his chair. His hands still gripped the edge of the table. They continued to grip it. After a moment he said, 'You've been about a quarter of an hour in the house. Are you telling me that you've found this out for yourself? I'm sorry, but I don't believe it. I want to know what Mark and Lydia have been telling you. I don't want to be offensive, but you must see that if either of them knew that my blueprints had been taken, well, it points to one of them as the thief. Only three people knew that the prints were missing – the person who took them, Mr Paradine, and myself. If Mark or Lydia knew—'

Miss Silver coughed.

'Very well put, Mr Wray. It is a pleasure to deal with anyone who can take a point so quickly. I can, however, assure you that neither Mr Mark nor Miss Lydia so much as hinted at the possibility that Mr Paradine's accusation had anything to do with your papers. Miss Lydia merely informed me that there had been a serious breach between you and the Paradine family, but that your business relations were not affected. Mr Mark added that your present visit was on government business of a confidential nature. My deductions were drawn from these and a number of other small facts. I gather from what you have said that they are correct.'

He let go of the table and leaned back.

'Oh, yes, they are correct.'

Miss Silver opened the green copybook and wrote in it. Then she said, 'Mr Paradine told you that he knew who had taken the papers?'

'Yes.'

'Did he give you any indication of who that person was?'

'No, he didn't.'

She looked up at him, pencil in hand.

'Mr Wray, you can help me here. You are shrewd and observant. I want to know the impression made on you at the time by his voice, his look, his manner. To what extent did they betray feeling – emotion – shock?'

Elliot gave a short laugh.

'It wasn't Mr Paradine's way to show his feelings.'

'Still, you might have received some impression, and you must subsequently have gone over that impression in your own mind. The discovery of the loss must have been a shock to Mr Paradine. Did you think then, or do you think now, that this shock was a personal one?'

Elliot looked at her, first with surprise and then with attention.

'He was in very good spirits. If you ask me, I should say that he was enjoying himself. He told me I'd got to stay, and told me I should have the papers back in the morning. Since you know so much, I may as well tell you that he was perfectly right – I did get them back. They were here on his table.' He leaned over to indicate the corner on her left. 'I took them, but I didn't mean to say anything about it. I thought that Mr Paradine's death was an accident – we all did at first. When it seemed that it was murder, I had to consider my position. As a result I didn't feel justified in holding my tongue, and when the Chief Constable came out here this afternoon I told him what you've just been telling me.' On the last words his lips twisted into an odd one-sided smile.

Miss Silver said, 'Thank you, Mr Wray. You did quite rightly. Let us return to Mr Paradine. He was not, you think, emotionally affected by his knowledge of the thief's identity?'

Elliot grinned suddenly and said, 'Mr Paradine didn't have emotions.'

Miss Silver looked as if he were evading the issue.

'I will put it another way,' she said. 'Mr Paradine had ten guests last night. From your own observation, for which of those ten people had he most affection?'

Elliot said bluntly, 'I'm not really stupid, you know – I can see what you're getting at. You want to know whether the person who took the papers was someone he was fond of, and whether he was upset about it on that account. Well, offhand, I should say he wasn't. I'm not saying this to the police, and I'm not swearing to it in any conceivable circumstances, but if you want that impression you were talking about just now, I don't mind giving it to you. I thought he'd caught someone out and he was going to enjoy scoring him off. But that may have been a put-up show. I don't think it was, but that's just my opinion. I've known one other person who could look as pleased as Punch and be in a perfectly foul temper underneath. I don't think Mr Paradine would have given himself away whatever he felt. He didn't show his feelings – you wouldn't even know whether he'd got any. He had a very detached, sarcastic manner. But if you want my own personal impressions about him and the family, here they are. I think he was fond of my wife. And I suppose he was fond of his sister – she'd kept house for him for twenty years. But that's supposition, not impression. I believe he thought a lot of Mark. He's in the research department, and he's done very good work. He wanted to go off to the RAF a couple of years ago, and Mr Paradine went right through the roof. I wasn't here at the time, but I believe there was an absolutely first-class row. I don't know what he felt about Dick Paradine. Everyone in the family is rather fond of him, so there's no reason to suppose Mr Paradine wasn't. Then there are Frank and Brenda Ambrose. They're steps – his wife's children. He thought a lot of her, and I suppose he thought a lot of them. He settled money on them when they came of age. Frank's in the business – solid, useful kind of chap, very thorough and methodical. Brenda is a bit odd-man-out in the family – a bit on the downright side.' His laugh informed Miss Silver that this was an understatement.

She looked from him to the portrait over the mantelpiece.

'Is that the late Mrs Paradine?'

'It is – covered with diamonds.'

Miss Silver gazed earnestly at the portrait. Fair and placid, Clara Paradine looked down upon the room. Ruby velvet and the diamonds of her husband's choice – a plump white neck and shoulders – fair hair of an even shade – blue eyes rather widely set under colourless brows – a kindly mien . . . Miss Silver considered her with attention, then turned again to Elliot.

'Was she English, Mr Wray?'

He looked at her.

'What makes you ask that?'

'It is not quite an English type. I wondered whether she had been Dutch, or German.'

Elliot said, 'German.'

'And her first husband, Mr Ambrose?'

'Oh, English.'

After a slight pause Miss Silver dismissed the subject. She said, 'Please go on with the rest of the party, Mr Wray,' and saw him frown.

'Well, that's very nearly the lot. You've seen Lydia Pennington. She's the sort you can depend on. Mr Paradine used to make a show of disapproving of her, but it's my opinion he liked her quite a lot – I just give it you for what it's worth. Miss Paradine will tell you that he loathed her. Her sister Irene is married to Frank Ambrose. Quite candidly, she's a bit of a fool – hasn't two ideas in her head. No, that's wrong – she has just two, little Jimmy and little Rena. She rams them down everybody's throat. I should say that Mr Paradine put up with her because he'd got to. That brings us to Albert Pearson – the perfect secretary and the perfect bore. He's some sort of third cousin. Mr Paradine found him about three years ago supporting a widowed mother and improving his mind at evening classes.'

'Very praiseworthy,' said Miss Silver in her most

decorous voice. 'May I ask how he was supporting his mother.'

'He was a jeweller's assistant, I believe. His mother died, and Mr Paradine brought him here as his secretary. He had mugged up shorthand and typing.'

'And was Mr Paradine attached to him?'

Elliot laughed.

'Nobody could possibly be attached to Albert,' he said.

TWENTY-SIX

MISS SILVER DINED with the family and afterwards sat with them in the crimson and gold drawing room, which she admired very much. A grandly proportioned room – such warm colouring – such rich brocades – such a deep-piled carpet – the crystal chandeliers too, the finest of their kind. She approved Mr Paradine's taste, and sincerely regretted his demise. Now, all too probably, these handsome and dignified furnishings would be replaced by chintz or linen.

Dinner had been a particularly trying meal. Since Miss Silver especially desired to see the entire family and Mark had made a point of this, they were all there, but nobody had dressed. The men were in their day clothes, Irene, Lydia and Brenda in coats and skirts, Phyllida in her grey dress, but Miss Paradine had put on a long black gown, plain and high in the neck. Miss Silver, as was her custom, had changed into a two-year-old summer dress – green artificial silk with a distressing pattern of orange dots and dashes, the front adorned by a large cameo brooch depicting an apocryphal Greek gentleman in a helmet. The removal of her hat showed her to possess a good deal of soft mousy hair done up in braids behind and tightly curled into a fringe upon her forehead, both braids and fringe controlled by a hair-net. In addition to the cameo brooch she wore small golden studs in her ears, a gold chain about her neck, and a bar brooch set with seed pearls to loop up the pince-nez which she occasionally required for reading. She still wore the warm ribbed grey stockings which she found so comfortable in winter, but had changed her laced outdoor shoes for a pair of black *glacé* slippers with beaded toes. Elliot's conviction that he had encountered her in an Edwardian film became intensified every time he looked at her – only the dress should have been longer – right down to her feet.

He had been placed as far from Phyllida as the table would allow – Grace Paradine had seen to that. She had seen to it too that he had never had five minutes alone with her all day. And she was trying to hoof him out. All right, let her try. He had been dragged in, and now he was going to stay, and Grace Paradine could pull all the strings she liked. It was Mark's house and not hers, and somehow he didn't think she'd get Mark to the point of telling him to go.

His preoccupation with this theme kept him silent through the greater part of the meal. Not that he was remarkable in this – Frank Ambrose spoke exactly twice, and Mark could not be said to have spoken at all. The meal was too much yesterday's party in caricature. Hashed turkey, fried plum pudding, the empty place at the head of the table which nobody cared to take. A detective sitting with them to watch how they looked, spoke, ate, drank, thought. These things were not conducive to conversation. Even Dicky's flow of talk had dried. Women have more social sense than men. Phyllida went on trying to talk to Frank on one side of her, and to Mark on the other, until it was so obviously useless to expect an answer that she gave it up. Lydia and Dicky exchanged a few low-toned remarks and then fell silent. Miss Paradine, at the foot of the table, was a dignified figure of grief. The long black dress with its high neck and falling sleeves enhanced the effect. There were dark shadows under her eyes, the line from brow to cheek had sharpened. There was no longer any anger in her look. Her eyes were sad. There was no resentment in her manner. She was the considerate hostess, anxious to make things easy for her guests, veiling her private sorrow. She spoke tenderly to Phyllida, with conventional courtesy to Miss Silver, kindly to everyone except Elliot Wray who might not have been there at all.

Miss Silver, placed beside Albert Pearson, received the full benefit of his conversation. It took more than a murder in the house to inhibit his passion for imparting information. But she was to learn that it must be information of his own choosing. Having received a sketch of his early history from Mark Paradine, she attempted to engage him upon a topic with which he might be supposed to be particularly conversant. She had herself an interest in curious and unusual jewels, but when she addressed a question upon the subject to Albert it met with no response. Instead she was favoured over the hashed turkey with a concise history of Birleton from Saxon times until the reign of Queen Elizabeth. The pudding afforded an opportunity of bringing the story up to date. The founding of the Paradine works by Benjamin Paradine – 'grandfather of the late Mr Paradine, and my own great-grandfather' – was interrupted by Miss Paradine giving the signal for the ladies to retire.

In the drawing room Miss Silver found herself engaged by her hostess.

'I hope you have everything you want.'

'Indeed yes, Miss Paradine.'

'You must tell me if there is anything I can do.'

Miss Paradine was being very gracious. If there was a hint of condescension in her manner, a trace of the pride that apes humility, it was very carefully restrained. Yet it is indisputable that Miss Silver was reminded of Royalty opening a bazaar. She took up her knitting bag, a Christmas present from Ethel, extracted her needles and a ball of dark grey wool, and said, 'You are very good.'

About half an inch of the nether part of little Roger's suit depended from three of the needles. Miss Silver inserted the fourth needle and began to knit with great swiftness and dexterity. After a slight hesitation Miss Paradine sat down in the opposite corner of the settee.

'We all hope so much that this terrible business may be cleared up as soon as possible.'

Miss Silver's needles clicked.

'Oh, yes, indeed.'

Miss Paradine's manner had undergone a change. It had become warm and sympathetic like her voice.

'These sudden bereavements are sad enough without the additional shadow of suspicion.'

'Yes, indeed.'

'My brother meant very much to us all. Miss Pennington, of course, did not know him well. She is my niece Mrs Ambrose's sister – not really a member of the family herself, though we are all very fond of her. And my nephew Mark is not, I think, very good at expressing himself – very clever in his own way, but very reserved, and just now, of course, very upset about his uncle's death. I feel that they may not really have given you any idea of how much my brother's loss will be felt.'

Miss Silver looked intelligently at her hostess and continued to knit.

Miss Paradine drew a long breath.

'My brother was a very remarkable man. He liked to do things in his own way. I suppose you have been given an account of what happened at dinner last night. It is most painful to us all that the police are placing a quite unwarrantable construction on what was said. I do ask you to believe that the whole thing has been grossly exaggerated. My brother had a vigorous and dramatic way of expressing himself, even about trifles. I am convinced that the whole thing meant very little. Something had vexed him, or rather someone, and he took this way of letting us all know about it. It was, I assure you, quite in his character. I thought so little of it myself that when the Superintendent questioned me this morning I really didn't mention it at all.'

Miss Silver said, 'Dear me—'

A very faint movement of Miss Paradine's dark brows suggested that she had controlled an incipient frown. She had a faint, sad smile as she said, 'I really made nothing of it at all. As I told Colonel Bostock this afternoon – he is the Chief Constable – it had quite gone out of my mind. The shock of my brother's accident – I still believe that it was an accident—' She broke off, held her hands tightly clasped together for a moment, and half closed her eyes. Then she got up. 'Forgive me – I should not have tried to speak of it – it is too soon. Perhaps you would like to talk to my niece Mrs Ambrose for a little, or to Miss Ambrose.'

Miss Silver gazed at the group about the fire – Irene, Brenda, Phyllida. She coughed and said, 'I should like very much to talk to Miss Ambrose, if I may.'

When Brenda, stolidly reluctant, was seated beside her, Miss Silver smiled affably and said, 'I asked to see you, Miss Ambrose, because I want someone observant and methodical to tell me just what happened after you came into the drawing room last night.'

Brenda stared with the light eyes which were like Clara Paradine's only not so blue. She had, altogether, a curious look of her mother, but without the kind comeliness and contentment of the portrait.

'In here – last night?'

'If you will.'

Brenda went on staring.

'Well, I don't know. We came in, and I said my stepfather must have gone mad. I suppose you've heard what he said at dinner?'

'Oh, yes.'

'Well, I said he must have gone mad to get us all here to a party and then say a thing like that. I said it was the limit, and my sister-in-law Irene – that's her on the left of the fire – well, she burst out crying and said she knew Mr Paradine was talking at her.'

'Dear me – did she say why?'

'No, she didn't. She made an exhibition of herself and kept on saying she hadn't done anything, and why should he think it was her. She's a very hysterical girl – no self-control at all. I don't know what she'd been up to, but if you ask me, I should say she'd got something on her mind – otherwise why go to bits like that? If it hadn't been for Miss Paradine, we'd never have got her quiet. Of course I'm no good because she can't stand me – wouldn't have me in the house if it weren't for Frank. Look here, I'll tell you one thing about Irene – she's vindictive. You wouldn't think so, because she's got that wishy-washy look and she'll talk about those kids of hers until everybody's sick of them, but if she gets a down on anyone she'll never let up on it. She's got one on me because I used to keep my brother's house and do it a damned sight better than she does. That's Irene all over – if she can't do a thing herself she hates the person who can.'

Miss Silver's needles clicked.

'An unamiable trait, but sadly common,' she observed.

Brenda laughed angrily.

'Irene only likes people who butter her up,' she said. 'Frank doesn't any more – he's found her out. I'm beginning to wonder if my stepfather hadn't too. That would account for a lot. You know, the reason she's all over those kids is because she goes down with them – they think she's wonderful. They'll get a nasty shock when they're a bit older, and then you'll see there won't be so much of the devoted mother. It makes me sick!'

'Dear me,' said Miss Silver, 'that is very interesting.' She gazed mildly at Brenda Ambrose. 'Pray continue. You were telling me what happened after dinner last night. Miss Paradine quieted your sister-in-law—'

'Oh, yes. She's clever – knows how to manage people. She had presents for us all. She went and got them. She didn't want Lane to notice anything when he came in with the coffee.'

As she spoke, the routine of the previous evening repeated itself. Lane came in with the great silver tray. Louisa followed with the cake-stand. Miss Silver considered these appointments very handsome, very suitable. She admired the robust Victorian decoration of the tray, the coffeepot, the milk jug, and deplored the absence of what would doubtless have been the equally handsome sugar basin. The bottle of saccharin of which Lane was so much ashamed was hidden from her view, but she would in any case have considered it a poor substitute. As a patriotic citizen she was prepared to drink her coffee without sugar, but not with saccharin. Still knitting, she observed, 'That was a happy thought of Miss Paradine's. You said she went and got the presents. Do you mean she went out of the room?'

'Of course. They were upstairs.'

'And how long was she away, Miss Ambrose?'

Brenda stared.

'Oh, no time at all. Just long enough to get the parcels.'

'Not long enough to have had a word with her brother?'

'No, of course not. He hadn't come out of the dining room.'

'You are sure of that?'

'Of course I am. I don't say things unless I'm sure about them. The men were still in the dining room. They came in after she had given us our presents. I had a torch, Phyllida had handkerchiefs, Lydia got bath salts, and Irene had snapshots of the children. The men came in after that.'

'And did they have presents too?'

'Elliot Wray didn't. Of course he wasn't expected. He and Phyllida have been dead cuts for a year. I must say he had a nerve to turn up like he did. Miss Paradine was wild. She wouldn't have given him anything anyhow – she's always loathed him. She gave the others a pocket diary each. It's frightfully difficult to think of anything you can give to a man, isn't it?'

'Yes indeed, but a diary is always useful. Had Miss Paradine managed to get them in different colours?'

Brenda nodded.

'Yes, she had. She's clever at that sort of thing – takes a lot of trouble.'

'She must do so. What colours did she manage to get?'

'Oh, brown – red – blue – purple.'

Brenda was becoming bored. She thought Miss Silver a futile old maid. She said abruptly, 'I'll get you some coffee.'

But as she rose, Miss Silver had another question.

'Blue would be my preference. I wonder if it was Miss Paradine's. To whom did she give the blue diary, Miss Ambrose?'

Brenda turned back. She felt she was being clever as she said, 'I'm afraid you can't make anything out of that. Mark got the blue diary. Richard is Aunt Grace's blue-eyed boy. He got the red. Some people prefer red, you know. Miss Paradine does.'

TWENTY-SEVEN

IN THE COURSE of the evening Miss Silver managed to converse with most of the members of the Paradine family. She found Mrs Ambrose deeply interested in little Roger's leggings, and consulted with her as to whether they should be left plain or enlivened with stripes of the emerald green. She also exchanged stories of Johnny, Derek and Roger for anecdotes of Jimmy and little Rena. Irene became quite animated and told her all about not being able to wake Rena last night, and going out to find Dr Horton, and how angry Frank had been – 'Men are so *unreasonable*.'

Miss Silver replied that they could not be expected to understand a mother's feelings. After which there was no ice left to break and she was told just how difficult Brenda was, and what a pity Lydia didn't make up her mind to marry Dicky and settle down in Birlcton – it would be so nice to have someone to leave the children with. Even a slight knowledge of Miss Pennington discouraged Miss Silver from believing that this would prove an inducement, but she took care not to say so.

With a little tactful prompting Irene's tongue flowed on. Miss Paradine was wonderful – 'Look how she's keeping everything together. You wouldn't think anything dreadful had happened. She has such self-control – I don't know how she does it. I do envy people who have a lot of self-control. Aunt Grace is wonderful that way. I remember at Phyllida's wedding, nobody would have guessed that she was simply broken-hearted, only of course she was. I don't think she would have liked Phyllida marrying anyone, but of course if it had been anyone in Birleton it wouldn't have been so bad. We used to think it would be so nice if she married Mark. He's a very distant cousin really – Phyllida is adopted, you know – so it would have been quite all right. But marrying Elliot Wray meant a complete separation for poor Aunt Grace – I don't wonder she felt dreadful about it. I don't know what I shall feel when Rena marries – I don't like to think about it.'

Miss Silver was soothing on the subject of Rena.

'Of course I *like* Elliot,' said Irene, 'and Phyllida was dreadfully in love with him. You know they are separated. I don't know what happened – Aunt Grace didn't talk about it. They were only just back from their honeymoon, and we all thought how happy they were, and then all of a sudden Aunt Grace said Elliot had gone and he wouldn't be coming back. Poor Phyl looked exactly like a ghost. You can't think how surprised everyone was when he walked in on Wednesday night just as if nothing had happened.'

'I can well imagine it,' said Miss Silver.

She conversed presently with Phyllida, who told her quite simply that she had come down to the study and talked with her uncle after the others had gone to bed.

'Elliot didn't want me to tell anyone, but that wouldn't have been right, would it? It hadn't anything to do with what my uncle said at dinner. Elliot was afraid the police might think it had. I wanted to see Uncle James about something quite different.'

Miss Silver looked at her kindly.

'That was very natural, Mrs Wray.'

Phyllida seemed startled.

'But I didn't tell you—'

Miss Silver coughed.

'You would naturally wish to find out why Mr Paradine had invited Mr Wray, and why Mr Wray had accepted his invitation.'

Phyllida's colour brightened. She did not quite know what to say. While she hesitated she met Miss Silver's gaze. There was something about it which made her feel that it wasn't any good to pretend or cover things up. She had a feeling of release. You don't talk about your own very private feelings to strangers. What gave her the feeling of release was the sense that Miss Silver was not a stranger at all. She came in and sat down by your fire and made herself at home, and all as a matter of course. She said, 'I had to talk to someone.'

'And Mr Paradine was able to help you?'

'Yes, I think so.'

Miss Silver had stopped knitting, the needles rested for a moment upon her lap. She said gently, 'I am very glad about that. Misunderstandings should never be permitted to continue.'

'I know. It wasn't just a misunderstanding.'

Miss Silver smiled. All at once Phyllida felt as if she and Elliot were in the nursery again. They were being told not to quarrel, and they were being encouraged to kiss and be friends. She returned the smile a little shakily, and heard Miss Silver say, 'When you came away from the study, did you see anyone?'

She was taken off her guard. She was thankful that she could say no. Plainly, she was startled.

A second question came quickly, 'Or hear anything, Mrs Wray?'

This time her colour changed. She looked down, she looked distressed. She said in a fluttering voice, 'Oh, no – there wasn't anything—'

Miss Silver did not press her. She thought there had been something, and she thought that presently she would know what it was.

The men coming in at this moment gave Phyllida a chance of escape. She caught Dicky as he passed, and left him to be talked to, or to talk to Miss Silver. She thought he bore up very well. He rather fancied himself with elderly spinsters, who invariably spoke of him as 'that charming boy'. A small cold thought like a snake moved suddenly in the shadows of her mind. A shudder went over her and she looked so white that Miss Paradine threw her an anxious glance.

'Come and sit down, darling, and get warm. You've been too far from the fire.'

She smiled faintly in reply, but instead of approaching the coffee tray she crossed to the other side of the hearth and stood there half turned from the room in a graceful bending attitude as if she were warming herself, foot raised to the marble kerb, hand resting lightly on the cold whiteness of the marble slab.

Elliot came over to her, coffee cup in hand. He set it down on the mantelpiece and said, 'I want to talk to you.'

The words pushed in over the thought that had robbed her of her colour. They were like someone coming into the room and banging the door. She knew Elliot in this mood. At the moment she found it heartening. Anything is better than being left alone in the dark with a snake. Still looking into the fire, she murmured, 'I don't see how—'

He took up his cup, drained the black coffee at a draught, and set it down again.

'What's to stop our walking out of the room together?'

Her colour rose.

'I couldn't.'

Elliot laughed.

'Afraid of the scandal?'

'I couldn't. Tomorrow – I'll find a time tomorrow.'

He said in an angry undertone, 'She's kept you running all day. It'll be the same tomorrow, with plenty of the family handy to make sure we don't get a minute alone.'

Phyllida went on looking into the fire. Elliot was in a very bad temper. Unreasonable to feel a pleasant glow creeping into the cold frightened place where she had been. She didn't say anything at all. An immemorial instinct prompted the thought that it wouldn't do Elliot any harm to wait.

Grace Paradine's voice called her with some insistence.

'Phyl darling!'

This time she went over, her own cup in her hand, and put it down on the massive silver tray.

'Yes, Aunt Grace?'

Miss Paradine beckoned her nearer and spoke low.

'Darling, if you could just keep Brenda with you and away from Irene. Both their nerves are in such a state, and I don't really feel I can bear much more.'

Impossible to refuse. Impossible to do anything except comply affectionately. She settled down to an evening of innuendo mounting by sharp degrees towards open accusation. Attempts to divert the conversation were useless. Whether you talked about the North Pole, the war in the East, or the latest film, Brenda managed to drag Irene in somehow. It would have been amusing if it had not been frightening. Phyllida began to wonder why Brenda and Irene should be allowed a monopoly of nerves. There was nothing in the world she would have liked better than to slap Brenda's face and burst into tears. Only of course she couldn't.

She went on talking about as many different things as she could think of, and Brenda went on talking about Irene.

TWENTY-EIGHT

THE DRAWING ROOM of the River House was not the only place where Irene was being discussed. Colonel Bostock, relaxing pleasantly in the society of his daughters, tossed a log on to the fire and, still leaning forward, remembered that there was something he had meant to ask them. He addressed himself to Janet, a healthy, well set-up young woman with a pleasant, sensible face.

'Remember the Pennington girls – Irene and, what's her name, Lydia?'

'Of course. Why?'

'Old Paradine's dead. One of them married the stepson, didn't she? What's his name – Ambrose?'

Alice Bostock said, 'There'll be pots of money. I wonder if Irene comes in for any of it.'

'She wasn't the red-headed one, was she?' said Colonel Bostock.

Both girls spoke together.

'Oh, no – that's Lydia.'

Colonel Bostock leaned back. Contemplating his girls, he felt well content with them. They weren't beauties, and they wouldn't set the Thames on fire. They were just decent young women who could work hard and enjoy themselves when they got a holiday – reasonably good-looking, reasonably intelligent, no kinks, no frills. Janet was the pick of the bunch. Very sensible girl Janet. Alice, a little fairer, a little slighter, not quite so much ballast, but a good girl too. And Milly – Milly took after him, the quickest of the three. Pity she couldn't get home this time.

He said in rather an abstracted voice, 'Irene – now wasn't there something about that girl Irene?' Alice looked at Janet and then looked away again. Neither of the girls said anything.

Colonel Bostock repeated his remark rather more directly.

'There was something about that girl Irene, wasn't there? You were at school with her, Janet. What was it?'

Janet said, 'It's a long time ago—'

Her father jerked an impatient shoulder.

'I suppose so. You're twenty-five. She'll be about your age. There was something about her. What was it? I want to know.'

Janet said reluctantly, 'I mean it's a long time ago – it doesn't seem fair to rake it up.'

Colonel Bostock's face displayed a lively interest.

'Rubbish! It either happened or it didn't happen. If it did, there'll be dozens of people who can tell me. Do you want me to go round asking them? I'm asking you two. That's better, isn't it? Make less talk.'

Janet looked at him seriously.

'It wouldn't be fair to rake it up – it's almost twelve years ago. And it wasn't anything really. I mean, nothing happened – Mina wasn't any the worse.'

Colonel Bostock grunted. He fixed bright sarcastic eyes upon his daughter's face.

'Nothing happened! Go on – tell me about it!'

'It was Irene's kitten,' said Alice. 'At least it wasn't really hers – it was a stray. And of course we weren't allowed to have pets at school, so Irene hid it in the toolshed.'

'She gave all her pocket money to the garden boy not to tell – the gardener was away ill,' said Janet. 'And she saved bits for it in a handkerchief, at lunch and tea, you know.'

'Of course she couldn't have kept it up, but she was awfully set on that kitten. It was a hideous little thing, too.' This was Alice again. 'And Mina Cotterell said she was going to tell Miss Graham. She was a perfectly odious girl – we all loathed her. She said she was sure the kitten had fleas.'

'Probably had.'

Alice said, 'Oh well . . . Anyhow Irene got perfectly wild. I don't honestly think she knew what she was doing. And she pushed Mina into the river.'

'She wasn't hurt,' said Janet quickly.

Alice made a face.

'Well, she might have been. It was an awfully dangerous thing to do. You know the bit of the grounds where we weren't allowed to go – they were definitely out of bounds because of the high bank over the river – well, I don't know how Irene got Mina to go there with her, but she did, and then she pushed her over.'

Colonel Bostock said, 'God bless my soul!' And then after a minute, 'Yes, yes – I remember. The Penningtons were in a dreadful way about it. The girl had a narrow escape. Couldn't swim, could she?'

Janet said, 'No. There was a man fishing, and he got her out. There was a most dreadful row. Irene would have been expelled if the Cotterells hadn't begged her off. It seems Mina had said the kitten would be drowned. I don't think Irene knew what she was doing. She's like that, you know – if she's set on a thing she can't think about anything else. It was that wretched kitten then. Now it's the children. She just can't think or talk about anything else. It's frightfully boring.'

Colonel Bostock nodded. After a moment he said, 'Well, well, who'd have thought it?' And then, 'Better not talk about it. Not to anyone.'

A little later on Superintendent Vyner came up to see his Chief and was had into the study.

'Sorry to interrupt you, sir, but there are one or two points—'

'All right, Vyner, sit down. What is it?'

Vyner sat down, filling the big chair. The light struck sideways on the thick fair hair which was turning grey and the solid bony structure of forehead and chin. His very bright blue eyes had a look between hesitancy and amusement.

'Well, sir, Miss Pennington wasn't there at the River House this afternoon, and I thought I'd just like to see whether she heard Mrs Ambrose go out or come in last night. We want to be able to fix the time if we can, so I went to Meadowcroft, found the whole party were at the River House, and went on there.'

'Get anything?'

'Not out of Miss Pennington. But I also saw Mr Mark Paradine, and he told me he'd called in a private detective.'

Like everyone else to whom this news had been imparted, Colonel Bostock said, '*What!*'

'Yes, sir. Did you ever hear of Miss Silver?'

Colonel Bostock said, 'God bless my soul! What's she doing here?'

'You've heard about her, sir?'

Colonel Bostock jerked.

'Met young Abbott when he was up for Christmas. Fellow who's a detective sergeant at the Yard. He's a cousin of the Abbotts at Huntersgrange. Met him there. He raved about the woman. Funny thing was I'd have bet my boots he wasn't the sort to rave about anyone. Cocksure young fellow. Cool hand. Brains.'

'Well, sir, she's done some very remarkable work – I happen to know that. She doesn't get into the papers, but these things go round. I heard about her first from Superintendent March at Ledlington. He was in on the Poisoned Caterpillars case, and he swears she saved his life.' Vyner laughed. 'It's a queer start, sir – she used to be his governess when he was a kid, and I believe that's just what she looks like, a little old maid governess. March told me a lot about her. There was the Chinese Shawl business last winter. Then the other day when I was in London I was seeing Detective Inspector Lamb, and he told me about the Vandeleur House murders – that's where they got that Mrs Simpson, you remember. Well, he gave Miss Silver the credit for that – fairly handed it to her.'

'Mark Paradine's called her in?'

'Yes, sir. And the point is, what are we going to do about it? I don't mind saying that I think she might be very useful. You see, she's there in the house – called in by Mr Mark himself – living with the family. It stands to reason she gets an angle that we don't get – a kind of a personal angle, if you take me, sir. And that's just what she's good at, according to Lamb. He says people talk to her, and she's a wonder at sizing them up. There's no doubt people do talk freer to someone who isn't in the police, and she's not tied up with rules like we are either.'

'What do you want to do?'

'Well, sir, I'd suggest that we let her see the statements. Lamb says she can be trusted not to give anything away.'

'Some women can.'

'Yes, sir. March and Lamb both say she's as safe as houses, so with your permission—'

Colonel Bostock jerked his shoulder.

'Oh, have her in, have her in! Tell you what,

Vyner, it's a damned awkward case – damned awkward. Look here, it isn't fair to keep you in the dark. I told you there was something about that girl Irene. Well, here it is.'

TWENTY-NINE

AS ON THE previous evening, the Ambrose party went home early. With the exception of Frank Ambrose, who had remained taciturn to the point of rudeness, Miss Silver had had a very pleasant conversation with each of them. Soon after their departure she excused herself and went up to the room which had been prepared for her. It was just before she said goodnight that she asked Miss Paradine about the diary.

'You will forgive me if I touch upon a painful subject, but I think your niece mentioned that you had given pocket diaries as New Year's gifts to your nephews.'

Grace Paradine smiled.

'There is nothing painful about that,' she said.

Miss Silver coughed.

'No, of course not. But I was going to enquire whether you also presented one to your brother.'

'Oh, no.' Miss Paradine sounded surprised. 'He didn't care for that sort of thing. He never used any calendar except a large plain card.'

'Those little diaries are so very convenient. I thought he might have liked one for his pocket, and it is so difficult to find a suitable present for a man.'

'He wouldn't have used it. He did not care for anything of that sort.'

Miss Silver perceived the subject to be distasteful. She thought it was time to say goodnight.

Her bedroom was comfortable – very comfortable, very cosy, with a floral carpet in which red was the predominant colour, curtains, bedspread and covers of chintz brightly patterned with poppies, cornflowers and ears of corn, red tiles in the fireplace glowing in the light of a small electric fire. The room, as she was aware, was almost opposite the one occupied by Mr Pearson and next door to Elliot Wray. On the other side, a bathroom – most convenient, most comfortable.

She removed the rather chilly dress of artificial silk and put on a sensible warm dressing gown crimson in colour. It was trimmed at the neck with hand-made crochet and fastened about her waist by a woollen cord rather reminiscent of an antique bell-pull. Comfortable black felt slippers having replaced the *glacé* shoes with their beaded toes, she sat down in a chair by the fire, and propping the green exercise book on a cushion laid across her knees, proceeded to make notes in it, using a fountain pen.

She had filled several pages, when there was a knock on the door. She said, 'Come in!' and looking up, saw a girl of about sixteen in a short black dress, white apron, and frilled cap. She had fat legs, a plump figure, apple-red cheeks, and bright blue eyes, for all the world like a china doll. She bore a hot-water bottle, and when she saw Miss Silver in her dressing gown she said, 'Beg pardon, miss,' and stopped dead.

'That will be quite all right,' said Miss Silver. 'You have come to turn down the bed? What is your name?'

'Polly, miss – Polly Parsons.'

'And this is you first place, I suppose?'

'Oh, yes, miss.'

'This is a sad New Year,' said Miss Silver.

Polly began to take off the chintz bed-cover and fold it up, disclosing a crimson eiderdown.

'Oh, yes, miss – it's ever so dreadful, isn't it?'

Miss Silver agreed.

'It must have been a dreadful shock to you all.'

'Oh, yes, miss, it was. I come over ever so funny.' She laid the folded bed-cover across a chair and came back to the bed.

'Does your work take you into the study at all, Polly?'

The girl had her back to her, bending forward to turn the bedclothes down. Right round to the roots of the short brown hair with its curled ends Miss Silver saw the colour run in a hearty blush.

'Only to make the fire up, miss, when they're at dinner. Mr Lane's busy then.'

'Mr Paradine used to sit in the study after dinner?'

'Oh, yes, miss.'

'And you went in as usual last night to make up the fire?'

Polly was sliding the hot-water bottle into the bed.

'Yes, miss.'

'And what time would that have been?'

Polly turned round.

'I couldn't say, miss.'

She met a kind look and an authoritative, 'Try, Polly.'

Hardly ever had she wanted to get out of a room as badly as she wanted to now. But it couldn't be done. She could no more have got past Miss Silver to the door than she could have disobeyed Louisa to her face. It just couldn't be done. Words came tumbling out in a hurry.

'I was a bit late – I'd to help outside because of the party.'

Miss Silver smiled.

'Then you probably looked at the clock. You would if you were afraid of being late. What time was it?'

'Just on nine, miss.'

'Was everyone still in the dining room then?'

Polly looked all ways.

'Well?' Miss Silver was gently insistent.

'The ladies came out as I got round by the door going through to the study.'

Miss Silver went on looking at her, quite kindly, quite firmly, sitting up prim and straight in her crimson dressing gown with the cushion across her knees.

'And how long were you in the study?'

Polly's cheeks turned from apple to beetroot. She said in a choked voice, 'I'd the fire to see to, miss.'

Miss Silver continued to look at her. Polly continued to blush. At the sound of a step in the passage she gulped and made for the door. On the threshold she stumbled out something that was evidently meant for an apology. The words 'Louisa' and 'the other bottles' were intelligible. The door shut on her. She could be heard running down the passage.

Miss Silver said, 'Dear me!'

THIRTY

COLONEL BOSTOCK, SUPERINTENDENT Vyner, and Miss Silver were in the study next morning. A fire burned brightly on the hearth. The crimson curtains were drawn back to their fullest extent, leaving in view the terrace, grey in the shadow of the house, and the scar on the parapet where James Paradine had struck against it in his fall. The night had been stormy, but the clouds were rifting. Every now and then a gleam of pallid sunshine touched the river.

Superintendent Vyner sat at the table. The statements which he had allowed Miss Silver to read lay where she had just placed them at his left hand. She had selected the most appropriate chair in the room, high and narrow in the back and straight in the seat, with a pattern of little shiny knobs all round it. Miss Silver sat up as straight as the chair back with her hands in the lap of her brown stuff dress. She wore her bog-oak brooch and an expression which combined a decorous self-respect with the deference due to authority, for which word she would undoubtedly have used a capital A.

Colonel Bostock had drawn an upright chair to the far side of the writing table. It had arms upon which he rested his elbows. As far as it is possible to lean back in a chair of that kind, he leaned. Occasionally, when Miss Silver was not looking in his direction, he contemplated her in a quizzical manner. The words 'God bless my soul!' might have been shaping themselves upon his lips. The bog-oak brooch intrigued him. Somewhere in the past he had encountered its twin. The association was with a wedding festivity – Jane's wedding – his wife's cousin Jane, the one Janet was named after. One of the bridegroom's aunts had had a brooch like that. Stiff old lady in a bonnet and feathers. Left all her money out of the family to endow a home for friendless parrots. He would not have sworn to the parrots in a court of law, but it was something like that. Anyhow Jane and her husband didn't get a penny. Monstrous.

Miss Silver said in her clear ladylike voice, 'You were very kindly going to tell me about the finger-prints, Superintendent.'

Vyner said, 'Yes.' He turned in his chair to face her across the corner of the table. 'Of course in a family business like this you're liable to get everybody's finger-prints everywhere, and you can't say there's anything proved by your finding them. Take the handle of this door for instance – it's just a smudge. Lane, Mr Pearson, Mr Wray, and Mrs Wray all handled it that evening, besides Mr Paradine himself.'

Miss Silver coughed.

'And the girl who made up the fire.'

Vyner said, 'Oh, yes.'

Miss Silver continued, 'She was in here at about nine o'clock.'

'Hm! Too early to be of any value. All the others were after nine,' said Colonel Bostock. 'We know that.'

'Well then,' said Vyner, 'it's the same pretty well everywhere. Lane, this girl Polly, Mr Paradine, Mr Pearson, Mr and Mrs Wray – there are prints from all of them. And all we get out of that is that the girl had been at this drawer. Mr Paradine kept sweets there, and I should say she's been at them.'

So that was why Polly had blushed and fled – or was it? Miss Silver turned this over in her mind as Vyner went on.

'I haven't said anything to her about it. But there we are, we're out to catch a murderer, and all we get is a kid stealing sweets. Well, not quite *all*, because there are Mr Mark Paradine's prints, and they're not quite so easy to explain. There are his and Mr Richard's on the chair the Chief Constable is sitting in, and on the edge of the writing table, and Mr Mark's on the little pocket diary. Now Mr Richard, he dropped in to see Miss Paradine in the late afternoon – that's certain. And he says he looked in on his uncle in the study when he was going away. We've only his word for it, but it's likely enough, and it would explain his prints. But Mr Mark Paradine – well, there's no explaining his. He wasn't here all day Wednesday, or the day before, or the day before that. He arrived for dinner on New Year's Eve, but he didn't see his uncle then because Mr Paradine was closeted with

Mr Wray, and he says, and everyone else says, that he didn't go anywhere near the study after dinner. He went away with Mr Richard at a quarter to ten, and he went back to his flat in Birleton Mansions. But after that, he says, he went out for a walk. Queer time of night to choose. The constable on duty at the bridge saw him cross over in the direction of the River House at about ten-twenty. It was bright moonlight then, and he knows him by sight. Mr Mark says he walked a bit along the road and then came back. He wasn't seen coming back, but Harding came off duty at half-past ten, and the man who relieved him is a newcomer and wouldn't take that much notice. It seems to me the only time Mr Mark could have made those prints was after ten-twenty, when Harding saw him going in the direction of the River House.'

'Who let him in?' said Colonel Bostock. 'Lane didn't.'

'The door wasn't bolted, sir. Mr Mark and Mr Richard lived here until a few years ago. Nothing more likely than that they still have latchkeys. Or if he hadn't, Mr Mark could have come round on the terrace and knocked at the glass door. Everyone in the family knew that Mr Paradine was waiting up till twelve.'

Colonel Bostock said, 'Shocking business.'

'Yes, sir. But that's when those prints were made – sometime after ten-twenty on Wednesday night. There's no other time they could have been made.'

Miss Silver coughed.

'Has he been asked for an explanation,

Superintendent? He told me frankly that he was under suspicion when he called me in. I informed him that I could be no party to any concealment of evidence, and that my sole obligation would be to do my best to discover the truth. He replied that this was his object in asking for my professional services. Are you aware that this pocket diary belongs to him?'

Colonel Bostock said, 'What!'

'A New Year's gift from Miss Paradine,' said Miss Silver. 'Mr Ambrose, Mr Pearson, and each of her two nephews had one. They were distributed in the drawing room after dinner on Wednesday night. There were four different colours. The blue one was Mr Mark's.'

'God bless my soul!'

'Well, I should say that just about puts the lid on,' said Vyner.

Miss Silver picked up the diary.

'One moment, Colonel Bostock. This is quite a new book, but you will see that it opens of its own accord. If you and the Superintendent will examine it, I think you will agree that the binding had been pressed back so as to keep the diary open at this page – and the date is February 1st.'

Vyner said, 'Yes, we noticed that. As a matter of fact we got a very good fingerprint there as well as on the outside. I was coming to that, because it's bit odd there are Mr Mark's prints both inside and out, and Mr Paradine's as well, and where they overlap Mr Paradine's are on top. Looks as if there'd been some talk about the date and Mr

Mark had handed him the book to see for himself. As to asking him for an explanation, I thought we might have him in now. I shall have to ask him if he objects to your being present, but seeing he called you in, he won't have much of a leg to stand on. Then if he's willing for you to be here, it gives a kind of a lead to the rest of the family, if you take my meaning.'

Miss Silver took it. She inclined her head and murmured graciously, 'That is very kind of you.'

The bell was rung, and Mr Mark Paradine's company requested. He came in with the look of a man who hasn't slept, and who rides himself on a strict curb. There was less gloom and moodiness in his aspect than there had been yesterday, more evidence of stern control. If he thought himself to be facing arrest he bore himself well.

Colonel Bostock said, 'How do you do, Paradine? Come and sit down.' Vyner said, 'Good morning.' Neither of the men rose, and neither offered to shake hands. From the outset it was perfectly obvious that the interview was of an official nature.

Mark sat down facing Miss Silver. Four people at a table – three in the service of the law, and one in what might very well prefigure the dock.

Colonel Bostock's expression suggested that he was mentally repeating the words, 'Very awkward business – very.' He cleared his throat and said aloud, 'Any objection to answering a few questions?'

'Oh, no.'

'No objection to Miss Silver being present? I believe you called her in.'

'No, I've no objection.'

Colonel Bostock looked across the table and said, 'All right, Vyner, go ahead.'

The Superintendent turned towards Mark with the diary in his hand.

'Is this your property, Mr Paradine?'

Mark looked at it, frowning.

'What makes you think so?'

'We are informed that Miss Paradine gave four of these small diaries as New Year's gifts on Wednesday evening. The blue one is said to have been given to you. Is that correct?'

Mark stiffened a little. He said, 'Quite.'

'These diaries were given in the drawing room after you had joined the ladies there?'

'Yes.'

'You did not come in here between that time and leaving the house at about a quarter to ten?'

'No.'

'Then, Mr Paradine, will you explain how it came about that the diary was found on this table when the police arrived at a quarter past eight on the following morning? It has your fingerprints and those of the late Mr Paradine on the cover and on the page dated February 1st, at which place the book had been bent open. Have you an explanation which you would care to give us?'

Mark found himself looking at Miss Silver, who was looking at him. Her gaze was steady and cheerful. It held the encouragement which a teacher extends to a diffident pupil. In some way which he could not explain he found himself encouraged.

'Yes, I think I have. I think I had better tell you just what happened,' he said.

Colonel Bostock cleared his throat again.

'It is my duty to tell you, Paradine, that anything you say may be taken down and used in evidence against you.'

Mark looked at him with something that came quite near to being a smile.

'Thank you, sir – but I'm explaining, not confessing. I went back to my flat in Birleton Mansions and I went out again, just as I told the Superintendent. I wasn't anxious to tell him where I went, but I suppose it was bound to come out. I came back here because I wanted to see my uncle, and owing to what he had said at dinner I didn't want the rest of the family to know.'

'God bless my soul! You came back here and saw Mr Paradine?'

'Yes, sir.'

'How did you get in?'

'I used my old latchkey.'

Colonel Bostock made a slight explosive sound. Vyner said, 'Why did you want to see Mr Paradine? Do you care to tell us that?'

Mark frowned.

'Yes, I'll tell you. I've been wanting for a long time to be released from the firm in order to join the RAF. My uncle has always refused to let me go. That is to say, the decision didn't rest with him, but there wasn't much chance of the government's releasing me unless he said he could do without me here.'

Colonel Bostock looked at him sharply.

'On research work, aren't you?'

'Yes, sir.'

'Go on.'

'My uncle wouldn't let me go. I came here last night to tell him he'd got to. That's all.'

'Why?'

'For personal reasons.'

'Going to tell us what they were?'

'No, sir. My uncle's death has altered everything. I can't hope to get away now.'

Vyner had been looking at him attentively. He said, 'What sort of interview did you have with Mr Paradine? Was it friendly?'

'Yes. He agreed to let me go. That's why the diary had been opened at February 1st. There's something I've been working on – I said I'd be through with it in about a month. He asked me to wait a month and see him again. I said, "Four weeks from today?" and he said, "No – a calendar month." I remembered the diary my aunt had given me earlier in the evening, so I took it out of my pocket and looked up February 1st – I wanted to see what day it was. Then I handed it over to him, and he said, "All right – if you're still of the same mind then."'

'What happened after that?'

'I went home. I didn't know I'd left the diary here. I didn't think about it again.'

'What time did you leave?'

'I don't know – about half-past eleven, I should think.'

'No one saw you come or go?'

'Not as far as I know.'

Vyner paused for a moment. Then he said, 'Mr Wray and Mr Pearson came down for a drink at eleven-thirty. Mr Wray says he got an impression that the front door was closing as he entered the hall. That would fit in with your time.'

'Yes.'

'Mr Paradine – on what sort of terms did you part with your uncle? Were they friendly?'

Miss Silver saw a muscle twitch in the dark cheek. The black brows drew together. He said, 'Yes.'

'He was alive when you left him?'

Under the frowning brows the eyes blazed for a moment. There was a noticeable pause before Mark Paradine got out his second, 'Yes.'

THIRTY-ONE

MISS SILVER BROKE the ensuing silence with a little cough.

'Mr Paradine, can you tell us just what was on the writing table when you were here on Wednesday night?'

A faint surprise showed itself in his face.

'What do you mean?'

She said, 'Just try to visualise the table as you saw it then, and tell me as many of the things on it as you can remember.'

His frown this time was one of concentration.

'I don't know – I wasn't noticing. I should say it was all very much as it is now.'

'Pray go on, Mr Paradine. Just name the things. You may find yourself recalling something.'

The frown deepened, contradicted by a half humorous, half impatient lift of the lip. He said, 'Well, all the things you see – inkstand – pen – pencils – blotting pad – writing block—'

'That is something which is not here now.'

'The writing-block? He had one in front of him whilst we were talking – I am sure about that. There wasn't anything written on it.'

'Pray continue.'

'I can't think of anything else.'

'A calendar? Miss Paradine happened to mention that he always used a plain card calendar.'

Mark shook his head.

'No, there wasn't any calendar, otherwise I wouldn't have got out mine. Of course it was the last day of the year. I expect he had thrown the old one away and the new one hadn't been put out.'

'Was there nothing on this corner of the table between myself and the Superintendent?'

'Only the newspaper.'

Miss Silver said, 'Dear me! There was a newspaper all across this corner?'

'Yes – *The Times*. He must have been reading it.'

'Mr Paradine, can you remember whether the paper was lying flat? In your recollection would there have been room under it for, let us say, Mr Wray's blueprints? I understand that they were contained in a cardboard cylinder. Would there have been room for it under the newspaper?'

A look of consternation came over his face. His eyes went to Vyner, to the Chief Constable.

'They're not missing! Was *that* what my uncle meant?'

Colonel Bostock said, 'Only just occurred to you?'

Mark had made a movement to rise, but it did not get him to his feet. He came down again, leaning forward across the table and looking from one to the other.

Colonel Bostock said sharply, 'Come, Paradine! What did you think your uncle meant by saying one of you had betrayed the family interests? Not a pleasant thing to say – not a pleasant thing to hear. What did you think he meant?'

'He'd missed the prints? It was that?'

'I asked you what you thought at the time, Paradine.'

Mark straightened himself up again.

'I'm sorry, sir. I never thought about the prints.'

'Indeed? Then I'd like to know what you did think.'

Mark was silent for perhaps half a minute. It seemed like a long time. Then he said, 'I'll tell you, sir. The whole thing was a shock, naturally – not pleasant to listen to, as you say. I never thought about the prints. I didn't know what to think. I was a good deal taken up with my own affairs, and when I came to think things over I wondered if he was referring to me. It sounds a bit exaggerated, but he always did go off the deep end at the idea of my leaving the firm. The last time we talked about it he said things that weren't very different to what he said on Wednesday night.'

'Remember any of them?'

'Well, he said I was willing to let the firm and the country down to snatch a little tin-pot glory.'

'So you thought it was you he meant on Wednesday night?'

Mark shook his head.

'It wasn't as definite as that. It just seemed to me that everything had boiled over. I felt I couldn't go on, and I went back to tell him so.'

Colonel Bostock's eyes held a bright sceptical twinkle.

'And you stick to it that the conversation was a pleasant one?'

The colour came up suddenly in Mark Paradine's face.

'Well, sir, it was. I got him to understand my point of view. I told you he'd agreed to let me go in a month if I still wanted to.'

'Yes, that's what you said.' The tone was as sceptical as the look had been.

Mark stiffened noticeably. Vyner said, 'You didn't know the blueprints were missing? When did you see them last?'

'I never saw them at all.'

'Sure about that?'

'Quite sure.'

'But you knew about them – you knew Mr Wray had brought them up?'

'Oh, yes.'

'You were in the late Mr Paradine's private office on Wednesday afternoon?'

'Yes.'

'At what time, and for how long?'

'I came in with Frank Ambrose a little before four o'clock, and I was there for about a quarter of an hour.'

'And were you alone in the office at any time?'

'Yes. My uncle was away most of the time. Ambrose left before I did. I just waited to see my uncle, then I came away too.'

'Did you notice an attaché case on the office table?'

'Yes, I think so – it would have been there. My uncle used it to take papers to and fro.'

'Did you touch the case?'

Mark frowned.

'I might have done – I was leaning against the table.'

'And what was Mr Ambrose doing?'

'I really don't know. We talked a bit.'

'You were leaning against the table. Did you stay like that all the time he was in the room?'

'No – I was over by the window part of the time.'

'What were you doing there?'

'I was looking out. We were killing time – waiting for my uncle. In the end Ambrose didn't wait for him.'

'Then you had your back to the room for a part of the time?'

'Yes.'

'And after Mr Ambrose left, you were alone?'

'For a minute or two.'

'You were alone with the attaché case?'

'I was.'

'You might have opened it? Did you open it?'

'Of course not.' The tone was half casual, half scornful.

'You didn't open the case – you didn't take the prints?'

'I didn't even know they had been taken.' Scorn predominated now.

Vyner looked at the Chief Constable. Colonel Bostock said, 'You didn't know that the prints had been taken. Did you know that they had been put back?'

Mark Paradine's expression changed. Something broke the stiffness. He leaned forward and said eagerly, 'Have they been put back?'

Colonel Bostock nodded.

'When, sir?'

Miss Silver said, 'That, Mr Paradine, is what we are trying to find out. We should be glad of your assistance. The prints were contained in a cardboard cylinder. This cylinder was found by Mr Wray when he entered the study early on Thursday morning after being informed of Mr Paradine's death. It was then lying on this corner of the table. Do you think it is possible that it was already there when you visited your uncle on Wednesday night?'

Mark looked, hesitated, frowned, and said, 'It might have been . . . But there must be fingerprints – if you've got the cylinder, there'll be the prints of the person who took it.'

He turned from one to the other, and got a very straight look from Vyner.

'I'm not saying anything about the prints on the cylinder, Mr Paradine.'

Mark pushed back his chair and stood up.

'Well, you wouldn't get any of mine on it,' he said.

THIRTY-TWO

WHEN THE DOOR had shut a little abruptly Colonel Bostock looked across the table at Vyner and said, 'What do you make of that?'

'Well, sir, the bother about the cylinder is there are too many prints on it – too many – too faint except for Mr Wray's own. Same with the papers inside. Mr Wray says Mr Paradine told him that he and Mr Moffat and Mr Ambrose had what he called a session over them. I take that to mean they had them out and passed them round. We haven't got Mr Moffat's fingerprints to compare, but the other two are there all over the place, and another lot which are pretty sure to be his. The outside of the cylinder is very confused indeed – just a jumble, as you might say, which is what you'd expect with that amount of surface and all those people handling it. There's one of Mr Paradine's pretty clear, and a finger and thumb of Mr Wray's.'

Colonel Bostock turned to Miss Silver.

'Got any ideas?' he said. 'Seems to me it lies between Mark Paradine and that girl Irene – Mrs Ambrose.'

Miss Silver said, 'Dear me—' She folded her hands in her lap, turned her head a little on one side, and gazed at him with bright expectancy.

Colonel Bostock, who had been prepared to cope with a fluent female, found himself relieved and stimulated.

'Take Mark,' he said. 'He admits to coming back and seeing his uncle. Won't say why. Admits he thought the remark about betraying the family interests might have been meant for him. Queer sort of story when you come to think about it. Anyhow he came back. Says so. Says the interview was a pleasant one. Admits the subject discussed had always previously put his uncle in a rage. This time no rage – everything very pleasant. Uncle agrees to let him go. Story full of discrepancies. What do you make of it?'

Miss Silver smiled faintly.

'Since you ask me, I think that Mr Mark would have made up a better story if he had been inventing one.'

''Hm! The calendar tripped him. Had to say something. Didn't have time to think it out.'

Miss Silver shook her head.

'He knew that he was under suspicion. It was one of the first things he told me. He was aware that he must have been seen and recognised by the constable on duty at the bridge. He could have provided himself with a much better story. As it is, the calendar corroborates him in a manner which he could not have anticipated. His statement that he produced it to look up a date and then handed it to his uncle is substantiated by the position of the fingerprints. The fact that there was no other calendar on the table also supports his story.'

'It's thin!' said Colonel Bostock explosively. 'Paradine tells the family that one of them's a criminal. Says he knows which of them it is. Says he expects a confession. Says he'll be here till twelve o'clock. Now I ask you, is it reasonable to suppose that Mark first covers up his tracks by saying goodnight and going away with his cousin, and then comes blinding back for any other reason except to confess?'

Miss Silver shook her head again.

'I think he did come back to confess, but not to the theft of Mr Wray's blueprints.'

Colonel Bostock stared. Miss Silver smiled.

'There is really a very simple explanation. Mr Mark is in love with Miss Pennington. I think he has been in love with her for some time, but I do not think he has ever told her so. These are my own impressions after seeing them together. From Mrs Ambrose I gather that the family expects Miss Pennington to marry Mr Richard Paradine, who has proposed to her repeatedly. They were seated together at dinner on Wednesday night, and in one of the toasts Mr Paradine made some glancing allusion which appeared to couple their names. I think it may easily be imagined that all this brought Mr Mark to the point of feeling that his position was unendurable. Mr Richard may have said something on their way home – there is no means of knowing this – but I can well imagine that Mr Mark was in no mood to sleep. You say no innocent man would have sought an interview which might compromise him, but you must remember that an innocent man would have no idea that a theft had been committed. He might easily have a confused impression that his uncle's words applied to his desire to leave the firm, upon which it would be natural that he should decide to return and settle the matter. If, as I think probable, he told Mr Paradine his true reason for wishing to be released, the fact that the conversation was of a friendly nature is no longer surprising. From the circumstance that Mr Paradine asked him to wait a month before making a final decision I am of the opinion that he did not take so dark a view of Mr Mark's prospects with Miss Pennington as Mr Mark did himself. You see, Colonel Bostock, this would explain the whole thing – would it not?'

Colonel Bostock said, ''Hm!' in the tone of a man who prefers to keep his counsel. Vyner, meeting Miss Silver's enquiring gaze, remarked, 'There's something in it.'

He received a darting glance from his Chief Constable.

'What's the good of that? Trying to say something without saying anything! Plain fact is we don't know. On his own showing Mark was here till half-past eleven. He may have gone away and left his uncle alive like he says, or he may have pushed him over.'

'He comes in for most of the property—' said Vyner in a dubious voice.

Colonel Bostock turned again to Miss Silver.

'It'll be him, or it'll be that girl Irene. Shocking thing, but when a girl's pushed one person off a cliff, you can't say she mightn't do it again. Happened when she was at school with my girls. She'd got a stray kitten. Against rules. Meddling busybody of a girl said she'd inform and get the kitten destroyed. Irene pushed her in the river. Might have been drowned. Fortunately wasn't. Very unpleasant affair.'

Vyner took up the tale.

'Mrs Ambrose is said to be wrapped up in her children. Suppose Mr Ambrose took those prints – he was one of the people who knew all about them. He certainly handled them. He had the opportunity of taking the cylinder out of Mr Paradine's case while Mr Mark was looking out of the window. It isn't nice to think of these things, but it seems his mother was a German – he may have been got hold of. The talk in the town is they live above their means. She's no manager. There's a good bit of money owing – bills that have been let run on. I don't mean to say there's anything they couldn't pay, but they don't. Well then, suppose he'd taken the prints – he might have been offered a big price for the chance of getting them photographed. He might have reckoned on being able to put them back on Wednesday night and nobody any the wiser. But before dinner's over Mr Paradine gets up and says his piece – says one of the family's a criminal and he knows which one it is. That's torn it as far as putting them back unbeknownst goes. If you will turn to Mr Ambrose's statement you will see that he says less than any of them. And that's him all through. From what I can make out nobody's had a word out of him about any of it.'

Colonel Bostock grunted.

'Can't say a man's guilty because he don't talk.'

'No, sir. I'm not saying he's guilty – I'm putting a case. If he had taken the prints he'd have had to think what he was going to do, and think quick. The only thing he could do would be to throw himself on Mr Paradine's mercy. We know he took his party away at a quarter to ten. We know he and his wife both went out again. She says she went for Dr Horton. He says he went to look for her. Nobody knows when either of them came in. Suppose Mr Ambrose went to the River House and Mrs Ambrose followed him – he might have told her something, or she might have guessed. The Ambroses are in Meadowcroft just across the river from here – a long way round by the driving road, but not more than seven or eight minutes' walk by the footbridge and the cliff path. Say they went that way – Mr Ambrose wouldn't go round by the front door and risk being seen. At least I wouldn't if I'd been in his shoes. I'd have come up on the terrace and knocked on this glass door behind me. Say Mr Ambrose did that – his stepfather would have let him in and they'd have had their talk. If Mrs Ambrose was following her husband, there'd have been nothing to stop her unlatching the door and listening to what was said. There's no proof in the way of fingerprints, because everybody had handled that door before we got here. Suppose she did that, suppose she found her husband was going to lose his job – and that would have been the very least of it if he'd been caught out selling a military secret. Whichever way you look at the thing, it was nothing less than ruin. Well, on what we know of Mrs Ambrose, she'd think first about her children. When she was twelve years old and another girl threatened her kitten she pushed her into the river. What do you suppose she'd do now if she thought her children were threatened?'

'God bless my soul!' said Colonel Bostock. 'What's the good of talking like that? There's no evidence.'

'No, sir – only a very strong probability. I'm not saying it was Mrs Ambrose. Mr Ambrose may have done it himself. I don't go farther than to say that one of them might have done it. They were both out – a few minutes' walk would have got them here. Either of them had a very strong motive if it was Mr Ambrose who took the blueprints. Everyone in the family knew that Mr Paradine was sitting up. Everyone seems to have known that he always went out on the terrace the last thing before he went to bed. Either of them could have waited around for him and pushed him over.'

'So could half a dozen other people! I'm not saying one of them didn't do it. Irene for choice. All I say is, there isn't any proof.'

'No, sir,' said Superintendent Vyner.

Miss Silver coughed and asked an irrelevant question.

'I should be glad to know just where you found Mrs Wray's fingerprints.'

'God bless my soul – you're not suspecting her!'

Miss Silver smiled in a very noncommittal manner.

'If the Superintendent would be kind enough to inform me—'

Vyner was quite ready.

'Well, she sat in that chair the Chief Constable's in now. Mr Mark sat in it too. There were his prints and hers on the back and arms – Mr Richard's too, but he says he was in after tea.'

'Were there any more of Mrs Wray's, Superintendent?'

Vyner frowned.

'As a matter of fact, yes – and in two or three odd places. Seems she must have gone out through what I'm told was the late Mrs Paradine's bedroom. That's the door, between the fireplace and the inner wall. There are prints of hers on the handle both sides of that, and the same with the door leading to the passage. There's also a full handprint high up on the inside panel of the second door. Looks as if she'd groped her way out in the dark. I haven't asked her about it yet – haven't had time.'

'Has any reason occurred to you for her going out that way?'

'I can't say it has.'

Miss Silver coughed delicately.

'If she was talking to her uncle and someone else came to the study door, Mr Paradine may not have wished her to see who it was. He may have indicated the other way out. That is a possible explanation?'

Vyner looked at her with respect.

'It might have been that.'

'I think it was.'

'You think she may have heard Mr Ambrose?'

'I would not say that. I received the impression that she had heard something. After speaking freely of her interview with Mr Paradine she became very reserved – she was afraid to go on. She made an excuse to leave me. I did not press her then, but if you will permit me to do so, I should like to talk to her again.'

Vyner looked across the table. Colonel Bostock nodded.

THIRTY-THREE

A LITTLE LATER Miss Silver met four people. Each was encountered in the most natural and casual manner. To each she addressed the same question.

Albert Pearson was passing along the passage when she came out of the study. He appeared to be on his way to the back stair leading to the bedroom floor above. At the sound of Miss Silver's slight cough he looked round. When she said, 'Oh, Mr Pearson—' he turned back and came to meet her.

'Can I do anything for you, Miss Silver?'

'Oh, no, Mr Pearson – I was just wondering if you knew what had happened to Wednesday's *Times*. There was something I wanted. But it does not really matter. I do not wish to be troublesome.'

Mr Pearson was all that was polite. He thought Lane would know – 'I will ask him.'

'Oh, pray do not trouble. I only wondered – do you happen to know whether Mr Paradine had the paper on Wednesday night?'

Albert gazed through his thick lenses with an air of industrious concern. Miss Silver was reminded of an ant. La Fontaine's fable floated through her mind as he said, 'Why, yes, I believe he did – in fact

I am sure of it. It was on his table when I said goodnight.'

'He was not reading it when you went in?'

'Oh, no. It was on the table.'

'On the left-hand side?'

'Why, yes, Miss Silver.'

He received a gracious smile.

'Thank you, Mr Peason. Then I think Lane will have it. No, pray do not trouble – I will ask him myself.'

She encountered Lane in the hall. He produced *The Times* of the 31st without any delay. The sight of it appeared to affect him and Miss Silver in quite opposite ways. Whilst a gratified expression showed itself upon her face, Lane came near to being overcome. The fact that the paper did not seem to have been unfolded was the text of a mournful homily.

'Dreadful, isn't it?' he said. 'I never knew him not to read his *Times* before. Regular as clockwork he'd sit down to it after dinner.'

'Then did nobody else read it?'

Lane shook his head.

'No, madam. The ladies had their own papers. *The Times* was special for Mr Paradine – he didn't like anyone else to touch it. He must have been very much put about not to have thought about it on Wednesday.'

'Did you see it when you went into the study after dinner?'

'Oh, yes, madam. It was laying on the table on his left.'

'He wasn't reading it?'

'Oh, no, madam – it wasn't unfolded.'

'Can you remember whether it was lying flat on the table?'

'No, madam, it wasn't.'

'Are you sure about that?'

Quietly and with decision Lane was sure.

'You see, madam, I couldn't help wondering why it didn't lay flat. There seemed to be something under it, and I couldn't help wondering what it was, Mr Paradine being a gentleman who kept his table very neat.'

'Thank you, Lane.'

The Times in hand, Miss Silver ascended the stairs. She met Phyllida Wray just at the top and enquired without more ado, 'Did you see this paper on the study table when you were talking to your uncle on Wednesday night?'

Phyllida looked vague for a moment, then collected herself and murmured, 'Yes, I think so – oh, yes, I did.'

Further questions elicited that she hadn't noticed particularly, but now she came to think of it the paper was sort of pushed up as if there was something underneath it. She really hadn't thought about it at the time, but looking back, that was how it was.

Miss Silver proceeded to her bedroom, where she found Polly Parsons, in lilac print with a duster. Shutting the door behind her, she said, 'You can go on with your dusting in a moment, Polly. I only want to ask you a question.' She held out *The Times*. 'Was this paper lying on the study table when you went in to make up the fire on Wednesday night? Think carefully before you answer.'

Polly stared round-eyed at *The Times*. Then she said, 'Oh, no, miss, it wasn't.'

'Are you sure, Polly?'

'Oh, yes, miss. It wouldn't be on the writing table – Mr Lane would never have put it there. There's a table special for the papers. I'd have noticed at once if it was out of its place.'

There was none of the embarrassment of the night before – not a stammer, not a blush. The colour in the rosy cheeks varied as little as if they had really been apples. The blue eyes met Miss Silver's with the blankest innocence.

She said, 'Thank you, Polly,' and went out, closing the door behind her.

Mr Wray was in his room next door. She could hear him moving.

At her tap he said 'Come in!' with just a touch of impatience in his tone.

He must have been walking up and down in the room, for he now stood at the window looking out. When the door shut he looked over his shoulder and appeared surprised. He said, 'Miss Silver!'

She said, 'I would like to talk to you, Mr Wray. Shall we sit down?'

'What is it? All right, you have the chair – I'll sit on the bed. What do you want to talk about?'

She was regarding him with grave attention. She

still held *The Times* of December 31st. She offered it now for his inspection.

'Did you see this paper on Wednesday night when you went in to say goodnight to Mr Paradine?'

'Yes – it was on his desk – I thought he had been reading it.'

'Oh, no, Mr Wray, it had never been unfolded.'

He gave a half impatient laugh.

'Then I suppose he was going to read it.'

'It has never been unfolded, Mr Wray.'

He leaned his elbows on the brass foot-rail of the bed, propped his chin on his hands, and said, 'All right – where do we go from there?'

Miss Silver coughed, not exactly in reproof but, as it were, to recall her own attention to the matter in hand. A strange idiom but really quite expressive – she must remember it . . . She wondered what dear Lord Tennyson would have said about modern slang. Something intolerant, she feared . . . The cough recalled her.

She said crisply, 'Mr Paradine was accustomed to read *The Times* every evening after dinner. On Wednesday night he was in his study from nine till twelve o'clock, and he did not even unfold it. What does that suggest to you?'

Elliot looked at her very straight.

'Suppose you tell me what it suggests to you?'

'Very well. In someone else the reason might have been distress of mind, but from your observation of Mr Paradine you assert that he was not distressed. Mrs Wray gives me the same impression, and so does Mr Mark. Mrs Wray was helped and comforted by her interview. Mr Mark was treated with sympathy and affection. "The heart at leisure from itself to soothe and sympathise" is not usually met with in anyone who is under a severe personal strain.'

Elliot grinned.

'You know, that doesn't sound awfully like Mr Paradine to me.'

Miss Silver coughed.

'We have different ways of expressing ourselves, Mr Wray. It is a fact that Mrs Wray and Mr Mark received sympathetic treatment.'

'Mark?'

'Yes. He was with Mr Paradine between eleven and eleven-thirty on Wednesday night. I think you just missed him when you came downstairs with Mr Pearson. There is a perfectly satisfactory reason for this interview, but we need not go into that now. Pray let us return to *The Times*. I believe there were two reasons why it remained unopened. The first is that it was used to conceal something, and the second that Mr Paradine was too fully occupied.'

'And how was he occupied?'

Miss Silver looked at him with bright intelligence.

'I think he had a number of visitors.'

'A number?'

'I believe so. There were, first, Mr Pearson and yourself. Then Mrs Wray, for about twenty minutes between ten and ten-thirty. Mr Mark could not have arrived much before eleven, but I have reason to believe that there was another visitor at half-past ten, since Mrs Wray seems to have left the study in some haste and by way of the late Mrs Paradine's bedroom.'

Elliot looked at her.

'I suppose you were there.'

Miss Silver smiled. In the manner of one who instructs a backward class, she explained.

'She left her fingerprints on both doors of that room. She would hardly have gone out that way if she had not wished to avoid someone who was coming in by the study door.'

Elliot said, 'Well, well. She's one of the unfortunate people who can't tell a lie, you know. Don't be too hard on her.'

Miss Silver's cough appeared to deprecate this levity. She said, 'I do not, of course, know who the visitor was.'

'You surprise me.'

'But I am quite sure that Mrs Wray knows. However, we will leave that for the moment and come back to the other reason why *The Times* remained unopened. It is the more important of the two.'

Elliot's face went grim.

'You said it was put there to cover something. Did you mean that it was put there to cover the cylinder with my blueprints?'

'Yes, Mr Wray.'

'What makes you think so?'

Miss Silver had brought her knitting bag with

her from her room. She now extracted little Roger's leggings and began to knit. Above the dark grey wool and the clicking needles she continued to look at Elliot.

'It is very simple, Mr Wray. At nine o'clock, which was just as the ladies were coming out of the dining-room, the under-housemaid, Polly Parsons, went into the study to make up the fire. *The Times* was then on the paper table. At round about ten minutes to ten, when you and Mr Pearson and Lane were all in the study within a few minutes of one another, *The Times* lay on the writing table at Mr Paradine's left hand. Lane says he noticed particularly that it had not been opened, but that it was not lying flat. He seems to have wondered what was under it. It was still there and still unopened when Mrs Wray came down just after ten, and when Mr Mark arrived at eleven.'

'For the matter of that it was still there in the morning.'

'And it was covering the cylinder with your blueprints?'

'Yes.'

He made an abrupt change of position, shifting away from the foot-rail and sitting up straight.

Miss Silver said, 'There is a strong probability that the cylinder was placed there between nine o'clock, when Polly came in to do the fire, and about ten minutes to ten, when Lane saw *The Times* in position to cover it.'

Elliot put his hands in his pockets and said, 'That's not possible.'

Miss Silver's needles clicked. Little Roger's leggings revolved.

'Pray, why do you say that, Mr Wray?'

'Because no one in the family had the opportunity of putting it back between those times. Nobody was alone.'

'Mr Pearson?'

Elliot frowned.

'Lane was already in the study when he got there. Besides—' He finished the sentence with a shrug.

'I agree that the time would be a very unlikely one for anyone to choose, the Ambrose party having just left, and the family separating for the night.'

'An incredible time,' said Elliot. 'Besides Lane was there first. As you say, he noticed *The Times*.'

'Yes. I was not seriously considering Mr Pearson. Everything points in another direction. You say that no one had the opportunity of replacing the cylinder between nine and a quarter to ten because no one was alone. I think myself that the time may be narrowed down to the quarter of an hour which elapsed before the men joined the ladies in the drawing room and Mr Paradine went to his study. I feel sure that the cylinder was placed there during this period, and there is only one person who had the opportunity of doing so.'

'None of the men left the dining-room, Miss Silver.'

'I am aware of that, Mr Wray. But one of the ladies did leave the drawing room.'

Elliot's fair brows made a rigid line above a gaze of singular intensity. He said, 'Who?' and kept his voice so quiet that the word had a toneless sound.

Miss Silver returned the look for a moment with a very steady one of her own. Then she said, 'Miss Paradine.'

THIRTY-FOUR

ELLIOT TIPPED BACK his head and laughed. The sound was not a pleasant one.

'You're a brave woman! Have you any idea what sort of explosive you're handling?'

Miss Silver coughed.

'I am giving you the result of what I have observed and deduced, Mr Wray. I should be glad to continue.'

'I should be glad if you would.'

She went on knitting.

'If you will consider the facts quite impartially you will admit that Miss Paradine was the sole member of the family who had the opportunity of replacing your cylinder. Unless you prefer what you have yourself stigmatised as the absurd proposition that Mr Pearson chose the moment when Lane was bringing in drinks, and the members of the family were exchanging good-nights, to rush into his employer's presence and confess to a theft.'

Elliot shook his head.

'You can wash that out. Albert is the soul of caution.'

'So I imagine. We therefore return to Miss Paradine, who left the drawing room at a few minutes after nine with the avowed object of bringing down the New Year's gifts which she had prepared for her guests. She was away for a very short time, but it would not have taken her long to do what I believe she did do. I think she came along this passage and down the stair at the end of it, and so into the study. It would really hardly delay her at all. Having deposited the cylinder upon Mr Paradine's table, she had only to set the baize door ajar and listen, to make sure that there was no one in the hall before she crossed it and returned to the drawing room with her gifts.'

Elliot gave a long, low whistle.

'Grace Paradine!' he said. 'Why?'

'Don't you know why, Mr Wray? I think you do. Forgive me if I speak plainly. She hates you – she is jealous of you. She has separated you from your wife. She has a very intense nature, and it is wholly set upon Mrs Wray. It is quite impossible to be in the same room with the three of you without becoming aware of this. I have been very acutely aware of it. Mrs Wray is aware of it too. It troubles her deeply. She is pulled in one direction by upbringing and by what she thinks of as loyalty and duty, and in another by all her natural instincts and feelings. Now consider Miss Paradine's position. She has achieved what I think she set out to achieve – a separation between you and your wife. I do not know how she effected it, but she is a woman of considerable force of character and, I think, quite unscrupulous where her feeling for Mrs Wray is concerned. She is very dominant, very possessive, very sure of her own claims. And then you come up here on a business visit. She is afraid of a meeting between you and Mrs Wray – she is afraid of future visits. She casts about for something that will prevent them. It occurs to her that if valuable plans were lost the breach between you and the Paradines might be rendered complete. I do not know whether such a result would have followed, but she might have supposed that it would. You will remember that Mr Richard Paradine had tea with her on Wednesday. It seems from your statement of what Mr Paradine told you that Mr Richard was aware that his uncle was bringing home papers of such importance that he would not leave them in the office unguarded whilst he went to wash his hands, but desired Mr Richard to remain there during his absence. Mr Richard has struck me as an amiable and rather talkative young man. I think we shall find that he mentioned the papers to his aunt. I am persuaded that she then found some opportunity of abstracting them, and that Mr Paradine was perfectly well aware that she had done so. He told you that he knew who had taken them, did he not?'

Elliot nodded.

Knitting rapidly, Miss Silver proceeded.

'I have been very specially struck by the fact that Mr Paradine seems to have felt no uneasiness about the loss of these important blueprints. You would agree on this point, would you not?'

Elliot's look had sharpened.

'Yes.'

'You described him as being in very good spirits.'

He said grimly, 'Oh, yes – he was enjoying himself.'

The needles clicked briskly.

'Don't you see what that implies, Mr Wray? A valuable secret was missing. If Mr Paradine was able to enjoy the situation, it means he was perfectly persuaded that there was no military reason for the theft. He must, for instance, have been quite certain there was no danger that the blueprints might be photographed. Think for a moment, and you will see it was incredible that he should temporise as he did if he had the slightest doubt on this point.'

In an expressionless voice Elliot said, 'Yes.'

Over the revolving needles Miss Silver's eyes were as bright as those of a bird – the proverbial early bird with the worm in view. The slight sideways tilt of her neat head was quite in keeping.

She said crisply, 'Mr Paradine knew that your blueprints had not been taken because they were blueprints, but for the purely personal and private reason that they were yours. After living with her for the last twenty years, we may suppose that he had a tolerable knowledge of Miss Paradine's frame of mind and of the situation in the house. We don't know how he knew that she had taken the cylinder, but he certainly did know. He may have been fond of his sister, but there is no doubt that he was very angry, and quite determined to punish and humiliate her. I think we may allow that she was punished. That speech of his at the dinner table must have been a dreadful experience for Miss Paradine. The family has always regarded her with great affection and respect – one cannot help observing that at every turn. Even Miss Ambrose had no criticisms.'

'They put her on a pedestal,' said Elliot bitterly. 'I've been up against that – Aunt Grace can do no wrong. It's the great family myth. I'm the sole blasphemer.'

Miss Silver nodded.

'Few characters can support the weight of infallibility. But once you have grown accustomed to a pedestal it is very hard to step down – harder still to be pushed down, and perhaps in public. When Miss Paradine sat at the dinner table on Wednesday night and heard her brother say he knew who had committed that still unnamed offence she must have suffered very deeply indeed. She could not be sure that his next words might not inform the whole family that she was the offender. I think you may feel sure that she had her punishment then.'

Elliot's face was colourless and set.

'She'd asked for it, hadn't she? Do you expect me to be sorry for her? You know what she has done – to me – to Phyllida. Even if I beat her now – even if that damned pedestal of hers is smashed so that she never gets on to it again – it's robbed us of a year.'

He got up, walked to the window, stood there a moment, and came back again, hard and controlled.

'Did she murder her brother?'

Miss Silver's clicking needles stopped. Her hands rested in her lap.

'I don't know, Mr Wray.'

THIRTY-FIVE

THERE WAS A silence which lasted until Elliot said with an effect of suddenness, 'How do you mean, you don't know?'

She began to knit again.

'Just what I say, Mr Wray. I am sure that Miss Paradine took the blueprints and afterwards replaced them. I am not sure that she pushed Mr Paradine over the parapet. She had the motive, and she might have made herself the opportunity, but there is at present no evidence that she did so.'

Elliot said, 'Look here, Miss Silver, you say she took those blueprints. I'm not saying she didn't. Then you say she put them back, and the only time it could have been done was somewhere between nine and nine-fifteen. All right, that goes with me. Now will you explain why Mr Paradine should have gone on sitting there in his study waiting for someone to come and confess? On your showing the blueprints were back and on his table. He knew who had taken them. What was hc waiting for?'

Miss Silver smiled.

'I think you can answer your own question, Mr Wray.'

'He wasn't letting her off? He meant her to come and confess?'

'Exactly. It was, I think, a trial of wills between them. I am not prepared to say which of them won. They were two determined and obstinate people. She may have come down at the last, or she may have decided to her own satisfaction that, having recovered the papers, he would not proceed to extremities. She may have persuaded herself that he did not really know who had taken them.'

Elliot said, 'Yes. All right, I'm with you.' He fell silent for a moment. Then he said, 'I can't remember just what I told you when we talked before. I'm going to say it again. There's something – I don't know whether it's important or not—'

'Pray tell me what it is.'

'I told you Albert Pearson was with me in my room. We came down for a drink soon after half-past eleven. We came down the stairs into the hall. Just at that moment the front door shut. I heard another door shut upstairs.'

'On which side of the house, Mr Wray?'

He gave her a grim smile.

'There was no one on this side to shut doors. Albert and I had the only two bedrooms occupied before you came.'

'It was on the other side?'

'It was. And as you know, my wife and Miss Paradine occupy the only two bedrooms there.'

Miss Silver's gaze dwelt upon him with intelligence.

'This was at half-past eleven?'

'A bit later. I don't know whether it's important or not. She may have been meaning to come down, and went back again when she heard the front door and our footsteps. I just thought I would tell you.'

'Thank you, Mr Wray.'

He made a movement as if he were throwing the whole thing off and said, 'What happens next?'

Miss Silver coughed.

'I should very much like to have a conversation with Mrs Wray. I should like you to be present. I propose that Polly should be sent to ask her if she could spare me a few minutes. We will adjourn to my room and wait for her there.'

They adjourned.

Polly was in the bathroom polishing taps. When she had been despatched on her errand and Miss Silver had arranged three chairs to her liking she addressed a question to Elliot.

'When you went in to say goodnight, Mr Wray, what did you say to Mr Paradine, and what did he say to you? Can you remember?'

She thought he stiffened slightly.

'None of it was of the slightest importance.'

She had taken an upright chair and was knitting placidly with her back to the light. Elliot, and presently Phyllida, would have perforce to face both it and her. She smiled kindly.

'That is as may be, Mr Wray. I should like very much to know what Mr Paradine said when he saw you. Did he give you the impression that he was expecting anyone else?'

'It was too early for that – too much coming and going. If you want to know, he asked me if I'd come to confess, and then told me to get out because he hadn't the time to tell me just what kind of a fool he thought I was. That was one of the times I thought he was enjoying himself.'

Miss Silver's expression became brightly interested, but she said no more. Her needles clicked. Eight or nine inches of dark grey legging now depended from them. She had presently to extract another ball from her knitting bag and join the thread.

Phyllida's knock elicited a cheerful 'Come in!' She had shut the door behind her and was well into the room before she became aware of Elliot propping the mantelpiece. A murmur of words about Polly and her message tripped up and came to nothing. She flushed vividly and stood still. Miss Silver said in a reassuring voice, 'Come and sit down, Mrs Wray. I won't keep you for long.'

Phyllida sat down. She faced Miss Silver, but she could see Elliot too. He did not speak, and he took no notice of the chair which had obviously been provided for him. He just stood there and looked. Curiously enough, she found this reassuring.

Miss Silver addressed her in an indulgent tone.

'Mrs Wray, why did you leave the study by way of the bedroom next door on Wednesday night?'

Phyllida said 'Oh—' and said no more.

Elliot laughed.

'It's no good Phyl – you'll never make a criminal. You left fingerprints on both the doors.'

She looked from him to Miss Silver and said, 'I – I just went out that way.'

'It was because someone else was at the study door, was it not? Mr Paradine sent you out through the bedroom?'

Phyllida said 'Oh—' again.

Miss Silver leaned towards her.

'That is what I think. You can correct me if I am wrong. I also think that you know who this someone was. You went into a dark room – there is no switch by that door. You would not have moved at once. There would naturally have been a moment when you were close enough to the room you had just left either to hear the newcomer addressed by name or to recognise the voice which addressed Mr Paradine. That was so, was it not?'

A flush showed in Phyllida's cheeks. She did not speak.

'I am sorry to distress you, Mrs Wray, but it will be better if you tell me what you know. At the moment Mr Mark Paradine is under suspicion.'

'Mark? Oh – but it wasn't Mark—'

Miss Silver nodded.

'Mr Mark did come back to see his uncle, but he did not reach the study until just before eleven.'

Phyllida's eyes were wide and troubled.

'It wasn't Mark. I was back in my room by half-past ten.'

'Will you tell us who it was, Mrs Wray?'

Phyllida turned those troubled eyes on Elliot.

'I think you'd better, Phyl.'

She said only just above her breath, 'It was Frank.'

'Mr Frank Ambrose?'

'Yes.'

'Will you tell us what you heard? You did hear something, did you not?'

Phyllida's hand went to her cheek in an unconscious gesture like a child's.

'Yes. Uncle James said, "Hello, Frank – come to confess?" and Frank said something, but I didn't hear what it was. I didn't want to hear. I wanted to get away.'

Miss Silver's needles clicked.

'Very natural, Mrs Wray.'

Elliot said in an astounded voice, '*Frank?* I don't believe it.'

Miss Silver coughed.

'You mean, Mr Wray, that you do not believe Mr Ambose to be the guilty person. You do not mean to imply any disbelief in Mrs Wray's statement?'

'Admirably put. I told you Phyl couldn't tell a lie. She can't, so it isn't any use her trying. She just has to make the best of a bad job and stick to the truth.'

Phyllida said 'Elliot!' in a tone of protest. And then, 'Miss Silver, *please* – it doesn't mean anything – it really doesn't. I mean Uncle James saying that, because he said exactly the same thing to me – about confessing, you know. I knocked at the door, and he said, "Come in!" And I said could I come and speak to him, and he said, "Come and sit down". And then he said, "Well, Phyllida – have you come to confess?" – just like that. So you see it didn't mean anything. Please, *please*, don't think it did.'

'He said pretty much the same thing to me,' said Elliot. ' "Come to confess, have you?" A bit grim, but it seems to have been his idea of a joke.'

Miss Silver opened her lips to speak and shut them again. Her mind was for the moment so brightly illuminated that it required all her attention. Having dealt with what she perceived there, she turned to Phyllida, who was saying earnestly, 'Everyone trusts Frank. He isn't always easy, but he's the solid kind – everybody trusts him. If he came back like that, it would be because he wanted to talk things over with Uncle James and find out what was wrong. It couldn't be anything else – it simply couldn't.'

Miss Silver looked at her with a kind of grave attention. She said, 'No doubt he will be able to explain the nature of his business with Mr Paradine. I think he will have to do that.' She folded her knitting, put it away in the bag which had been Ethel's Christmas present, and got up. 'There is something that I want to ask Lane. He will be busy later on, so I will see if I can find him now.' She went over to the door with the bag slung on her arm. With her hand on the knob, she turned and looked again at Phyllida. 'Pray do not be troubled, Mrs Wray,' she said. 'The truth hurts sometimes, but, believe me, it is always best in the end.'

THIRTY-SIX

ELLIOT AND PHYLLIDA were left alone. Neither of them moved, until suddenly she lifted her eyes and gave him the same troubled look as before.

'Why didn't you write?' she said.

He had been leaning back against the mantelpiece. Now he jerked upright.

'Why didn't I write?'

She kept her eyes on him. The blue had gone out of them. They were dark, like water under a cloud. The colour had gone from her skin too. She had a lost, white look which would have gone to his heart if it had not made him almost too angry to speak. She said, 'I thought you would write – but you didn't—' Her voice trailed away.

He said, 'You didn't get my letters – is that what you're saying?'

There was a very faint movement of her head which said 'No.' His face had gone so bleak that it frightened her.

He said, 'I wrote you two letters. In the first one I told you just what had happened about Maisie Dale. In the second I asked you to let me know whether you had got that first letter, and when I could come and see you. I suggested meeting you in

Birleton as I didn't want to come to the house. I got an answer to that by return, a quite explicit telegram – "Cannot meet you now or at any time. Please accept this as final." So I did.'

Phyllida sat quite still. Everything in her was too cold and stiff to move. She went on looking at Elliot because she couldn't look away.

He said very harshly and angrily, 'What are you looking like that for?'

She made her lips move then. She said, 'I didn't get the letters.' And, after a pause, 'I didn't send the telegram.'

Suddenly his face frightened her. The stiffness broke. She began to shake. Her shaking hands came up and covered her face. She said in a small piteous voice, 'Don't! Oh, please don't! I didn't get them – I really didn't.'

She felt his hands on her wrists, pulling her up. She had to face him. The look that had frightened her was gone. He said in a controlled, gentle voice, 'Don't be an idiot, child – unless you want me to beat you. Did you think I was angry with you? We've got to have this out. If you pull yourself together and listen to me, I'll tell you what I wrote in the letter you didn't get. Can you do that?'

His grip was hurting her wrists. She had a feeling of security – of being held up. She said, 'Yes.'

Elliot put her back in her chair, pulled Miss Silver's chair round a bit, and sat down facing her.

'Are you all right?'

She nodded.

'Yes. I was silly.'

'You've said it! All right, no recriminations. Now listen! Going back to the smash-up – I quit because I was afraid I should murder somebody if I didn't. I've got a foul temper – I expect you know that. I can keep the upper hand of it as a rule, but that time it got away. I'd just enough sense to get out. I went back to London, and when I'd cooled off a bit I sat down and wrote to you. I'll tell you the whole thing now. There isn't a great deal in it. I'm not particularly proud of it, but it isn't what you've been told. I can tell you what really happened, but I can't make you believe it. I can just say this – I can prove part of what I'm going to tell you, but if you can't believe me without that proof, it's all up between us.'

He waited.

Phyllida lifted her eyes and said, 'I'll believe you—'

'All right, then here goes. The June before we were married – we've got to get back to that. We hadn't ever met. We didn't meet until September, when Mr Paradine suddenly asked me to dine, I don't know why. I didn't even know you by sight. I was working pretty hard and not taking much time off. Cadogan said I was working too hard. He wanted me to take a weekend off and get right away. Well, I bumped into a chap I used to know. He'd got a spot of leave, and he asked me to join a weekend party at a place he'd got on the river. In the end we didn't go there. We went to a road-house instead – himself, and me, and a couple of girls – Doris for him, Maisie for me. It was a pretty rackety party. We kept it up late and we went the pace a bit. There wasn't anything more in it than that as far as Maisie and I were concerned. She was the sort of girl that's out for a good time and can't get enough of it. She wasn't very old, and she was just cram full of vitality – you could almost see the sparks flying. She was a good sort . . . Well, that's that. We started back. I'd a bit of a hang-over – I can't say whether that had anything to do with what happened. I don't drink as a rule. I suppose my reactions may have been affected – I don't know. Anyhow we had a smash. A lorry came blinding out of a side road, and I wasn't quite quick enough. We turned over. The car wasn't damaged, but Maisie was knocked out. We took her into the nearest house, and of course we had to give our names and addresses. Maisie came round all right, and when the police had finished with us we went on. I drove her home, and that was the end of it as far as I was concerned.'

Phyllida's lips parted. She took a quick breath, but she did not speak. Her eyes never moved from his face.

He jerked with his shoulder and said, 'All right – I'm coming to the rest of it. It didn't happen for another three months. I met you, and I began to fall in love with you. After I came up here at the end of September I was pretty sure it was the real thing. I was rather walking on air. Then I bumped into Doris – the other girl. She was in a restaurant with a fellow I knew – not the same fellow. I went over and spoke to them. She was a bit tight, and she went for me tooth and nail – said I'd a nerve to come and speak to her after what I'd done to Maisie. I wanted to know what I'd done, and she said didn't I know, and I said no I didn't. After that she calmed down a bit and told me I'd better go and see for myself. So I did. She was paralysed – something gone wrong with her back after the accident. She didn't feel it for a bit, then it went on getting worse. I asked her why she hadn't let me know, and she said it wasn't my fault and why should she. I told her she'd got a claim against my insurance and I'd fix it for her. I put a solicitor on to it, and she got her compensation. I went to see her once or twice. She was grateful and very plucky. She and Doris were living together. I went into it all with Doris. I arranged to pay part of the rent. Maisie hadn't any people, and she wanted to stay where she was. She said the girls came in and out, and she'd rather die than go into a hospital. So I fixed it up with Doris.'

Phyllida took another of those quick breaths. This time it carried a word.

'Elliot—'

He gave her a frowning look.

'You see, Miss Paradine was perfectly right when she told you I was paying Maisie's rent. She was perfectly right in saying that I went to see her after we got back from our honeymoon. I did. What I should like to know is how she found out.'

Phyllida moistened her lips.

'Mrs Cranston wrote and told her – about the

accident. She wrote when she knew we were going to be married. The letter was delayed – it didn't arrive until we had gone away.'

'Cranston? I remember – the woman at the house . . . Face like a horse—'

Phyllida nodded.

'She said she thought it was her duty. She's like that. I used to put my tongue out behind her back when I was little, and feel dreadfully wicked about it afterwards in bed.'

Elliot went on frowning.

'Mrs Cranston told her about the accident. Who told her I paid the rent, and went to see Maisie on Boxing Day? Did she hire a detective?'

The colour ran up to the roots of Phyllida's hair. She bent her head and heard Elliot laugh.

'I thought so! Now, Phyl, stop blushing and listen! This is where you've got to have a look at things as they are. I'm afraid you're not going to like it, but here it is. If Miss Paradine put a detective on to find out about Maisie he'd get her address from Mrs Cranston – she was listening in all right whilst the policeman was taking our statements. Well, he couldn't have found out about the rent and not have found out that Maisie was a cripple. If Miss Paradine hired him he'd have reported back to her. In plain words, Phyl, she knew she was telling you lies. She wanted to separate us, so she took a chance and hoped for the best. As it happened nothing could have gone off better. You flattened out, and I played into her hands by banging out of the house. Then she watched for my letters and suppressed them, and topped it all up neatly by sending me a telegram to say you never wanted to see me again, or words to that effect. These things are quite easy to do if you mean to have your own way and don't give a damn. She didn't. She doesn't. Miss Silver will tell you that she took my blueprints, and she's right – dead right. She's got to have what she wants. She wants you. She'll do anything to keep you, and get rid of me.'

The shamed flush had died away. She was as pale as she could be. She said, 'Elliot—'

'Look here, Phyl – did she ever suggest a divorce?'

Phyllida shook her head.

'Then don't you see that proves it? She knew damned well that there was no evidence. Besides she wouldn't want you free. You might marry someone else, and she wanted you all to herself.'

'Elliot – *please*—'

'Isn't it true? You know it's true!'

She looked at him again.

'Yes—'

He took hold of her and pulled her up.

'Well then – what about it? We can't both have you. She's made it that way. She's taken everything and twisted it – it can't be put back again. You're either my wife or her daughter. It's not your fault or mine that you can't be both. It's something she's done herself.'

'*Elliot*—'

He gave that short angry laugh.

'That's not going to get us anywhere!' He let go of her and stepped back. 'I could make you choose me. I know that, and you know it. But I'm not doing it – I'm not even touching you. You've got to choose for yourself. If you want time to think about it you can have all the time you want.'

'I don't want any time—' The words were just a murmur.

'Well then, choose!'

There was a silence. When it had lasted quite a long time, Phyllida said, 'You sound so angry—'

'I am angry.'

Another silence. Then, 'Is Maisie very pretty?'

'No!' The word was jerked out impatiently.

Phyllida said, 'You look as if you hate me. Do you?'

'Probably.' His face twitched. He reached out and pulled her into his arms. 'Stop being such a damned fool, Phyl!'

THIRTY-SEVEN

MISS SILVER WENT briskly to the dining room, where she found Lane laying the table for lunch. Her slight cough having attracted his attention, he straightened up and turned towards her.

'Do you require anything, madam?'

'Thank you, Lane, I should be glad if you would answer one or two questions. I think you are aware that Mr Mark Paradine has asked me to enquire into the circumstances of his uncle's death.'

'Yes, madam.'

'I should be glad to know what time it was when you took the tray of drinks into the study on Wednesday night.'

Lane looked worried.

'I don't know that I could say – not to be exact, madam. It was after the quarter to, but it was some way off ten o'clock, I should say.'

'Would that be your usual time?'

'No, madam. Ten o'clock was my time, but if Mr Paradine wished for the tray earlier he would ring. On the Wednesday night his bell went at a quarter to ten. I'd just come back from letting Mr Ambrose and his party out, when Mrs Lane told me that the bell had gone.'

Miss Silver said, 'Thank you.' And then, 'Mr

Paradine was alone in the study when you went in with the tray?'

'Why, no, madam.'

Miss Silver looked brightly expectant.

'Indeed? Pray, who was with him?'

'Well, madam, it was Mr Pearson. But I don't want to give any wrong impression. He was just going into the room as I came through the baize door from the hall with my tray.'

'And did he see you?'

'I hardly think so. He was going into the study as I came through.'

'Did he shut the door behind him?'

'He had no time to do so, madam. He must have heard me coming before he could close the door.'

'Did you hear him speak to Mr Paradine, or Mr Paradine speak to him?'

The worried look became intensified.

'I hardly like to say.'

Miss Silver looked at him steadily.

'You were with Mr Paradine for a great many years?'

'Yes, madam.'

She said, 'He was murdered.'

Lane had been holding a cut-glass decanter in his hand. It shook. He set it down.

Miss Silver went on speaking.

'Innocent people are under suspicion. There is one guilty person. I hope to find out who it is. Everyone in this house knows something that may help. If everyone will tell me what they know, those innocent people can be cleared. Was it Mr Pearson who spoke, or Mr Paradine?'

He had turned a little away to put down the decanter. He remained like that, looking down. He said in a very low voice, 'It was Mr Paradine.'

'Did you hear what he said?'

'Yes, madam.'

'Will you please tell me what you heard.'

'Madam—'

'Yes, Lane? It will be better if you tell me.'

He said, 'Mr Paradine said – well, madam, he said, "Hello, Albert, have you come to confess?" But if I may say so, I took it to be one of Mr Paradine's jokes. Being with him as long as I've been, I wouldn't say that it was meant seriously. That was the way Mr Paradine talked – he'd sound very angry, and be laughing at you all the time. I've told you what he said, but I wouldn't like to think I'd given a wrong impression.'

Miss Silver coughed.

'You have not done so. How long did you remain in the study?'

'No longer than it took me to set down the tray and retire.'

'And where was Mr Pearson whilst you were doing this?'

'He stayed near the door, madam. If I may say so, he seemed to be rather upset, which I put down to his not being so well accustomed to Mr Paradine as to relish his way of joking. I can remember being very much taken aback myself when I first came to the River House. Very unexpected, Mr Paradine could be, when you were not accustomed to his way of putting things.'

Miss Silver smiled.

'I can quite understand that. Perhaps it will make you feel easier to know that Mr Paradine addressed a very similar remark to Mrs Wray that evening.'

Lane appeared to be very much relieved.

'Then there would be no doubt about its being a joke, madam. Very fond indeed of Mrs Wray, Mr Paradine was.'

Miss Silver nodded.

'Well then, Lane, that was all? You came out of the study, leaving Mr Pearson with Mr Paradine?'

'You may put it that way, madam. In point of fact Mr Pearson left the room before me, but just as I was going out Mr Paradine called him back. I could not avoid hearing what passed. He said, "Don't post that letter to Lewis – I may want to alter it. I'll see you about it some other time." And Mr Pearson said goodnight and came out and shut the door.'

THIRTY-EIGHT

EMERGING FROM THE dining room, Miss Silver was aware of Mark Paradine on the stairs. He was coming down two steps at a time. He looked like a man driven hard on a road which is none of his choosing. Until Miss Silver pronounced his name, which she did very clearly, it is to be doubted whether he was aware of her presence. In the concentration of his mind upon its own bitter thoughts he might very well have brushed against her as he passed without noticing that she was there. But her 'Mr Mark—' halted him. He turned, looked vaguely in her direction for a moment, and came to.

'Oh – Miss Silver! Did you want me?'

'Just for a moment, if you will be so good.'

After a brief pause of indecision, during which he was remembering painfully that the police were in the study, he opened the first door on the left-hand side of the hall and ushered her into the billiard room, an enormous room with half-drawn blinds and the hot, stuffy feeling of a heated place to which no fresh air has been admitted. Miss Silver thought it a very fine room, but she would have liked to have opened a window. This not being the moment for such digressions, she gave her whole attention to the matter in hand. But before she had time to speak Mark said in hard, flat tones, 'Well – are they going to arrest me?'

'Are you not rather jumping to conclusions?'

'I think not. I don't quite see how they can help it. The only question seems to be whether it will be before lunch or afterwards. My uncle's solicitor, Mr Harrison, is coming in to see the safe opened at half-past two. I thought they might wait till then, though I really don't know why they should. As far as I know, the only things he kept there were a few private papers and my aunt's diamonds.'

Miss Silver displayed interest.

'The ones she is wearing in the portrait?'

They had remained standing. Mark leaned against the near end of the billiard table, hands driven deep into his pockets. He nodded.

'That's it. Nobody's worn them since she died. They ought to have been in the bank, but he liked having them handy. He used to take them out and look at them. I found him doing it one night, and he told me all about them – what he'd paid for them, how much they'd risen in value, and how well Aunt Clara had looked in them.'

Miss Silver picked out the word value and repeated it with a slight monitory cough.

'They must be of considerable value, Mr Mark.'

'I suppose they are—' His voice was wearily indifferent.

Miss Silver coughed again.

'To whom are they left?'

'They are divided between my cousin Richard and myself.'

Miss Silver appeared preoccupied. She said, 'They will be valued for probate. Would you object to an earlier valuation?'

'I? Why should I? I don't take any interest one way or the other.'

She hesitated very slightly.

'Then you would have no objection to a valuer being present when the safe is opened?'

She saw his face change. Eyes and mind seemed to focus upon her for the first time.

'What for?' His voice had a startled sound.

She said gravely, 'Mr Paradine was murdered. I am not yet sure of the motive behind the murder.'

'I thought you said Elliot's blueprints had been taken.'

'They were taken – and they were put back again. The only time that they could have been replaced was between nine and a quarter past. The only person who had an opportunity of replacing them was Miss Paradine. I concluded that it was she who took them. But I do not know whether she returned later and caused her brother's death by pushing him over the parapet.'

Mark's hands came out of his pockets. He stood up straight.

'What are you saying? What possible motive—'

'She wished to make a complete breach with Mr Wray. She expected this to follow upon the loss of the blueprints. I imagine that it might very easily have done so. The thing she wishes most in the world is to prevent a reconciliation between Mr and Mrs Wray.'

Mark looked at her in horror, but it was the horror, not of incredulity, but of most unwilling conviction. He got out a handkerchief, wiped a sweating brow, and said, 'Did she – do it?'

'I have told you that I do not know. She had a very strong motive. Her brother knew what she had done – if he chose he could ruin her credit with the family. You are in a position to know what that would mean to her.'

He said, 'For God's sake, don't! It's too horrible. She couldn't have done it!'

Miss Silver glanced at him compassionately.

'Then we must look for another motive in some other person. Will you tell me what Mr Paradine said to you when you entered the study on Wednesday night?'

He appeared surprised, startled, relieved.

'How do you mean?'

'I want to know what he said when he saw you.'

Mark frowned. A spark of comprehension came and went, a muscle twitched in his cheek. He said, 'How do you know?'

Miss Silver smiled.

'He said the same thing to three other people who went to see him that night. I was curious to know whether he also said it to you. Now will you tell me what he said?'

Mark went back a step. He took hold of the edge of the table above the corner pocket and gripped it hard.

'He asked me if I had come to confess.'

Miss Silver beamed.

'That is just what I thought. He addressed the same remark to Mr Pearson and, separately, to Mr and Mrs Wray.'

'Why?'

Miss Silver coughed.

'According to Mr Wray, Mr Paradine was enjoying the situation he had created. To a man of his ironical turn of mind there would be entertainment in watching the response to a question of this nature. He had just startled you all very much by saying that one of you had betrayed the family interests. He had in mind the theft of the blueprints, but only one of those present would be aware of this. I believe that one to have been Miss Paradine. The rest could not know what he meant – they could only surmise. It is, unfortunately, true that most people have something to hide. There are privacies of the heart and mind. There are dilemmas, faults, failings, sins, which we would not willingly expose to view. Mr Paradine's accusation shocked more than the criminal into a hasty search of conduct and conscience. I wonder how many confessions were made on that Wednesday night. I think you made one, did you not? I think it was very kindly received. But suppose, Mr Mark, that one of the confessions he invited was of such a nature that it could not be made without ruin? Why, then we would have a second motive for the murder. That is what I meant when I said that we must ascertain whether there was anyone who had such a motive – anyone, that is, other than Miss Paradine. We know what her motive was. If *she* did not murder her brother, there must be someone else with a motive as strong or stronger. To find the murderer we must find that motive. It may not even exist – there may be no other motive. But the fact that these very valuable diamonds were kept in the house does suggest a possible motive. Since every possibility should be explored, I suggest that these jewels should be examined by a competent person. Do you happen to know whether there is a detailed list of them, and where Mr Paradine would have been likely to keep it?'

Still in that indifferent manner, Mark said, 'The list is in the safe. I don't think there's an earthly chance that anything is missing. My uncle was always having the things out to look at – he liked handling them. We'll have a valuer in if you want one, but he won't find anything wrong. You'll have to look somewhere else for your motive, and the police aren't going to look any farther than me. If you ask me, they'll arrest me just as soon as Harrison tells them the extent to which I benefit under my uncle's will. I get about three-quarters of everything, you know – Uncle James's idea of supporting the family dynasty. That's the sort of motive a policeman likes – plain straight-forward murder for a sizeable lump of cash. Just as soon as it occurs to them to ask Harrison about the terms of the will my number will be up. They'll probably let me open the safe before they arrest me, but that's about as much rope as I'll get. It's now half-past twelve – Harrison is to be here at half-past two. I've got about two hours. Any suggestions as to what I should do with them?'

Miss Silver chose to regard this as a pleasantry, though as a rule pleasantries are not delivered in so bitter a tone. She smiled and said, 'I think you might find it helpful to talk the matter over with Miss Pennington.'

THIRTY-NINE

THE NEXT HALF hour was a busy one for Miss Silver. After spending ten minutes in the study with Colonel Bostock and Superintendent Vyner she returned to her bedroom and found it empty. Polly Parsons, having answered the bell, was asked some questions which resulted in heartfelt sobs and some interesting admissions. Having been bidden to dry her eyes, hold her tongue, and summon Louisa, she departed, still gulping and unfeignedly glad to get away.

Left alone in the billiard room, Mark stood for some moments looking moodily at nothing. His inward vision was, however, obsessed with the picture presented in Miss Silver's last words. If he was going to be arrested he had this next half hour in which to see Lydia again. After that the domestic business of lunch would intervene, and then the police would be coming back – if indeed they intended to go. Harrison would arrive, and at any time the balloon might be expected to go up.

Lydia was at Meadowcroft. Normally it took seven minutes to get there by the river path and the footbridge. He could cut the seven to five. He went out of the front door and down the steep cliff path at a run.

Meadowcroft stood among the fields on the farther side of the river – a converted farmhouse, mellow and comfortable. He had always considered it wasted on Frank and Irene, who had filled it with jangling modern furniture bought in suites.

He wasn't thinking about furniture as he let himself in. If Lydia was not in the drawing room, he would ring the bell and say he wanted to speak to her. Anyone was at liberty to think anything they pleased. He had to see her once more before he stopped being a free man and became the accused.

He walked through the hall without meeting anyone, opened the drawing-room door, and saw Dicky on the far side of the room with his hand on Lydia's shoulder and his head bent to kiss her. At any other time this would have halted him. It did not halt him now. He came in, shut the door behind him, and crossed to where they stood together in front of the fire.

Dicky said, 'Hello, Mark!' And then, 'Well, I'll be getting along.'

The words, and the manner in which they were said, went by as if they had not been spoken. As far as Mark was concerned they did not penetrate his consciousness at all. Lydia looked vaguely, smiled, said something which was just an indistinguishable murmur, and fell silent. Dicky went down the room and out.

As the door shut, Mark moved to the mantelpiece and leaned there, looking down into the fire. After the first moment when he had seen her face lifted for Dicky's kiss he had not looked at Lydia. He had come to see her, but now that he was here he couldn't look at her. There was too much to say between them, and now it would never be said. She would marry Dicky and be happy. The family had always planned it that way.

Lydia's voice broke in upon these cheerful thoughts.

'Mark – what's the matter?'

He said without looking up, 'I wanted to see you,' and then frowned desperately, because what was the good of saying that now? The impulse which had brought him here had expended the last of its energy as he spoke. It failed, and left him drained.

Lydia said, 'Darling, if you want to see me, it's no good looking obstinately into the fire. You've got the direction wrong.'

He straightened up at that, looked down at her, and found her noticeably pale. In a stumbling sort of way he said, 'Why do you look like that?'

'Like what?'

'Pale.'

'Darling, my colour comes out of a box, you know. Make-up isn't done before the funeral – at least, I gather, that's the idea.'

'I see—' His tone was quite abstracted now.

'Mark, why did you come?'

'I think they are going to arrest me. I wanted to see you again.'

'Why should they arrest you?'

'I told you. I went back. I left a pocket diary on

the study table – the one Aunt Grace gave me. Someone recognised it. I was with him till half-past eleven, and he was dead before twelve. I come into most of what he'd got to leave. They are bound to arrest me. I don't see what else they can do.'

'Why did you go back?'

'I wanted to get away – from the firm – from Birleton, I'd told him so before. We had a row about it. I thought I'd try again. I told him why I wanted to get away. He said all right, if I still wanted to go in a month's time he'd do what he could about it.'

'Have you told the police that?'

'More or less.'

'Have you told them why you wanted to go?'

'No.'

'Will you tell me?'

He shook his head.

'I don't think so. It doesn't matter now. I just came – to say goodbye—'

There was a pause. Lydia looked at him, and looked away.

She looked into the fire. It dazzled and shimmered in a very bewildering way. She couldn't remember when she had cried last, but she thought she was going to cry now. Her voice was hot with anger as she said, 'Do stop being stupid! Why should you say goodbye?'

'I told you. I'd better go now. I don't want to see anyone else. Are you going to marry Dicky?'

Colour that was not out of a box came back in two bright patches. She looked at him and said, 'Why should I?'

'He was kissing you when I came in.'

'Darling, I should be put in prison if I married everyone who kissed me. It just can't be done.'

'Why was he kissing you?'

Lydia's very lovely eyes were as innocent as a baby's. The slight moisture which had made the flames dazzle deepened the green in them.

'Do you really want to know?'

'Yes.'

Her voice fell to a modest murmur.

'I was promising to be a cousin to him.'

'*What!*'

She nodded. Black lashes veiled the sparkling green.

'A first cousin – by marriage. He'd just been putting a pistol to my head. He said he had asked me to marry him eleven times and he didn't mind making a round dozen of it, but if I said no again he was through. He's awfully fond of Daisy Carter and he thought they'd be very happy together, but he'd give me one more chance. So I said, "All right, darling, it's no." The kiss was a fond farewell. No hearts broken, and every prospect of Daisy endowing him with the Carter moneybags.'

'You're not going to marry him?'

The lashes swept up again.

'A little slow on the uptake, aren't you, darling?' She came up close, stood on tiptoe, and put up her face.

'You love me, don't you?'

'Yes.'

'Terribly?'

'Terribly.'

'For a long time?'

'Always.'

'That's why you wanted to go away?'

'I thought you'd marry Dicky – I couldn't stand it.'

'Never thought of asking me yourself? You seem to have an inhibition or something. You might get Dicky to show you how it's done. It's quite easy really.'

He looked at her without speaking. She reached up, put her arms round his neck, and said between laughing and crying, 'Have a stab at it, darling!'

FORTY

ABOUT TEN MINUTES later Irene opened the door, said 'Oh!' in a very startled voice, and hung undecided whether to go or stay. Lydia, with a firm hold upon the arm which Mark had just removed from her waist, observed with modest pride, 'It's all right – we're engaged. Come along and say "Bless you, my children." And I'm going back to lunch with him at the River House, so you'll get a chance of saving on my rations. Hurry up with the congratulations, because we're going to be late, and you know how much Aunt Grace likes that.'

Irene stared, caught her breath, and made the most admired gaffe of her life.

'I thought it was Dicky!'

'Dicky didn't,' said Lydia crisply. 'Mark on the other hand did, but he doesn't now. You can think up something a little more effusive over the sago pudding, darling. I shan't be back for ages, so you've got plenty of time.'

Lunch was in progress at the River House when they walked in, but it had not got very far. Grace Paradine raised her eyebrows very slightly, Lane set a place beside Mark's, and the meal went on.

It was whilst he was handing the vegetables that

Miss Paradine asked in a low voice, 'Where is Louisa?' and received the equally low reply,

'She is not very well, madam.' The hand under the dish from which she was helping herself to potato shook slightly.

Her eyebrows lifted again.

Nobody wished to prolong the necessary business of eating, but in the absence of Louisa the service dragged. Phyllida and Elliot Wray were placed at opposite ends of the table. Elliot looked at no one, ate what was set in front of him, and confined his conversation to Mark, who on more than one occasion answered at cross purposes. Phyllida kept her eyes on her plate. She had a pretty colour, and every now and then her lips trembled into a smile. Grace Paradine, catching one of these looks, stiffened and ate no more.

Mark and Lydia sat side by side. They did not look at one another. Each felt the other unendurably dear. Each experienced an almost terrifying happiness which might at any moment be snatched away. For Mark to be silent was nothing new, but if everyone else had not been equally preoccupied, the fact that Lydia scarcely opened her lips could not have failed to attract attention. Miss Silver alone appeared to be perfectly at her ease. She conversed pleasantly with Albert Pearson, who for once had very little to say.

Everyone was glad when the meal was over. Mark went to make a telephone call. Lydia left the room with Phyllida. Miss Silver, Albert, and Elliot

Wray were following, when Miss Paradine, who had walked over to the window, turned back and addressed herself directly to Elliot.

'Will you remain behind for a moment? There is something I want to say.'

He shut the door upon the others and waited.

'What is it, Miss Paradine?'

'I would like to know when you propose to leave this house.'

His look had been so hard before that it did not seem as if it could harden any farther, yet this happened. He said, 'I came here at Mr Paradine's invitation – his very urgent invitation. I am staying at Mark's. I shall probably stay until after the funeral. Is that all?'

'No. I should like you to go. You are not welcome here.'

'I am not your guest, Miss Paradine.'

She had been pale, very pale indeed, but now the colour flooded into her face.

'Have you no consideration for Phyllida?'

'Have *you*?'

'That is insolent.'

Elliot laughed.

'You can't have it both ways, I'm afraid. If we are being polite, you don't order me out of Mark's house. If we revert to the comfortable state of saying just what we think, I can say things too. Do you want to hear them? Or shall we go back to being hostess and guest again?'

With the angry colour in her face she went to the door, but suddenly checked and turned, standing against the jamb. The flush died down, leaving her pale again.

'What have you got to say?'

Her movement had brought them so close together that there was not the stretch of an arm between them. It was too near for Elliot. His anger came up in his throat. He went back until the table stopped him. From this safer distance he said, 'You won't like it.'

'What have you got to say?'

He stood looking at her for a moment before he answered. All the lines in her face had deepened. Every muscle was tense. Her eyes blazed at him. He said, 'I think you know. You wanted Phyllida for yourself. You tried to separate us, and you thought you'd brought it off. You knew perfectly well that what you told her was a lie. You couldn't have known that I was helping Maisie without knowing that she was a cripple. You suppressed the letters I wrote to my wife – you sent me a forged telegram in her name. You thought you'd won. Then I came up here on business, and you couldn't leave well alone. If you had you might have gone on winning – I don't know. You had the bright idea that the loss of my blueprints might add a breach of business relations to the personal breach with the family. I don't know what put it into your head. Your brother may have mentioned the blueprints, or Dicky may have told you that Mr Paradine had brought them home with him – probably Dicky. Anyhow you took them. I don't know how Mr Paradine knew it was you, but he did. He sent for me and made me stay. Then he cast his bombshell at dinner, and you knew you weren't going to get away with it. You put the blue-prints back before we came out of the dining-room – you had the opportunity when you went upstairs to get your presents for the girls. You didn't see your brother then – he was still in the dining room. Did you see him later? I heard a door shut upstairs when Albert and I were coming through the hall round about half-past eleven. Were you meaning to come down and see him then? If you were, you would have heard us crossing the hall – you would have gone back and waited until we were out of the way and come down later. Did you come down later?'

She stood there and listened. When he had finished she said, 'Is that all?'

'Isn't it enough?'

She turned stiffly and went out of the room.

FORTY-ONE

POLLY OPENED THE door of Miss Paradine's sitting room and saw her at the writing-table. Without turning her head Grace Paradine said, 'Is that you, Louisa?'

'No, ma'am, it's me.'

'Where is Louisa?'

'She's not very well, ma'am.'

Miss Paradine sat with a pen in her hand, but she had not been writing. The nib was dry, and the sheet in front of her blank. She said in an abstracted voice, 'Yes – I forgot—' And then, 'Go down and ask Mrs Wray to come up here to me. If she is in the drawing room, just go to the door and ask if you can speak to her for a moment. Then when she has come out of the room you can give her my message. Can you remember that?'

'Oh, yes, ma'am.'

'Very well.'

She had not turned her head or looked at Polly. She sat there with the pen in her hand, and did not write. Her body was stiff and motionless. Her mind had never been clearer, or her will more resolute. Behind it there was an anger like ice. Never in all her life had anyone spoken to her as Elliot Wray had just spoken. Never had she felt such determination, such inward power.

When the door opened again and Phyllida came in she was ready to turn to her with a welcoming smile.

'My darling – did I disturb you?'

Phyllida's 'No, Aunt Grace' was soft and fluttered. She looked distressed.

Grace Paradine said quickly, 'What is it, Phyl? Has he been upsetting you?'

'Oh, no.'

'I think he has. That's what I wanted to talk to you about, my darling. This situation can't go on. It is most distressing for you – for all of us. God knows, we have enough without that.' She took a handkerchief from her loose sleeve and touched her eyes with it. The hand which held it shook a little.

Phyllida said, 'Please, Aunt Grace—'

The hand came down and lay upon the other one, still clasping the handkerchief.

'Forgive me, my darling – this has all been such a shock. I did not think that even Elliot Wray would choose this moment to make things worse for me.'

Phyllida said nothing. What was there to say? She didn't know. She stood looking at Grace Paradine as you look at something in a dream – something which isn't real.

Grace Paradine got up and came to her.

'I could bear his insulting behaviour if it only affected me, but I can't and won't have you exposed to it. I asked him to go – for your sake, my darling – and he told me that he was Mark's guest, not mine. So I must speak to Mark, but I wanted to tell you first. I don't want you to think that I would do anything behind your back.'

A shiver went over Phyllida. If it is a dream, you can wake up. If it isn't a dream, you have to bear it. She said, 'Please, Aunt Grace – it isn't any good—'

'What do you mean, Phyl?'

Phyllida looked away.

'It isn't any good. I know. Why did you do it?'

If she had been watching Grace Paradine she would have seen her eyes brighten and a little colour come up in her cheeks. She meant to fight, and she meant to win. She felt the glow which the fighter feels. She made her voice very gentle.

'Phyl, darling, what do you mean? Won't you tell me? Is it something that he has been saying? If it is, I think you will have to tell me.'

Phyllida looked, and looked away. She could not meet what she saw in Grace Paradine's face. It had meant love and shelter as long as she could remember. It had meant sympathy, kindness, protection. She couldn't meet it. She said almost in a whisper, 'Please, Aunt Grace—'

And then suddenly courage came to her. When you have to face something, you can.

'Yes, I'll tell you – I must. Elliot and I have talked. I know he wrote to me – twice. I know what was in the letters. I didn't get them. I know why. I know all about Maisie,' she said.

'You know what he has told you.'

'Yes.'

'My darling, do you suppose that he has told you the truth? Do you suppose that any man tells the truth about that sort of thing? He is tired of this girl now – I believe she has been ill – and he wants you back. Why shouldn't he? You are young and pretty, and you come in for a comfortable sum of money under James's will. Naturally, he wants you back.'

Phyllida said steadily, 'You say Maisie has been ill. Don't you know that she has been paralysed for months?'

'Is that what he told you? Did you believe him? Oh, my darling, do you want him to break your heart all over again? He wants you now – how long would he want you if you were ill like this poor girl? He throws her over – he isn't ashamed to come and tell you about it. What have you got to trust to? I suppose she thought she had something. What will you have?'

Phyllida lifted her eyes. They had a look of immeasurable sadness. She said, 'It's no good. It wasn't like that – I think you know that it wasn't. We love each other. You mustn't try to separate us any more.'

There was a silence. Then Grace Paradine said in her deep, tragic voice, 'Is that how it is?'

Another silence.

Grace Paradine turned away. After a moment she said, 'I want to make you understand. Will you listen to me, Phyl?' The words were gently, even tenderly spoken.

Phyllida's breath caught in her throat with pity.

'Of course.'

Grace Paradine was not looking at her. She stood half turned away, and she looked down at the papers on her table.

'It is so hard to make anyone else understand. That is the tragedy of the older people – they have suffered themselves – sometimes they have suffered horribly. Very often it has been their own fault. They have expected too much, trusted too much, made mistakes because they were ignorant, because they thought they knew everything. The one thing they want in all the world is to save the children they love from making the same mistakes and suffering in the same way. What do you think it feels like when the children won't listen, won't believe – when they have to stand aside and see them walking towards a precipice?'

'You can't live someone else's life, Aunt Grace, however much you love them – you have to let them live their own.'

Grace Paradine turned her head. She was shockingly pale, but she smiled, 'Your voice, but not your words, Phyl. Come here a moment, my darling.' Then when Phyllida had come to her she put a hand on her shoulder. 'Look, Phyl – here is the first photograph I had taken of you after you came to me. You were eighteen months old. I did everything for you myself. You were the dearest little baby. Later on I got a nurse for you, but I nearly always washed and dressed you myself. Here's the miniature I had done when you were five. It's very like you still. Here's your first school photograph – in that hideous gym tunic, but you were so proud of it. Here's one in the dress you had for your coming-out dance. It was a pretty dress, wasn't it? There are dozens and dozens more. I've kept them all. Most of them are somewhere in this room. Everyone laughs at me about them – Dicky calls it my Phyllida gallery. But I've never minded their laughing. Every bit of you has been too precious to part with – I've wanted to keep it all. You see, you've been my life.'

Phyllida made some movement, some sound as if she would speak, but the words wouldn't come. With a new vibration in her voice Grace Paradine went on.

'It's the only life I've had. You can't understand that, can you? I'm telling you, my darling, because I want you to understand. You have always been loved and wanted, but I haven't.'

'Aunt Grace!'

Grace Paradine said low and steadily, 'Whatever place I have now I have made for myself.' She looked into Phyllida's face. 'Has anyone ever told you that I was an adopted child?'

Phyllida was most unfeignedly startled.

'Oh, no.'

'I suppose most people have forgotten it – it's so long ago. James's mother lost a baby girl, and they adopted me. I believe she was very fond of me, but she died before I was five. The others were quite kind, but I was nobody's child. I set my heart on having a place of my own. When I got engaged I thought I was going to have one. I suppose you know that I was engaged to Robert Moffat?'

'Yes.'

'A month before my wedding day I found out that there was a girl over at Birstead – somebody told me. He didn't deny it – he just said it was all over. James and his father wanted me to marry him – they didn't seem to think it mattered. Phyl, my darling, I'm not telling you this to distress you, but to show you why I felt as I did about Elliot Wray.'

Phyllida said in a low voice, 'Yes, I see that. But it's different—'

'Is it? I don't think so. My life was broken, and there wasn't anyone to make it easier for me as I have tried to make it for you, there wasn't anyone to surround me with love and tenderness. There were ten dreadful, empty years. And then there was you. Everything began again. It was like a new life. You can't let go of any part of your life without dying a little. That is why I kept all your clothes, all your photographs. I couldn't bear to part with any of them – it would have been like parting with some of my life. And then Elliot came.'

It was when she said Elliot's name that Phyllida began to feel as if she couldn't bear it. She was gentle, but she wasn't stupid. All this emotion, this pain, was being used as a weapon against Elliot. Emotion which you do not share can become intolerable. To be so near to Grace Paradine, to be actually and physically under the weight of her hand, had become intolerable. But to draw away now – she couldn't do it.

Grace Paradine had paused as if Elliot's name had halted her. Now she went on.

'He came – James invited him. If I hadn't been away, he would never have had the chance of hurting you – I should have taken good care of that. But when I came back it was too late – you were engaged. And James backed him up – I've never forgiven him for that. I didn't like him, and I didn't trust him, but there was nothing that I could lay hold of. I wanted a longer engagement. James took his side again. Then when it was too late and you were married, I got Agnes Cranston's letter. I can't tell you how terrible it was to get it like that – too late.'

The hand on Phyllida's shoulder was cold. She could feel it through the stuff of her dress, heavy and cold. For all her pity she couldn't bear it any longer. She stepped back. The hand fell. A slow, dull colour came into Grace Paradine's face.

Phyllida said in a voice which she tried to keep from shaking, '*Please*, Aunt Grace – I came here to say something. Won't you let me say it? It's no good going over what has happened. We started wrong – we've got to begin all over again. Elliot and I are going to. Won't you? People can begin again. It isn't wrong to get married and have a home of your own. My real mother would have been glad—'

She could have said nothing more disastrous. An old smouldering jealousy caught and flamed. Phyllida saw a face she had never seen before – control breaking into fury, lips moving over words which came to her in a low, dreadful mutter. She hardly knew what they were. She was aghast and shaken.

When Grace Paradine said 'Go!' she ran out of the room with only one thought in her mind, to get out of sight and sound of the storm which she had raised.

FORTY-TWO

DOWNSTAIRS IN THE study Frank Ambrose said in a tired voice, 'Oh, yes, I came back. I don't mind telling you about it – I suppose it was bound to come out.'

He sat where Mark Paradine had sat, in a chair drawn up to the short side of the writing table. Miss Silver faced him across its length, placidly knitting. Bent over the blotting pad, Superintendent Vyner was taking notes. On the opposite side Colonel Bostock sat frowning, and wishing that he hadn't known all these people for donkey's years. Dashed awkward situation – dashed awkward case.

It was Miss Silver who coughed and said, 'I think it would be as well, Mr Ambrose.'

Frank Ambrose squared his shoulders. He looked like a man who hasn't much left to come and go upon. His big frame was kept upright only with an effort. His large impassive face sagged with fatigue. The fair skin looked grey. He said, 'It is really very simple, but because of my stepfather's death all the natural, simple things which happen in a family have become suspicious. So you see, I can tell you what happened, but I can't make you believe it. There is nothing to corroborate my statement.

There is only my own unsupported story. I came back because I was greatly disturbed and distressed by what my stepfather had said at dinner. The more I thought about it, the more I felt that I couldn't just leave it at that. I made up my mind to go back and talk the whole thing over with him. If you ask anyone who knew us both they will tell you that we were on very intimate terms. In some ways he treated me as a son, in others as a friend. I mean that he would discuss things with me. That's why I came back. He had a strong, sarcastic temper. I didn't want him to do anything that would make a permanent breach in the family.'

'How did he take your coming back?' said Colonel Bostock.

Frank Ambrose was silent for a moment. Then he said, 'We talked. I was with him for about twenty minutes. Then I went away.'

Vyner looked up and said, 'Did he tell you that Mr Wray's blueprints were missing?'

There was again that moment of silence. Then Frank Ambrose said, 'Yes.'

'Did he tell you who had taken them?'

'I'm afraid I can't tell you that.'

'You can, of course, refuse to answer any questions now, but you may be asked them in another place, when you will be on your oath.'

'Of course I realise that. I'm afraid I can't tell you anything more at present.'

When the door had shut behind him, Miss Silver said 'Dear me!' Colonel Bostock blew his nose loudly.

'Well, what do you make of that? He knows something.'

Vyner was shutting his notebook.

'There isn't much doubt about that.'

'Looks as if he hasn't slept for a week. By the way,' – the Chief Constable turned to Miss Silver – 'his wife's out of it – that girl Irene. Glad about that. Nasty thing for a young woman, murder. Not at all the thing. Vyner'll tell you.'

The Superintendent turned his pleasant blue eyes upon Miss Silver.

'I had some enquiries made at Dr Horton's house. The two maids share an attic room to the front. Well, one of them says she looked out somewhere after eleven and she saw Mrs Ambrose walking up and down like she said she did. You will remember that it was bright moonlight until the rain came on at twelve. She is quite sure about its being Mrs Ambrose. She made a joke of it to the other girl. It seems she was always ringing Dr Horton up about the children, and this was the girl who would take the messages, so they made quite a joke of it, and looked out several times to see if she was still there. They were up late because the other girl was going to her sister's wedding next day and she was finishing her dress. They say Mrs Ambrose was still there at ten minutes to twelve. I think that's good enough.'

Miss Silver nodded.

'Oh, yes.' Over the clicking needles she looked brightly at the two men. 'I think we may say that most of the time between a quarter to ten and midnight is now accounted for. It might be helpful to have a timetable before us. Perhaps the Superintendent will be kind enough to take one down—'

9.45 – Departure of Mr and Mrs Ambrose, Miss Ambrose, and Miss Pennington.

9.50 or so – Departure of Mr Mark Paradine and Mr Richard.

9.52 or 53 – Mr Pearson to the study to say goodnight, followed immediately by Lane, who saw him both enter and leave.

A few minutes later – Mr Wray to the study to say goodnight. His visit was brief. Coming out, he found Mr Pearson waiting for him. They proceeded to Mr Wray's room.

10.10 – Mrs Wray to the study to talk to her uncle.

10.30 – Mr Ambrose knocks on the study door and is admitted – Mrs Wray having gone out by way of the unused bedroom next door.

10.50 – Mr Ambrose leaves. Between that time and

11.00 – Mr Mark Paradine to the study. Some time before

11.30 – Mr Mark Paradine leaves. Mr Wray and Mr Pearson come down to the dining room to have a drink. Mr Wray hears the front door close. He also hears a door shut upstairs on the corridor occupied by Miss Paradine and Mrs Wray.

11.53 – Mr Wray and Mr Pearson return upstairs. They separate immediately. Mr Wray goes to have a bath.'

Superintendent Vyner stopped writing and looked up with an extremely startled expression on his face.

'Did you say eleven-fifty-three, Miss Silver?'

Little Roger's dark grey leggings revolved beneath the busy needles.

'That is what I said, Superintendent.'

Vyner's eyes remained fixed upon her face.

'Mr Wray and Mr Pearson have both stated that it was eight minutes past twelve by the clock in Mr Wray's room when they came upstairs.'

Miss Silver coughed.

'The clock had been tampered with.'

'God bless my soul!' said Colonel Bostock.

Miss Silver continued to knit.

'Mr Pearson's alibi naturally attracted my attention. It was, if I may put it in that way, so very determined. On the other hand, he made no secret of the fact that it had been carefully arranged. If you will refer to his statement you will see that he says quite plainly, "After the accusation made by Mr Paradine against a member of his family whom he did not name, I could not afford to have it supposed by anyone that it might be aimed at me. I therefore waited for Mr Wray and took care to remain in his company until well after midnight – Mr Paradine having stated that he would sit up in the study until twelve o'clock. It was just on ten past when Mr Wray and I separated at the door of his room." '

Vyner had been flicking over pages. He nodded.

'Word-perfect, Miss Silver.'

She inclined her head.

'You see he is quite frank, and that what he says is reasonable. He is not liked by the rest of the family. The cousinship is a distant one, and as far as any familiarity is concerned is more or less in abeyance. It is only the younger members of the family whom he addresses by their Christian names. It is Miss Paradine – Mr Ambrose – Miss Ambrose. Everyone would have been relieved if he had been the culprit. The desire for an alibi might therefore be natural and innocent. On the other hand it might not. If he had a motive for killing his employer, this innocent-seeming alibi might be very useful indeed. No motive has up to the present come to light, but if such a motive should be discovered, then the following points will be of interest.' She unrolled some more of the dark grey wool, turned her knitting, and continued. 'The first point is this. If you will turn again to Mr Pearson's statement you will see he says that Lane was in the study when he went in to bid Mr Paradine good-night. In Lane's statement there is what reads like a corroboration of this, but it is not quite accurate. Mr Wray, Mrs Wray, Mr Ambrose, and Mr Mark were all greeted by Mr Paradine with the same half sarcastic, half jocular remark, "Have you come to confess?" I wished to know whether Mr Pearson had been greeted in the same way. If he had, and if there were anything serious on his conscience, the question might very well have convinced him that his fault was known, and he may then have planned Mr Paradine's death. All this, of course, depends on whether he had some serious dereliction to conceal. On questioning Lane I discovered that he was not actually in the study when Mr Pearson entered it. He was coming through the swing door with a tray, when Mr Pearson, who had approached from the other end of the passage, passed before him into the study. He heard Mr Paradine say "Hello, Albert – have you come to confess?"

'God bless my soul!'

Miss Silver's needles clicked.

'It is not necessary to labour this point. We do not know whether Mr Pearson had anything on his conscience or not. He had no time to answer Mr Paradine, because Lane came into the room, and though he was called back for a moment as Lane was leaving again, he was out in the passage before the swing door had closed. I really do not wish to put too much stress on this small point, but I think it may have to be considered later on.'

Vyner said, 'The point being, why did Mr Pearson say that Lane was already in the room when he came in?'

'Yes.'

'It might be just part of his being nervous about his reputation.'

'That had not escaped me, Superintendent.' She coughed and continued. 'We now come to the second point. If Mr Pearson's alibi was a false one, the clock in Mr Wray's room must have been tampered with. I tried to think when it might have been done. Not before dinner, because there was no indication then that the room would be occupied, or that Mr Paradine would make the accusation which he did, in fact, make after dinner. Not between the time the accusation was made and a quarter to ten, because Mr Pearson was in company with the rest of the party during that time. The first opportunity would occur between the time when Lane saw him leave the study after saying goodnight to Mr Paradine and the time, a few minutes later, when Mr Wray found him waiting in the passage. He would have had time in the interval to run up the back stairs and alter the clock in Mr Wray's room.'

Colonel Bostock gave an expostulatory grunt.

'What the fellow might have done isn't evidence, madam!'

Miss Silver met his frown with undisturbed placidity. She hastened to agree with him.

'Precisely. There was no evidence. I am merely telling you what led me to enquire whether any evidence existed. I went to my room last night at a quarter to ten. A few minutes later the young under-housemaid, Polly Parsons, came in to turn down the bed. On thinking this over it occurred to me that she might, whilst performing the same office on Wednesday night, have noticed the clock in Mr Wray's room. I found an opportunity of questioning her just before lunch today, and this is what she told me. She had been helping with the washing-up on Wednesday night because of the party, but when Mr and Mrs Ambrose went away at a quarter to ten Louisa sent her up to turn down the two gentlemen's beds and put a couple of hot-water bottles in Mr Wray's because there hadn't been time to air it. She came up the back stairs on the kitchen side of the house and along past Mrs Wray's and Miss Paradine's rooms, and she saw Mr Pearson come out of Mr Wray's room and run along the passage towards the back stairs on that side. She said she wondered what he was doing in Mr Wray's room. She went in and turned down the bed and put in the hot-water bottles, and just as she was straightening up she saw the clock on the mantelpiece, and she thought, "Well, it *is* late!" because the hands were standing at ten minutes past ten. Then she went across the passage into Mr Pearson's room, and the clock there made it five minutes to. She thought how angry Mr Paradine would be, because all the clocks had to be just so, and she says she went down into the kitchen and talked about it to the other girl, Gladys, and to Louisa.'

Colonel Bostock pursed up his lips and whistled.

Vyner said, 'One of the first things we did was to check up on the clocks. The one in Mr Wray's room was right to the tick on the Thursday morning – but of course it would be.'

Miss Silver nodded.

'Mr Pearson would have set the hands back again whilst Mr Wray was in the bathroom. He strikes me as a very thorough young man.' She paused, gave her slight cough, and continued. 'There is just one other point. Mr Wray says that he and Mr Pearson came down to the dining room for a drink soon after half-past eleven. When I asked him if he could not be a little more exact he said oh, yes, he looked at the clock, saw that the hands were standing at sixteen or seventeen minutes to twelve, and proposed that they should go down to the dining room. As they came into the hall, he heard the front door close. But Mr Mark Paradine says he left the house at about half-past eleven, and it was he who shut that door. There would be a definite discrepancy if it were not that we now know that the clock in Mr Wray's room was a quarter of an hour fast. This discrepancy corroborates Polly's story.'

Colonel Bostock whistled again. Vyner said, 'There is a clock in the hall, and one in the dining room. Wouldn't Mr Wray have been likely to notice the discrepancy himself?'

Miss Silver shook her head.

'I think not. The hall has only one very dim light, and as to the dining room, Mr Pearson could have provided against any danger of the clock on the mantelpiece being noticed by only switching on the light over the sideboard. This would appear quite natural, as the drinks were there. In any case I do not think that Mr Wray was in a very observant frame of mind. He had just met his wife again after a year's estrangement, and his thoughts were very much taken up with his own affairs.'

Vyner nodded.

'That's true enough. Well, Miss Silver, Mr Harrison will be here any moment now.' His eyes were most intelligently bright. 'We'll have to get along with opening that safe. Are you thinking that we may come across a motive for Mr Pearson there?'

Miss Silver looked prim.

'I would not like to say that, Superintendent.'

FORTY-THREE

MR HARRISON ARRIVED very punctually at half-past two. At a quarter to three precisely he opened James Paradine's safe. The original intention had been that Mark and Richard Paradine should be present, but in view of recent developments it was decided that as many of the family as were in the house should be invited to attend. Miss Silver was there, and so was an inconspicuous Mr Jones, sent up by Birleton's leading firm of valuers. Miss Paradine raised her eyes at him and, leaning towards Mark, enquired in a low voice whether he was Mr Harrison's clerk. On receiving a negative reply she appeared faintly surprised, but asked no farther.

Mr Harrison, having opened the safe, stepped back and made way for Superintendent Vyner, who proceeded to lift out and lay upon the writing table the faded red leather cases which Mr Paradine had handled on the night of his death. He took hold of them with a carefully gloved hand, and as he set each one down he touched the spring and threw back the lid.

'We'll just check up on these before we go any further, Mr Harrison.'

Mr Harrison produced a list and read from it:–

'Diamond tiara – valued three years ago, £4,000.
Diamond solitaire earrings – ditto £1,000.
Solitaire diamond ring – £500.
Diamond cluster ring – £200.
Diamond marquise ring – £150.
Diamond half-hoop ring – £200.
Pair diamond bracelets – £1,000.
Corsage ornament – £2,000.
Diamond bar brooch – £100.
Diamond sunburst – £400.
Diamond butterfly – £150.
Diamond trefoil brooch – £200.'

'All present and correct,' said Vyner. He glanced over his shoulder in a casual manner. 'Mr Jones, will you be so good—'

Everyone had been looking at the diamonds. Grace Paradine had not seen them for twenty years. Strange to think of them shut up like that in the dark, keeping their beauty and their brilliance as they had kept their value. Clara's diamonds – the thought went through her mind slightingly. She had never really liked Clara. They took Frank Ambrose back to the last time he had seen his mother wear them. She had looked ill and frail. Over their glitter her eyes had been tired, and faded, and kind. Richard, Lydia, Phyllida, and Elliot Wray had never seen them before except in the portrait above the mantelpiece. Mark had both seen and handled them. His look passed over them without interest. He was wishing only that all this formal business should be over, for then he would know whether they were going to arrest him or not. The diamonds had for him at the moment about as much allure as chips of gravel. Albert Pearson, who might have been supposed to take a professional interest, appeared almost as indifferent. And yet that was perhaps not quite the right word. Hesitating on the outskirts of the group about the table, he seemed to experience some embarrassment at being there at all. As a relation he would hardly have a claim. As James Paradine's secretary then? But he was not being called upon for any professional duty. He blinked once or twice behind his thick lenses and pushed sweating hands deep into his pockets.

Mr Jones said 'Allow me—' and stepped past him.

Sitting primly upright at the far side of the table, Miss Silver watched him come. She was not knitting. Her hands rested in her lap. Her eyes were bright and very intent. They watched Mr Jones – a little man, fair-skinned and indeterminate, with old-fashioned pince-nez sitting rather crooked, and a set of gleaming artificial teeth which imparted a slight lisp to his speech. He came right up to the table, bent over the cases, looking into each with an effect of painstaking scrutiny, and said in his gentle, lisping voice, 'You are aware, I suppose, Mr Paradine, that some of these stones are copies?'

Shocked into immediate interest, Mark straightened up, came forward a step, and standing level with Mr Jones and the Superintendent, said in a startled tone, 'What do you mean?'

Mr Jones picked up a pen from the table, held it poised, and used the nib as a pointer. It hovered above the trefoil brooch.

'That is a copy – very good paste. So is the butterfly – and the bar brooch. So are the stones in these solitaire earrings and the solitaire ring. The large centre stone in the corsage ornament has also been replaced by paste.'

Mark said, 'What!' And then, 'Are you sure?'

Mr Jones showed his gleaming dentures in a slight pitying smile.

'There is no doubt of it at all, Mr Paradine.'

Silence descended on the room. Superintendent Vyner's eyes turned towards Miss Silver. As plainly as if he had spoken, they said, well, there's your motive.

Miss Silver coughed, and, as if by one consent, they both looked at Albert Pearson. It was not only his hands that were sweating now. His forehead glistened. Even to the most casual eye he was ill, and ill at ease.

Vyner turned to Mr Jones.

'The rest of the stones all right?'

Mr Jones produced a pocket magnifying glass and brought it to bear upon each piece of jewellery in turn. The process appeared to be interminable. But in time all things come to an end. The magnifying glass went back into a deep breast pocket. Mr Jones lisped his assurances, and was encouraged to depart. The door shutting behind him sounded to Albert Pearson like the crack of doom. His heart beat with sickening heavy thumps. His hair was clammy on his brow. Through the mist which clouded his glasses he was aware that everyone had turned in his direction. It was like the worst kind of nightmare. He heard Superintendent Vyner addressing him by name.

'Will you come up to the table, Mr Pearson? I should like to ask you one or two questions. At the same time it is my duty to warn you that what you say may be taken down and used in evidence against you.'

He came forward, stumbled upon a chair, and finding himself seated, began mechanically to polish his misted glasses. When he put them on again there was a smart young constable with a notebook almost at his elbow and everyone was looking at him – everyone except Phyllida, who looked as if she was going to cry. Of the others, Miss Paradine wore the kind of expression with which she might have dismissed a dishonest kitchenmaid. It was too much *de haut en bas* to be vindictive, but it held a very definite trace of satisfaction. He was not only outside the family circle now, he was judged and damned before ever a word was spoken. As he sat there he could feel the ring of circumstance closing in to damn him. He was to be what he had always known they would make him if they could – the scapegoat. Well, he'd got his alibi – let them see if they could break it. He'd been one too many for them there. He squared his shoulders, leaned forward with his arms upon the table, and said, 'I'm perfectly willing to answer any questions you like.'

They were all looking at him. The Superintendent and Mark standing together over the laid-out cases where the diamonds caught the light, Lydia Pennington on Mark's other side, moving closer, slipping her hand inside his elbow. Elliot Wray with an arm round Phyllida, who was shaking – and what had she got to shake about, damn her? Against the mantelpiece, directly under his mother's portrait, Frank Ambrose staring gloomily, not so much at him as past him down the room. Across the corner from the Superintendent, at the end of the table, Miss Silver, dumpy and dowdy, with her ridiculous bog-oak brooch, and the small bright eyes which looked you through and through. Across the other corner from her, Mr Harrison, grave and shocked. Beyond him, Miss Paradine, Richard, and right at his elbow here, the young constable with the notebook.

Albert Pearson set his mind, set that rather heavy jaw, met all those shocked, accusing looks, and said stubbornly, 'Well – what about it?'

FORTY-FOUR

VYNER SAID, 'MR Pearson, there are certain obvious reasons why this discovery is compromising for you. A substitution of stones such as has taken place is not everybody's job. It could also only have been done by someone who had access to this room and to the late Mr Paradine's keys. You happen to combine both these qualifications. It is therefore my duty to ask you whether you have anything to say.'

Albert had himself in hand. He said in his earnest, boring voice, 'Quite so. But I am afraid I can't help you. I know nothing at all about this.'

'The diamonds are gone, Mr Pearson, to the tune of something like two thousand pounds. They didn't go of themselves.'

'I suppose not, Superintendent. It doesn't occur to you that Mr Paradine himself may have had them replaced?'

'Are you going to say that you acted under his orders?'

'Certainly not. I am only saying you may find it difficult to prove that the work was not done by Mr Paradine's orders. You will naturally examine the cases for fingerprints, but I am afraid that you will be disappointed. You see, Mr Paradine handled them so constantly himself. He liked having the jewels out and looking at them – a fact which would have made it very difficult for anyone to tamper with them.'

There was a pause before Vyner said, 'You are very well informed, Mr Pearson.'

The large round glasses were turned upon him steadily. Albert said, 'What do you expect? I was his secretary.'

'Very well. I said there were obvious reasons for suspecting you. There are others not so obvious. Was it in your capacity as secretary that you put on the clock in Mr Wray's room by a quarter of an hour on Wednesday night?'

A dull, ugly colour came up in patches under Albert's skin. The skin was clammy. His hands lay in full view upon the table. It took all his will-power to keep them there unclenched. He said in a rougher voice, 'I don't know what you mean.'

'I think you do. The under-housemaid, Polly Parsons, saw you come out of Mr Wray's room when she came up to turn down the beds. She was surprised to find that the clock in that room put the time at ten minutes past ten, whereas the clock in your own room made it five minutes short of the hour. Fifteen minutes' difference, Mr Pearson. You were very careful indeed to have an alibi for the time that Mr Paradine was to be waiting in his study. He was waiting there to receive a confession. When you went in to say goodnight to him just after ten minutes to ten, Lane, who was immediately behind you, heard Mr Paradine say,

"Hello, Albert – have you come to confess?" You had no time to answer him because Lane came in with the tray. I suppose you were both there for a few minutes, which would bring the time right for you to run upstairs, alter the clock, and be down again to meet Mr Wray and stay with him until that altered clock gave you your alibi by pointing to eight minutes past twelve. But it was then actually only seven minutes to – there was still seven minutes of the time which Mr Paradine had set. You said goodnight to Mr Wray, who went immediately to the bathroom and turned on the taps. You knew that Mr Paradine would still be in the study – you had time to catch him there, and to answer the question which he had asked you. If you had a confession to make you had time to make it. If you did not mean to make a confession you had time to reach the terrace by way of any of those ground-floor windows. There is a print of yours upon the frame of the bathroom window. In common with everyone else in the house, you were aware that Mr Paradine invariably went out on to the terrace before he retired for the night. Someone waited there for him, Mr Pearson. Someone pushed him over the parapet. It is my duty to tell you—'

Albert Pearson jerked back his chair so violently that it crashed. The patchy colour had gone from his face, the dark skin had a greenish tinge. He leaned over with his hands on the table, propping himself. If ever a man showed the extreme of fear, he showed it. But there was something else –

something which made Miss Silver lay a hand on the Superintendent's sleeve. He was about to step back in order to pass behind Mark, but the hand checked him. She said, 'Wait! He has something to say'.

Leaning there, sweating, shaking, Albert said it. He looked straight down the table over Miss Silver's head to Frank Ambrose leaning tall and gloomy against the black marble of the mantel-shelf.

'Mr Ambrose – you can't let him do it – you can't let him arrest me! You can't go on holding your tongue, nor can I. I'm an innocent man, and you know it. If I was there, so were you, and we both saw what happened. You're not going to stand there and hold your tongue! I'd have held mine if it hadn't come to this, but I'm not holding it now – I couldn't be expected to! If you don't speak, I'm going to – and you may think it comes better from you!'

There was a startled silence. All the faces turned towards Frank Ambrose, whose face showed nothing except an impassive fatigue. When Superintendent Vyner said sharply, 'Mr Ambrose?' he straightened himself with an effort and answered the implied question.

'Yes – there is something that I must say. Pearson is right. I don't think I can let you arrest him. You see, I came back again.'

Miss Silver rose to her feet, moved her chair to one side, and sat down again. By turning her head either to the right or to the left she could now see both Albert Pearson and Frank Ambrose. For the moment her attention was engaged by the latter.

Vyner said, 'In a statement made this afternoon, Mr Ambrose, you said that you came back here to see Mr Paradine at about half-past ten. This is corroborated by Mrs Wray, who heard your uncle address you by name as you came in. You say further that you remained for about twenty minutes and then left the house and went home. Is that correct?'

'Quite correct – except that I didn't go home.'

'You left the house?'

'Yes, but I didn't go home. I will try to explain. I intended to go home, but I didn't want to get there too early. I was a good deal distressed at my stepfather's frame of mind. I was afraid of a serious breach in the family. He had told me what he meant to do, and I could see that it was likely to lead to a breach. The night was then fine. I wanted to think, and I set out to walk the long way round by the stone bridge – it's about three miles. When I got to my own door I looked at my watch. It was between a quarter and ten minutes to twelve. I didn't feel like going in – I felt that I must go back and find out what had been happening there. I knew that my stepfather would still be up, and I planned to go by way of the terrace and either catch him as he came out or knock on the glass door and get him to let me in. I went back by the footbridge and up the cliff path. In daylight I do it in seven minutes. I suppose I may have taken ten – I wasn't hurrying. I had made up my mind that it would be better to wait till he came out on the terrace – he might have had someone in the study with him. I came up on to the end of the terrace and about halfway along it. Then I stopped. The sky had clouded over behind me, but there was a little moonlight on the river. There was a good deal of diffused light. I could see the parapet against the line of the river, and I could distinguish the windows against the white wall of the house. I saw the window of my stepfather's bathroom thrown up. It is a sash window. Someone leaned out of the lower half.'

'Did you see who it was?'

'No. At the time I thought it might be Lane. It certainly wasn't my stepfather – there would be no mistaking his height.'

'It could have been Mr Pearson?'

Frank Ambrose said in a casual voice, 'Oh, yes, it was Pearson, but I didn't know that until afterwards.'

Miss Silver took occasion to look down the table in the direction of Albert Pearson. He was standing up straight with one hand in a pocket and the other on its way there. From the fact that it grasped a large white handkerchief she considered that he had been wiping his forehead. The greenish tint had gone from his skin. He had the air of a man who has been reprieved. She brought her glance slowly back again – the young constable, busy over his shorthand – Richard Paradine, standing up – Miss Paradine, very upright, very pale – Mr Harrison a little more shocked than before – Frank

Ambrose, with his look of a man at the end of his tether.

Behind her Vyner said, 'Will you go on, Mr Ambrose.'

Everyone in the room was to remember the pause that followed. What must be said next would be irrevocable, because here was an eye-witness of James Paradine's death. Whether confession or accusation, the words, once spoken, could never be recalled.

Frank Ambrose said in a tired, even tone, 'This room and my mother's room next door are alike. I saw the glass door of my mother's room swing open. Someone came out on to the terrace—'

'Not Mr Pearson?'

'No, not Pearson. I heard the first stroke of the hour on the Orphanage clock up the road. A moment later my stepfather came out from this room and walked across the terrace to the parapet. The person who had come out of my mother's room followed him. I didn't want to intrude. I stood where I was. I didn't guess what was going to happen – you don't think about things like that until they happen. I saw my stepfather pushed, and I saw him fall. The person who had pushed him ran back into my mother's room. It was all so sudden that I didn't move. It seemed to happen faster than I could think. Then the rain came. I had a torch in my pocket. I got it out and ran up, flashing it over the terrace. The beam swung wide and caught Pearson at the bathroom window. He knew that I had seen him, but I didn't know until just now that he had recognised me. I went and looked over the edge. It was pouring with rain – I couldn't see a thing. I went down to the river path, and found my stepfather lying there dead. When I was quite sure that he was dead I went home.'

There was another pause. Vyner said, 'You should have reported what you had seen to the police, Mr Ambrose.'

Frank Ambrose assented wearily.

'Naturally.'

'If you did not, it was because you had some very strong motive for keeping silent?'

This time he got no answer.

'Mr Ambrose – I have to ask you whether you recognised the person who came out of the late Mrs Paradine's room.'

Albert Pearson, standing stocky and obstinate at the end of the table, said in his most dogmatic manner, 'Of course he did. And so did I.'

Vyner turned a direct gaze upon him.

'You say that you recognised this person. Will you explain how? Mr Ambrose has just stated that the light was not sufficient for him to recognise you until he turned the beam of his torch upon you.'

Albert nodded.

'There was a light on in the room she came out of – that's how. I saw her when she came out, and I saw her when she went back. The light was right in her face.'

The pronoun was like an electric shock. Elliot Wray's arm tightened about his wife. Lydia drew in her breath sharply.

Vyner said, 'You say it was a woman?'

'Of course it was.'

'What woman?'

Frank Ambrose took a step forward. He said, '*Pearson—*'

But Albert shook his head.

'It's no good, Mr Ambrose – you can't cover it up. I'm not going to hang for her, and that's that. You'd all like it that way – I know that. That's why I monkeyed with the clock. I knew that if I hadn't an alibi, you'd all be saying that I was the one who'd done something he'd got to confess to. But there's nothing doing – not when it comes to hanging. I saw who it was that came out of that door, and you can't get from it.'

He turned to Vyner and said in a voice that was suddenly louder than he meant it to be, 'It was Miss Paradine.'

FORTY-FIVE

THERE WAS A shattering silence. Even the young constable lifted his head with a jerk and stared across his shorthand notes at the family amongst whom the bomb had fallen. His quick hazel eyes flicked over them. Mr and Mrs Wray, just opposite – gosh, he looked grim! – and she'd got her mouth open as if she was going to scream, only there wasn't any sound. Miss Pennington and Mr Mark Paradine – he looked bad, like a man looks when he's been hit and you don't know whether he'll drop or not. The Super – well, was he expecting that, or wasn't he? – you couldn't properly tell. That Miss Silver – well, you couldn't tell about her either – a queer little cup of tea if ever there was one. Mr Ambrose now – it wasn't any surprise to him – he'd known it was coming all right – bad case of strain – he'd known all along – tried to cover it up. Well, when it came to your own family, he supposed most of us would.

All this in the oldest medium of all – the thought-pictures which invention has never managed to overtake. All the pictures were there in the brief moment in which he turned, as everyone else had turned, to look at Grace Paradine. She was sitting in her upright chair, and she had not moved. She had been too pale before to lose any colour now. Her hands had been lying in her lap. They lay there still. There was no measurable change or movement, but there was a dreadful effect of tension, of the lack of movement being due not to weakness, but to implacable control. What it was that was being controlled showed for a moment in her eyes – an indescribable look of . . . He couldn't get any nearer to it than violence. He thought to himself with a kind of surprise, Gosh – she did it!

Miss Silver's cough came into the silence. She leaned forward and spoke down the table to Elliot Wray.

'Mr Wray – if I may make a suggestion – there is no need for Mrs Wray to be here.'

Grace Paradine moved. She looked where Miss Silver was looking and allowed her eyes to dwell upon the ashy face against Elliot's shoulder. Then she said in a deep, calm voice, 'Phyllida will stay.'

Elliot bent. His lips could be seen to move. Phyllida shook her head.

Grace Paradine said, 'Since she has heard this monstrous accusation, I should like her to hear me answer it.' She turned to the Superintendent.

Through the giddiness which hung round her like a mist Phyllida could hear him warning her. The words that had been said to Albert Pearson were being said again – 'anything you may say . . . taken down and used against you . . .' The room was full of that giddy mist. It came and went in waves. She couldn't see anyone's face. She let her head rest against Elliot's shoulder and felt his arm hold her up. Deep under all the dreadfulness was the feeling that he was there.

Miss Paradine listened composedly to the formal words. Then she said, 'Thank you, Superintendent. I am naturally most anxious to do anything I can to clear this matter up. I should have thought that such an accusation, coming from one who admits his own presence—'

Mr Harrison, sitting beside her, leaned forward and said something in a low voice. She did not turn towards him, but made a slight negative movement with her head.

'Thank you – I very much prefer to speak. The accusation is, of course, fantastic. Mr Pearson's motive seems obvious.' Her glance rested for a moment upon the diamonds. 'He admits to a manufactured alibi. He admits to being present when my brother fell. I really do not know what more you want.'

Vyner looked her straight in the face.

'There is another witness besides Mr Pearson.' He turned abruptly. 'Mr Ambrose—'

Grace Paradine turned too.

'Well, Frank, it seems to rest with you. You can dispose of all this in a moment.'

Their eyes met. There was command in hers. No anger now, no violence – a calm and smiling demand. It was the most horrible moment of his life. If she had been less sure of him, less sure of herself, it would have been easier. She smiled into his eyes and waited for him to clear her. As he could. He had only to say that the person who came out of Clara Paradine's room was a stranger – too tall, too short, too large, too small to be Grace Paradine. He had only to say that he had seen a stranger's face. His heart sickened in him. He couldn't do it. With that smiling glance on his, he couldn't do it. Cause and effect – the thing done and what it does, to yourself, to everyone else – the thing called justice, the thing called crime, the inevitable link between them – the dead man whom he loved more than most sons have loved a father – the stubborn core of his nature which would yield no farther – these things constrained him. He withstood that smiling demand, and saw the smile burn out in anger.

She said in that deep, full voice, 'Come, Frank – we're all waiting for you. Since I wasn't there, you couldn't have seen me. You have only to say so.'

He said, 'I can't—'

The words dropped into the hush which waited for them. They had been said – they couldn't be taken back again. He felt a kind of dreadful relief.

Vyner said, 'You recognised Miss Paradine?'

'Yes—' The word was only just audible.

Grace Paradine stood up.

'Just a moment, Superintendent. I think I have the right to ask you to test this extraordinary allegation. Since my nephew says that he saw me come out of my sister-in-law's room, I must suppose that he honestly thinks so. I can prove that he is mistaken, and I would like the opportunity of doing so. But perhaps before we go any further someone will tell me what motive I am supposed to have had. One does not, after all, commit a crime without some motive, and since I had none—'

Vyner said, 'There is a motive, Miss Paradine. When Mr Paradine told you all that one of the family had betrayed its interests he was alluding to the theft of Mr Wray's blueprints. They were taken from his attaché case some time late on Wednesday afternoon. They were put back on the corner of this table between nine o'clock and nine-fifteen – we have witnesses who can narrow the time down to that. You are the only member of the family who was alone even for a moment during that period. You were the only one who had the opportunity of putting those blueprints back.'

She looked at him with a touch of contempt.

'That is quite fantastic. I really cannot be troubled to deal with it now. What I should like you to do is to test what Mr Pearson and Mr Ambrose have said. I suggest that we should go out upon the terrace – or rather that Mr Ambrose should go out – and stand where he says that he was standing on Wednesday night. Mr Pearson should be in the bathroom looking out of the window. I will come out of my sister-in-law's room, cross over to the parapet, and return.'

Vyner was looking at her keenly.

'What do you hope to prove by that, Miss Paradine? Since it is now broad daylight, the test is without any value at all. There should be, and will be, a test carried out after dark.'

Grace Paradine smiled. It was the slight, almost

involuntary smile of the hostess shepherding her guests. It took acquiescence for granted. Her whole manner did that. Vyner was not insensible to it. She said graciously, 'Of course you will carry out your own tests, Superintendent, but I am sure you will not refuse me this one. It really will not take more than a moment, and I think that even by daylight I shall be able to show you that it was quite impossible that either Mr Ambrose or Mr Pearson should have seen the face of the person who came out of the bedroom.'

Had she been a shade less assured in her manner, Vyner might very well have refused. Her self-possession; the reasonable, even temper of her voice; the way in which she so assumed his consent that she had already taken a step towards the door – all these things swung the balance down. He said, 'Very well, Miss Paradine, I won't say no. But to my mind there's no value in it.'

Mr Harrison had risen to his feet. He stood, shocked and doubtful, looking after his client. He supposed that she would be his client. It was all quite unbelievable, quite dreadful. He didn't think his firm had ever handled a murder case before. He desired most ardently that they might avoid handling this one.

Miss Silver had risen too. Like Mr Harrison, she was looking after Grace Paradine, who had gone through into the bedroom closely followed by the young constable who had been taking notes. Their voices could be heard there, and after a moment the rattle of curtain rings.

Vyner said, 'Come, Mr Ambrose – we'd better get on with it.'

As the two men moved together towards the glass door, Miss Silver opened her lips and then without speaking brought them quickly together again. The room was emptying fast. Albert Pearson went out, presumably to take up his position at the bathroom window. Richard Paradine, Mr Harrison, Mark and Lydia had followed Vyner and Frank Ambrose to the terrace. The glass door remained open – Elliot and Phyllida just short of it.

Miss Silver came up with them, laid a hand on Elliot's arm, and said in a low, insistent voice.

'Keep her here, Mr Wray. Don't let her go out.'

He looked round at her, startled by her manner.

Vyner could be heard calling out, 'Now, Miss Paradine—'

All those on the terrace looked towards the windows of Mrs Paradine's room – two large windows and a glass door forming a bay. Across this bay the curtains had been drawn, but whereas in the study they cut the bay off from the room, in the bedroom they followed the curving line of the windows. The rose-coloured lining could be seen touching the glass.

They all saw the rose colour move and shimmer. A dark gap appeared in the middle of it. The handle of the glass door moved, the door opened, Grace Paradine came out. There were a couple of steps down. She took them, came half across the terrace, and looked first to her right where Frank Ambrose stood by the nearest of the drawing-room windows, and then to the left where Albert Pearson leaned from the window of the bathroom. Her glance swept the family group outside the study, and she turned.

Phyllida wasn't there. But Phyllida must be there. The dark dominant eyes went seeking till they found her, just inside the study. But not looking out – not looking this way. And she must look – she must see – she must remember. If they would give her time. But the young constable was at her elbow. Vyner was coming up. She called out in a ringing voice, 'Phyllida!'

There was no time – no time at all. She saw Phyllida move and turn to the terrace.

Vyner said, 'What is it, Miss Paradine?'

They all heard her say, 'It's nothing.'

But Phyllida was looking, Phyllida was coming out.

Now—

Phyllida had made no more than that one movement towards the terrace, when Elliot pulled her roughly back, turning her head against his shoulder and holding it there.

So she did not see what Grace Paradine had meant her to see – the quick step on to the parapet, and the quick step over it and down. She did not see, but she knew. She shuddered and went limp and cold in Elliot's arms.

FORTY-SIX

LATE THAT EVENING three people sat with Miss Silver in Phyllida's sitting-room – Mark Paradine, Lydia, and Elliot Wray. Phyllida was not there. She lay on her bed in the room beyond, her tears all cried away, her thoughts not taking hold of anything yet, but knowing that Elliot was there just on the other side of the door, and that he wouldn't leave her again. She could hear his voice, and Mark's, and Lydia's, and Miss Silver's – not as words but as sound. She liked hearing the sound, but she didn't want to hear the words. Presently she would be able to think about going away with Elliot, and about Lydia and Mark. She loved Elliot, she loved Lydia and Mark. Presently she would be able to think about loving them. Just now she could only lie there and let the sound of their voices go by.

On the other side of the door Mark said, 'I've been with Colonel Bostock and Vyner. They've fairly had the wires humming. It's like you said, Elliot – the Ministry wants everything soft-pedalled as much as possible. The blueprints are not to be mentioned. Everything is to be done to avoid publicity. They'll try for death by misadventure for Uncle James, and suicide whilst the balance of her mind was disturbed for her. There'll be a lot of talk, but it will go by.' He gave a heavy sigh. 'I suppose she was insane.'

Miss Silver coughed. Little Roger's leggings were almost completed. They dangled oddly from her needles by the last remaining toe.

'Not in the usual sense of the word. She knew what she was doing, and she was in control of her actions. But she had, I think, for many years allowed herself to be governed by a most fatal and inordinate desire to absorb the feelings and emotions of anyone she cared for. Her engagement to Mr Moffat was broken off not because of a moral recoil, but because of that desire to be the first, in fact the only one, in his affections. From what your wife told you of their last interview, Mr Wray, I think this is quite clear. A symptom of this is the terrible fact that she made that last effort to attract Mrs Wray's attention. She knew that she had lost her, but she still wanted to be a dominant factor in her life. She made that dreadful attempt.'

Elliot said harshly, 'Don't talk about it – it's damnable.'

Miss Silver looked at him with kind, bright eyes and continued as if he had not spoken.

'Fortunately, it did not succeed. You were very prompt, Mr Wray.'

Lydia was in one of the big chairs, her hair bright under the light, her face paler than anyone had ever been allowed to see it – dark shadows smudged in under the green eyes with their shading of dusky lashes. But for all its pallor the small pointed face was relaxed. There was a tremulous sweetness about the mouth.

Mark sat on the arm of the chair and kept a hand upon her shoulder. You could not look at them without seeing how much they were aware of one another, how deeply they were at peace between themselves. Mark said in a difficult voice, 'I went on and saw Frank. He's terribly cut up. He told me all about it. I said that I should tell you three. No one else. It was like this. When he went back the first time – he says he told the police about that—'

Miss Silver coughed.

'Yes, Mr Paradine – I was there.'

'He didn't tell them very much, I gather – only that he went back, and that they talked. Actually, Uncle James told him all about it. He thought a lot of Frank, and Frank thought a lot of him. He told him who had taken the blueprints. He saw her from Aunt Clara's room – he was just opening the door to go back into the study when she came in. He stood where he was because he didn't want to meet her. They'd had words some time earlier in the day – about Elliot – and he didn't want to start it all over again, so he just stood where he was. His attaché case was on the table. The cylinder with the blueprints was in it, right on the top. She went straight to the table, opened the case, took the cylinder, and was out of the room again in a flash. He let her go. Then he sat down and thought out how he could score her off. It was the climax of a long time of strain. He told Frank just what he thought about her – said she had separated Elliot and Phyllida and was doing her best to smash up his marriage with Irene. He said he had stood out of the ring for a year because he was afraid of making things worse, but he wasn't standing out any longer. He told Frank she had taken the blue-prints because she thought that would make a final breach between Elliot and the firm, and so keep him away from Birleton. And he said he was going to show her just where she got off. He said he'd had enough of it. Frank was awfully shocked and upset. He tried to soothe him down. The thing he was most anxious about was to prevent an inter-view between them that night whilst they were both worked up. In the end he got Uncle James to write to her giving his terms. He said he thought anything was better than letting them meet. Uncle James gave him a copy of the letter, and he handed it on to me. Here it is. I'm going to read it, and then we'll put it on the fire. The police have taken a copy, but they won't use it.'

He spread out a sheet of the firm's paper and read aloud what old James Paradine had written on New Year's Eve:

'MY DEAR GRACE,

I saw you take the cylinder with Elliot's blue-prints. I note that you have found an opportunity of replacing them, but that does not close the account between us. I think perhaps it is best that we should not meet tonight. I am therefore letting you have my terms in writing.

(i) You will cease to stand between Elliot and Phyllida. Whatever their differences have been, they are deeply attached to each other and should be allowed to settle their own affairs without further interference from you.

(ii) Within a reasonable time – not more than a couple of months – you will discover a desire to have a flat or a small house of your own. I shall offer this house as a hospital for the duration, and move into a flat in Birleton.

If you still wish to see me, I shall be in the study until twelve. But the terms are quite irrevocable. I advise you to sleep on them.'

Lydia drew in her breath sharply.

'He sent her that letter? How?'

'Frank took it up and slipped it under her door. Then he went away. I was coming in as he went out. We passed each other in the drive.'

Lydia took another of those quick breaths.

'Oh! You never said—'

He had a curious fleeting smile for that.

'Nor did Frank, darling.'

He got up, went over to the fire, dropped the sheet of paper on to a tilted log, and watched it blacken and burn. Standing there looking down at the curling ash with the sparks running to and fro, he said, 'I wonder what she was doing when Elliot heard her door shut at half-past eleven.'

Miss Silver's needles clicked.

'She may have intended to go down and see Mr Paradine then. Hearing the front door close after you, Mr Mark, and becoming aware that Mr Wray and Mr Pearson were crossing the hall, she would naturally go back to her room.'

Mark bent forward and pushed the log with his foot. The ash crumbled, the sparks flew up, the letter was gone. He said, 'That's what I can't get off my mind, you know. If she had come down and seen him then, it might have been different – she might not have done it.'

The needles clicked again.

'That is not for us, Mr Mark. We must not think about what might have happened. We cannot recall the past, but we can prevent its poisoning the future.'

He said, 'Yes,' and came back to the arm of Lydia's chair.

Elliot said abruptly, 'That's that. What about Albert?'

Mark lifted a hand and let it fall again upon his knee.

'I've been wrestling with the police about him. I said I wouldn't prosecute, and Vyner got a piece off his chest about compounding a felony. I pointed out we had no evidence to show that there had been a felony. Albert is perfectly right – Uncle James might have had the work done himself. We know he didn't of course, but we know that there isn't any proof of that, and you can bet Albert will have covered his tracks. Anyhow, suppose we did get the evidence – where should we be? Right in the middle of the sort of stink we're all doing our best to avoid. Old Bostock chipped in and said I was right and it was a damned awkward case, which struck me as a bit of an understatement. Anyhow he's called Vyner off, and Albert is for the army.'

Elliot gave a short laugh.

'The war is as good as won!'

Mark said, 'When I'd got that squared I came back and saw Albert. I told him he'd better come clean, and he did. I don't know how much he was lying. Not much, I think, but of course he was doing the best for himself. It makes quite a story, but I dare say it's true, or as near as makes no difference. His mother was ill, and they were awfully poor. He was working for a firm with a good solid connection. They got a lot of valuable stuff in for alterations and repairs. He began by picking out a stone here and a stone there and substituting something not quite so good – not paste but the real thing – lighter stones – inferior quality. He'd sell the stone he'd picked out and pocket the difference between that and the replacement. He says there's quite a lot of that sort of thing done – that's how he got to know the ropes. Then his mother died, and he came here. He says nothing was farther from his thoughts than to try any monkey business. He was going to be industrious and respectable, because he hoped it was going to pay a lot better than balancing on the edge of crime. Unfortunately, the past bobbed up – his friend Izzy in fact. Albert says that Izzy blackmailed him. I don't think I believe that part. I think Izzy suggested a deal over Aunt Clara's diamonds and Albert fell for it. There was quite a brisk market for stones just about then. Our leading moneygrubbers were feeling nervous about the prospects of a capital levy after the war, and were putting the stuff into diamonds. Aunt Clara's had just been valued, so the chances of a revaluation, even for probate, were remote. He fixed it all up with Izzy, and waited for an opportunity. Well, he got it when Uncle James was laid up last year. He was actually sent to get the cases out of the safe. It was as easy as falling off a log. He photographed everything, took careful measurements, Izzy supplied the imitations, and Albert substituted them for the real stones. He dwelt with pride on the fact that he is a very skilled workman – I had to head him off giving me a lecture on the subject.'

Miss Silver coughed.

'It was the fact that, whilst full of information upon every other subject and unusually eager to impart what he knew, Mr Pearson appeared unable or unwilling to converse upon anything connected with his former profession that first turned my attention in the direction of the diamonds.'

'It was frightfully clever of you,' said Lydia.

Miss Silver shook her head in a modest and deprecatory manner.

'Oh, no,' she said. 'You see, Mr Pearson's alibi was naturally a very suspicious circumstance, and yet in a young man so obviously determined to advance himself it really was capable of an innocent interpretation. What he said to Mr Wray is quite true. He is not an attractive person. He is not liked, and nobody would have been sorry to assume that it was he who had incurred Mr Paradine's displeasure. So then, it all came down to this – if he had a motive for murdering Mr Paradine, the alibi was compromising, and if it could be proved to be false, quite conclusive. Looking about for a possible motive, I naturally thought about the diamonds, and suggested that a valuer should be present when the safe was opened.'

'It was very, very clever of you,' said Lydia. 'We thought Mark was going to be arrested every minute. It was like standing on the edge of a most dreadful precipice and waiting for the fall to begin. I didn't think anything could be so frightful. And you saved us.'

Mark put his hand on her shoulder again.

Miss Silver beamed upon them.

'Praise is gratifying even when exaggerated. I do not think that Mr Mark was really in much danger. You see, he was innocent – that was quite plain from the beginning. He was shocked, and he was in grief. There was no trace of guilt or remorse. But my first evening in this house showed me two things very plainly. Mr Pearson was in a nervous state, and declined any approach to the subject of jewellery. Miss Paradine was in a highly charged condition of antagonism towards Mr Wray and possessive feeling for Mrs Wray. I am sensitive to such currents of feeling, and have found this very useful in my work. Strong emotions of this nature point towards a motive for murder even more conclusively than concrete evidence. I considered Miss Paradine, but I also considered Mr Pearson. Mr Paradine, having omitted to name the person he accused, left the way open for anyone who had been at fault in some other direction to accuse himself. I soon discovered that it was Miss Paradine who had taken the blueprints, but I still thought it possible that not she but Mr Pearson had committed the murder. The more I thought about his alibi, the more incriminating it appeared. After Polly's evidence it seemed very difficult to believe that he was innocent, and when Mr Jones declared that the diamonds had been tampered with it became impossible.'

All this time Elliot Wray had been silent. He said now, 'And yet he didn't do it. Or did he?'

Mark started. Lydia said, 'Oh!'

Miss Silver gave him a bright attention.

'That is a very interesting remark, Mr Wray. May I ask what prompted it?'

Elliot leaned forward.

'What was Albert doing in the bathroom?' he said.

Miss Silver coughed.

'I have asked myself that question.'

'He'd got no conceivable reason for being there, you know – unless he was waiting for Mr Paradine to go out on the terrace. He must have been there for at least five minutes. If he wasn't waiting for that, what was he waiting for? If he wanted to see Mr Paradine he had only to open the study door and go in. But he didn't do that – he hung out of the bathroom window and waited. I say there was only one thing that he could have been waiting for.'

Miss Silver inclined her head.

'That is so. But you are forgetting the direct evidence of Mr Frank Ambrose. He saw Miss Paradine come out of her sister-in-law's room, and he saw her push her brother over the parapet. That he did so is an extremely fortunate circumstance for Mr Pearson, whose presence in the bathroom had already been established by the discovery of one of his prints upon the window frame.'

'What was he doing there?' said Elliot obstinately.

Miss Silver resumed her knitting. The stitches were diminishing to the point of the dark grey toe.

'I can tell you what I think,' she said. 'I cannot tell you whether it is the truth or not. That will never be known to anyone except Mr Pearson. But I have read his character, and I have tried to put myself in his place. I can tell you what I think. Consider for a moment what his feelings must have been when Mr Paradine launched his accusation at dinner. He could not have doubted for a moment that it was aimed at him. His sin had found him out. Think what that meant to him. He had been an industrious boy and an industrious young man, he had attained a confidential position, he had good prospects, and in one moment he saw all these things about to dissolve and leave him ruined. I believe he went to the study in a desperate state of mind, resolved to know the worst. Mr

Paradine's 'Hello, Albert – have you come to confess?' must have removed his last lingering hope. But the immediate entrance of Lane put it out of his power to reply, and in the next few moments, whilst they were together in the room, I believe that a plan formed itself in his mind. Mr Paradine called him back to suggest an alteration to some letter dictated earlier in the day. This took only a moment. Before Lane was out of earshot Mr Pearson left the study and ran up the back stairs to alter the clock. The alibi was already planned. I do not know whether Mr Paradine's death was planned also, or whether that came later during the hours when he sat in your room, Mr Wray, and waited for midnight. I think he did plan Mr Paradine's death – like you I can see no other reason for his waiting at the bathroom window. But I do not think he would have carried out his plan. At any rate he made no move to do so. He remained at the window and watched while Mr Paradine stood by the parapet. He could not have expected him to stay there indefinitely, yet he made no move. He has, I think, no imagination. He made a plan, but he had no idea of what his feelings would be when it came to carrying it out. He has not the temperament of a murderer. His mental processes are orderly and balanced. I can only repeat that I do not believe he would have killed Mr Paradine.' The last stitch left the last needle. Little Roger's leggings dropped completed upon Miss Silver's lap. 'Let us think of pleasanter things,' she said. 'You will be taking your wife away, Mr Wray?'

'As soon as the inquest and the funerals are over.'

'That is very wise.'

She turned to Mark and Lydia.

'May I say how much I wish you every happiness.'

Lydia said, 'We owe it to you.' And Mark, 'She's going to leave her office and take on Albert's job here. Then as soon as all this ghastly business is over we can get married. I shall hand this house over for a hospital, or a convalescent home, or anything that's wanted, and we'll go and live in my flat. It will do to start with anyhow.'

Miss Silver rolled up little Roger's leggings and put them away in her knitting bag together with the needles and a half-finished ball of dark grey wool. Then she rose to her feet and smiled kindly upon the three young people.

'I wish you every happiness,' she said.

PATRICIA WENTWORTH

THE CHINESE SHAWL

'Miss Silver has her place in detective fiction as surely as Lord Peter Wimsey or Hercule Poirot'
Manchester Evening News

Tanis Lyle was one of those passionate women who always get their own way. Her cousin Laura hated her. Most women did. But men found her irresistible and she used them mercilessly.

So when Tanis was found murdered there seemed to be any number of suspects on hand.

But Miss Silver had her own suspicions . . .

PATRICIA WENTWORTH

THE CASE OF WILLIAM SMITH

'Miss Wentworth is a first-rate storyteller'
Daily Telegraph

Who was William Smith? And why was Mavis Jones so horrified to see him?

For seven years William had worked as a wood-carver for the local toyshop, ignorant of his true identity. The war had robbed him of his memory, and no one expected him ever to find out the truth. So when he took his work to Eversleys Ltd, why was his life so instantly in danger?

William makes the frightening discovery that there are people who will stop at nothing to ensure his memory does not return. And without knowing anything of his own past how can he and Miss Silver stop his enemies striking again?

HODDER

PATRICIA WENTWORTH

OUT OF THE PAST

James and Carmona Hardwick are spending the summer playing host to numerous friends and relatives in an old Hardwick family residence by the sea.

The arrival of Alan Field, a devastatingly handsome though shady figure from Carmona's past, lifts the holiday atmosphere from the ugly old house and replaces it with mounting tension, culminating in murder.

Fortunately for the Hardwicks and their guests, Miss Silver is present to unravel the secrets and lies and stop the killer in their midst.

PATRICIA WENTWORTH

MISS SILVER COMES TO STAY

'Miss Silver is marvellous' *Daily Mail*

When he was 21, James Lessiter told Henrietta Cray that he loved her before all things. Catherine Lee's heart was broken but James had a side to him that most people do not see. When their engagement breaks off noone is sure why and Rietta refuses to explain.

Twenty years later, James returns to the village an extremely wealthy man. Rietta is still unmarried and Catherine is a penniless widow living in a cottage on the Lessiter estate. Trouble is inevitable, for Catherine hides a shameful secret, a secret she is desperate to keep from James. However, James already knows and intends to have his revenge whatever the cost. But he does not realise the cost will be his own life.

When Miss Silver investigates, there are all too many people in Melling with a motive for murder.

PATRICIA WENTWORTH

THROUGH THE WALL

There are bitter scenes in the Brand family when Martin Brand dies and leaves his large estate not to his widowed sister-in-law but to Marion, his young niece whom he had only met once in his life.

For Marion, the prospect of sharing her new home with Martin's predatory relations is not a happy one, and when a battered body wearing a coat is found on the beach her unhappiness turns to panic. Will Miss Silver find the murderer before the next killing?

PATRICIA WENTWORTH

THE GAZEBO

'Miss Silver has her place in detective fiction as surely as Lord Peter Wimsey or Hercule Poirot'
Manchester Evening News

For Althea Graham, suffering the whims of her malevolent invalid of a mother, the old family home is a prison. So when two competitive offers for the Graham's house are made to her it suggests that the house may hold some dark rewarding secret.

Then old Mrs Graham is found murdered in the gazebo . . .

PATRICIA WENTWORTH

THE CASE IS CLOSED

The Everton murder case has long been closed. The culprit has been charged with the murder of his uncle and has served a year of his sentence already. Or has he?

The evidence against Geoffrey Grey is convincing but his wife believes in his innocence. And so does her young cousin, Hilary, who decides to solve the mystery herself.

But when Hilary herself is nearly murdered she turns in desperation to her ex-fiancé for help. Fortunately, he is acquainted with the singular Miss Silver, who is only too pleased to be asked to investigate.

PATRICIA WENTWORTH

THE BENEVENT TREASURE

'The room was dark. She had pulled back the curtains and could just see the shape of the window. She sat up straight in bed with her heart beating fast . . .'

Somewhere among the dust and cobwebs of the sinister Benevent Mansion lies the legendary Benevent treasure. But a terrible death has been prophesied for whoever uncovers it.

When Candida Sayle is invited to visit her elderly maiden aunts, she dismisses such gloomy thoughts. But as Candida begins to discover the family's dark secrets she puts herself in grave danger. Thankfully Miss Silver has investigative skills of her own.